W9-AYQ-073

Destiny's Embrace

Center Point
Large Print

Also by Beverly Jenkins and available from
Center Point Large Print:

The Destiny Series
Destiny's Surrender

The Blessings Series
Bring on the Blessings
A Second Helping
Something Old, Something New
A Wish and a Prayer

**This Large Print Book carries the
Seal of Approval of N.A.V.H.**

Destiny's Embrace

Beverly Jenkins

CENTER POINT LARGE PRINT
THORNDIKE, MAINE

The text of this Large Print edition is unabridged.
In other aspects, this book may vary
from the original edition.
Printed in the United States of America
on permanent paper.
Set in 16-point Times New Roman type.

ISBN: 978-1-62899-202-1

Library of Congress Cataloging-in-Publication Data

Jenkins, Beverly, 1951–
Destiny's embrace / Beverly Jenkins. — Large print edition.
pages cm. — (Center Point Large Print Edition)
Summary: "In late 19th-century California, Logan Yates, a self-
important ranch owner, must confront his feelings for his beautiful, free
spirited housekeeper, Mariah Cooper"—Provided by publisher.
ISBN 978-1-62899-202-1 (library binding : alk. paper)
1. Housekeepers—Fiction. 2. Ranchers—Fiction.
3. California—Fiction. 4. Large type books. I. Title.
PS3560.E4795D47 2014
813′.54—dc23
                                                      2014017388

To Queen Calafia and my orginal Cali crew:
Shareeta, Angie, Linda, Christine, and Fedelies.

Prologue

Nine-year-old Mariah Cooper was ecstatic. For the very first time, her mother was allowing her to deliver a dress to one of the customers of her dress shop. The lady, a Mrs. Ainsley, lived a few blocks away, and because her house wasn't far, Mariah had been trusted to get it there and herself back, undamaged, and in one piece. She and her mother lived on the Colored side of Philadelphia, and as she passed the homes of her neighbors and classmates, she didn't tarry because she wanted her mama to be proud of her.

Her steps slowed, however, when she saw Liam Anderson sitting with some boys on his front stoop. He'd gotten in trouble in school earlier that day and blamed her. Their teacher, Miss Worth, stepped out of the classroom for a moment and left Mariah in charge. Mariah was told to write down the name of anyone exhibiting unruly behavior, and that person or persons would be dealt with upon her return.

The moment Miss Worth exited and closed the door, Liam ran to the front of the room where Mariah was seated, hit her on the side of her head, and ran back to his seat. The kids laughed—not loud enough to be heard in the hallway, but the snickering only added to her shame. Liam was the biggest and oldest person in the class, and not a day passed by that he didn't bully someone smaller and younger. Mariah detested him because he seemed to set his sights on her more than anyone else.

Before she could recover from the sting of the first blow, he returned for an encore, and this time hit her harder. Blinking and determined to keep her tears in check while the children giggled, she snapped, "I'm putting you on the list, Liam Anderson."

"If you do, I'll get you after school, Witch Hazel." The derisive name was one she'd been given because of her gold-colored eyes. She thought the name as abominable as Liam.

To make certain Mariah took his threat seriously, he ran up and hit her again just as Miss Worth reentered the classroom.

When Miss Worth grabbed him by his ear and escorted him away to see the school principal, Mariah was admittedly pleased. Now, watching him leave the stoop and approach her wearing a nasty grin, she wasn't pleased; she was afraid. But running away wasn't an option, so she continued up the street where he stood blocking her path.

"Get out of my way, Liam. I have to deliver this dress for my mama."

"My papa whipped me because of you."

"It was your own fault."

He pushed her down. The dress in its brown

paper shroud landed beside her. She scrambled to retrieve it before it got wet from the puddles left by the afternoon rain. "Leave me alone!" She picked up the dress and prayed it wasn't damaged.

"Witch Hazel!"

He pushed her down again, and she landed in the muddy street, which stained her white stockings and the front of her blue dress. "Stop it!"

By then, people were stepping outside to see what was going on, and a man's voice rang out, "Leave her alone!"

Liam froze.

Trembling and trying not to cry, she picked up the dress. Her mother was going to whip her something fierce if it was ruined. Her rescuer was fast approaching. Beside him and hurrying to keep up with his determined stride was a new girl at school named Kathleen. Mariah assumed the man to be her father. She was so grateful to see them and wiped at the tears in her eyes. Liam, on the other hand, took off at a run and disappeared inside his house. His friends on the stoop scattered like rats.

"Are you all right, little lady?" The concern in the man's voice was mirrored in his kind gaze.

"I think so, sir."

"I'm Mr. Jennings. Kaye says you're in her classroom at school."

"Yes, sir."

"I'll make sure his parents know about this."

Mariah shook her head. "Please, don't tell them. He'll only pick on me more."

"She's right, Papa," Kathleen added. "He hit her three times today at school."

Mariah looked down at her precious cargo.

"What's that you have there?" Mr. Jennings asked.

"A dress from my mama's shop. I was on my way to deliver it to Mrs. Ainsley." The paper was bent and slightly crushed, but appeared to be intact.

"How much farther do you have to go?"

"Another block."

"Kaye will wait with you while I get my carriage. We'll drive you there and see that you get home safely. Not sure what this city is coming to when a youngster can't do an errand for her mother without being attacked by hooligans."

"I'll be okay now, Mr. Jennings."

But he hastened away.

"Your papa's nice," Mariah said to Kathleen.

"Yes he is. I'll bet your papa will be mad when you tell him about Liam."

"I don't have a papa. He died."

"Oh. I'm sorry."

"That's okay. Thank you for helping me."

"I didn't laugh when Liam hit you at school. Do you think we can be friends?"

"I'd like that."

Mr. Jennings returned and drove Mariah and her

new friend to Mrs. Ainsley's house. Once there, he explained what happened and why the paper was so dirty. She was appalled by the incident, and when she opened the paper the dress inside was undamaged. She was so pleased, she gave Mariah a few pennies for her trouble.

True to his word, Mr. Jennings drove her home and escorted her inside. Her mother looked from him and Kaye to Mariah and her muddy attire, and asked, coolly, "Who are you, and what happened?"

He opened his mouth, but she cut him off. "Mariah. Explain."

Seeing the ice in her mother's eyes, Mariah told the tale slowly, hoping she'd understand.

When she was done with the telling, her mother said in the same cool tone, "Thank you, Mr. Jennings. You can leave us now."

He appeared concerned by her attitude. "None of what happened was your daughter's fault. The dress wasn't damaged—"

"Good day, Mr. Jennings."

Anger filled his face, but he didn't voice it. "Good day, ma'am. Come Kaye."

Once they exited, her mother fumed, "How dare you come home covered in mud. Do you know how much time I spent making that dress you're wearing?"

"Mama, it wasn't my fault. I—"

"Did Mrs. Ainsley give you money?"

"Yes."

Her mother stuck out her hand. Mariah, fighting back tears, placed the two pennies in her palm.

"Now go get the strap. I'll teach you to come home full of mud."

"But, Mama—"

"Fetch the strap!"

Mariah swallowed her tears and hurried to retrieve the strap.

Chapter 1

Alanza Yates stood in the cool morning air on the verandah of her rancho and gazed out at the vast green landscape. Off in the distance, near the tree line that bordered the rising mountains, horses and colts destined for sale galloped leisurely under the watchful eyes of mounted ranch hands. To the west, slow-moving cattle, also destined for sale, fattened themselves on the open grasslands and drank at the clear stream that meandered down from the hills. Her orchards, with trees bearing lemons and oranges, shared space with tidy rows of grapevines budding with fruit. The rancho, originally established by her grandfather, and passed to her father upon his death was her birthplace. As a youngster, when the area was known as Mexico's Alta California, she'd ridden from one end of the estate to the other without a care in the world. Since then, many things had changed, and most importantly, so had she.

She was born Alanza Maria Vallejo, the pampered only child of the wealthy and well-

13

connected Don Francisco Vallejo, who traced his lineage back to the glory days of Spain. By the time she was fifteen, Alanza had been educated by the friars and nuns, traveled widely in Mexico and Europe, and promised in marriage to Don Jose Ignacio, a man thirty-five years her senior. She hated him. He and his sweaty hands were always trying to touch her when he found her in the hallways of her home alone, without her parents or *duenna*. His leering piglike eyes, and the way he licked his lips as if she were something he planned to eat, made her hate him even more, so she refused to honor the marriage agreement. Her father raged, her mother cried, and the neighboring Spanish families shook their heads at her scandalous insolence while whispering behind their fans about her reputation. To make matters worse, she was secretly in love with a man not of Spanish descent. His name was Abraham Yates. Her parents wouldn't have minded his African heritage; after all, there were many families in Mexico and Spanish California with the same blood, including more than half of the original settlers of the city of Los Angeles.

What they would've minded was that Abraham was an American. In their eyes, his ties to the Bear Flag Party, a group whose machinations opened the way for the American government to gain California from Mexico via subterfuge and then war, would've made them threaten to send their only daughter to a nunnery and never see or speak to her again. They demanded she marry Don Ignacio, but because she was stubborn and spoiled, she ran away to her secret love with the hope that he would take her in.

Being an honest man, Abraham immediately brought her back to her parents. But the damage was done; no Spanish man of good family would have her now, so a padre was immediately summoned, and after enduring the only beating ever meted out by her father's hand, Alanza was quickly married off to the widower Abraham Yates to become his wife and the stepmother to his six-year-old son, Logan.

Alanza sighed at the memory. She'd been so arrogant and full of herself at that time. Had she known then what life had in store for her, she would've thrown herself at her father's feet and begged for forgiveness and mercy. After the ceremony, she and Abraham returned to his small cabin. His admittance to not being in love with her shattered her world. He'd no idea she'd held such strong feelings for him, and told her had he known he would've gently pointed out the truth. Having had no experience with men, she'd assumed the soft smiles he sent her way when he came to the ranch to tend her father's horses meant something. Each time he visited, she found some nonsensical reason to speak with her father whenever the two men conversed, just to bask in Abraham's smile. But on the evening of her wedding day, she realized she was nothing more than a vain, spoiled child who'd brought shame down on herself and her family, and forced a stern but compassionate man to be yoked to her till death did them part. Her humiliation, guilt, and shame knew no bounds.

"Senora?"

Her reverie broken, Alanza turned to her Irish housekeeper. "Yes, Bonnie?"

"Mr. Logan and his men have returned. Do you wish lunch served before or after you welcome him home?"

"After, Bonnie. *Gracias.* And have my carriage brought around, *por favor.*"

Bonnie departed, leaving Alanza alone with her thoughts again. The knowledge that Logan had arrived home safely made her send up a silent prayer of thanks. Abraham lost his life in a rock slide eight years into their marriage. She knew better than to burden Logan with her fears that he'd suffer a similar fate, but whenever he was away, she slept restlessly and lit extra candles to the Virgin Mother on his behalf. Many second wives chose to distance themselves from children brought into a marriage by their husbands, but she'd loved Logan from the moment they'd met. The years following Abe's death were filled with despair and an abject poverty she never could have imagined while growing up in her parents' home, being waited upon by a small army of servants and sleeping beneath silken sheets. Logan became her touchstone and her light during that time. He talked with her, listened to her hopes and dreams, and worked tirelessly by her side. In many ways he still held that role. Although she hadn't given him birth, he was her son, and she loved him as fiercely as if she had.

Abraham might not have loved her, but he'd been tender in bed, and as a result, she gave birth to two sons who she loved just as much as her stepson. Andrew Antonio, or Drew—he of the godlike face—chose the law as his profession and women as his hobby. He bore the most resemblance to Alanza and her Spanish ancestors. Two years after his birth came Noah, her youngest. He grew up and chose the sea, or rather the sea chose him. On a trip to San Francisco, when he was eighteen years old, he was shanghaied. His family had no clue as to what had happened, and Logan and Drew turned the city upside down in their efforts to find him, but to no avail. It was as if he'd disappeared off the face of the earth. For two long, miserable years, Alanza prayed to the saints on behalf of her missing child, then finally a letter arrived informing them of his fate. In spite of all that had happened, the sea became his life and he now sailed his own ship, the *Alanza*.

No, Abraham never loved her, but love was what she wanted the most for them. Love with wives who adored them and children who loved them as much as Alanza did.

A weary Logan Yates was on his way to a bath and bed when he heard the door pull. Having just gotten home from six grueling weeks in the saddle rounding up wild mustangs in Montana, he wasn't in the mood for visitors. Going to the door, he had to step around saddles, spurs, braided lariats, chaps, boots, socks, discarded denims, union suits, and all the rest of the equipment and clothing belonging to him and his ranch hands. A quick glance through the dirty windows of his equally cluttered parlor showed Alanza's fancy black coach parked out front. He assumed she'd come to welcome him home. He loved her very much and was glad to see her, but he knew he was going to have to listen to her lecture him about the unholy mess that was his house. It was his hope the lecturing would be short because he was dead on his feet.

Alanza entered with a sweep of blue silk and fragrant perfume. "Welcome home, my son," she said warmly in her Spanish-inflected English. "I missed you."

He placed a kiss on her offered cheek. "Missed you, too. It's good to be back." She was in her late forties, only nine years older than he, and wore her age well. The first time they met, he remembered looking at her raven black hair and matching eyes and thinking her the most beautiful woman in the world.

"Any problems along the way?" she asked.

"None. We brought back a stallion, four mares, and seven yearlings. All in good shape. Eli and the men are getting them settled into the corral." He watched her discreetly glancing around at the mess that also covered what little furniture he had, and he sighed inwardly because he knew what would follow.

"When are you going to hire a housekeeper?"

When he didn't respond, her lips thinned, which made him attempt to come to his own defense. "I don't need one, and besides, it isn't as if I'll be entertaining guests."

"But you should be," she countered. "You are a leader here, just like your father was. It's a good thing I love you as much as I do."

"Why?"

"Because if I didn't, I'd've taken a torch to this place months ago."

Amusement filled his dark eyes. "A torch?"

"Fueled by kerosene. The smell in here alone is enough to make decent folks swoon. Please allow me to hire someone."

"Soon as we get the new bunkhouse built, things will be back to normal."

Logan and his men were forced to stow their gear in the house after the fire from a lightning strike destroyed the bunkhouse. That was a year ago. What with riding to Montana twice a year for horses and then breaking them for sale, there hadn't been time yet to get a new one built. Polite society might call his place a sty but he and the hands didn't mind the clutter or the smell.

Alanza was still staring around, her distaste muted but plain. "You'll never get a wife this way."

"Fine with me, because I'm not looking for one."

She raised an elegantly shaped eyebrow and warned, "If I am sent to my grave without grandchildren I will haunt the lot of you for eternity."

"Then you might want to speak with my brothers. I have my horses and the land."

"And Valencia," she stated coolly.

Valencia was his mistress. Logan met her statement without reacting.

She shook her head. "I'll put notices for a housekeeper in a few papers back East. Your reputation precedes you here. Any woman who applies will undoubtedly want to share your bed instead of making it. Back East, we may be able to find a true candidate immune to your manly charms."

"Up to you. Me, I've been in the saddle for weeks. Going to take a bath and sleep."

"You have my luck finding a place to do either."

"I love you, too," he chuckled.

Smiling, she squeezed his hand affectionately, gave his cheek a parting peck, then swept out of his house with another rustle of silk and the trailing scent of her sweet perfume.

After her departure, Logan took a good honest look around and supposed it could use some help. Although he'd never admit it aloud, she was right about the stink, too; it was the first thing he noticed upon entering. But the last thing he wanted was a dried-up, back-East biddy underfoot ordering him around. He gave the orders. He didn't take them.

"Dona Alanza still complaining about the house?"

Logan turned to see his partner and friend, Eli Braden, entering from the back of the house. The spectacle-wearing Texan was one of the finest horsemen Logan had ever met. "Were you hiding so she wouldn't see you?"

"Yep. Didn't want her lighting into me, too. Reminds me too much of my own mama." Eli took a long look around. "This place could use some cleaning, though. If we could bottle the smell, we'd make a fortune selling it as rat poison."

Logan rolled his eyes. Eli's digs were reminiscent of ones often flung Logan's way by his siblings, both of whom believed provoking him to be their main mission in life. "The horses settled in?"

"Yeah. Stallion still pitching a fit, but he'll come around. You really going to hire a housekeeper?"

"Alanza is."

"I wish her luck. If it were me, I'd take one look at this mess and hightail it out of here like my saddle was on fire."

"Go home."

"Going. See you tomorrow." He left, cheerily whistling "The Yellow Rose of Texas."

After his much longed for bath, Logan walked out to check on the white stallion. It was still angrily charging around the confines of the corral. After spending life unbridled and free, it wasn't happy being penned in, and reminded him in many ways of how angry his own stallion Diablo had been after capture. Logan understood the mustang's distress, but he didn't let empathy take precedence over the fine price the horse would bring when sold. He spent another few minutes marveling over its beautiful strong lines before leaving the horse under the watchful eyes of his hands and slowly making his way back to the house.

Logan was thirty-seven years old, and as he'd aged, recovering from the long rides to Montana and back seemed to take longer and longer. It wasn't something he admitted out loud; as it stood, some of the younger hands had already affectionately taken to calling him or Eli "Old Man." And at the moment he certainly felt like one. Five years ago, his left knee was nearly shattered by a kick from a stallion similar to the one now rearing and bellowing with rage in the corral, and although the knee healed, it never fully recovered. Long rides made it ache, as did the winter rains. Some of the other ranchers his age had long since turned their more arduous tasks over to the younger men in their employ but Logan refused to follow suit. Whether it stemmed from pride, arrogance, or just plain stubbornness he didn't know, but he'd been the man on the Destiny ranch since his father returned from a trip to Montana dead and laid across the back of his horse. Logan had been fourteen. He and the then twenty-three-year-old Alanza had worked their fingers to the bone to keep their land, but they'd known much less about ranching back then and as a result wound up so destitute that at one point, there'd been no money and even less food. When life finally got better, he'd vowed that as long as he lived, she and his brothers would never have to endure such hardship again. So far, that vow had been kept.

He made his way through the cluttered hallway and into his bedroom. The sight of the clean bedding brought on a smile because he knew Alanza's servants were responsible. Lying down, he thought about her wish for grandchildren. He supposed one of her sons would eventually have to tie the knot in order to make her dreams come true and to ensure Destiny's land stayed in the family, but he didn't see himself as a candidate.

He enjoyed the company of his mistress, Valencia. She was a fine woman, even if she was a bit hesitant in bed, and she'd made it plain that she didn't want to marry. He didn't see Andrew Antonio as a likely candidate, either. Drew lived in San Francisco and had a *remuda* of mistresses that snaked from the Bay to Mexico City. No way was he going to give Alanza her desired grand-babies. So that left his baby brother, Noah. Turning over to make himself comfortable, Logan made a mental note to send the captain of the *Alanza* a letter informing him of his duty. Smiling at the thought of Noah's probable reaction, the weary Logan closed his eyes and instantaneously fell asleep.

Chapter 2

On the other side of the country, Mariah Cooper was seated on the floor of her mother's dress shop in Philadelphia wishing the portly Mrs. Julia Porter would stand still. Every time Mariah tried to set a pin in the hem of the gown the woman was wearing, she'd swivel around to speak to the other customers in the shop, thus making it difficult to set the next pin evenly. Julia Porter was the biggest gossip in the city of Philadelphia, and when she wasn't spreading false, lurid tales, she was openly seeking information to spread more. Today's subject was the impending marriage of Mariah's friend, Kathleen Jennings, to Carson Wales, a wealthy, older gentleman. Mariah knew Carson worshipped the ground Kaye walked on, but Julia Porter had her own take on the impending nuptials. "She's after his funds. Plain and simple." Julia turned again and made the silk move before the pin could be set. "Heaven knows what he sees in her, besides the obvious. Those bosoms of hers have been drawing male attention since she was old enough to wear a corset."

Mariah wanted to speak up in defense of her friend, but kept her lips tightly sealed. Julia Porter, like the other women in the shop, was among her mother's best customers. Were Mariah to tell the old bat what she really thought, her mother, Bernice, would lose the business, and as it was, Mariah had a hard enough time staying in her mother's good graces.

"Mariah!" her mother called sharply. "Are you woolgathering or pinning that hem?"

"Pinning, Mother."

Julia Porter peered down. "Why on earth is it taking you so long?"

Mariah kept her head down so as to mask her reaction. "Almost done, Mrs. Porter."

The woman huffed with impatience. "And to think this dull-witted girl aspires to marry my Tillman. Can you imagine having a grandchild with her witch eyes?"

The ladies laughed.

The caustic remark made Mariah tighten with embarrassment. Her odd-colored eyes had been the subject of taunting for as long as she could remember. One would expect a mother to come to the defense of her child on the heels of such a nasty remark, but Mariah knew better than to expect that from her own. Tillman was Julia's only son. Although he'd professed his undying love for Mariah, his mother was having none of it. Witch Hazel Mariah was too old and lacked the social stature Julia preferred her future daughter-in-law to have. To Mariah's disappointment, Tillman refused to go against her wishes. "I'm done now, Mrs. Porter."

"It's about time."

Mariah gathered up the pins and got to her feet. "Mother, if you don't need me for anything else, I'll go start dinner."

Julia Porter drawled, "I hope she cooks faster than she pins, Bernice, otherwise you may starve to death."

Chin raised, Mariah ignored the chuckles and walked out of the room with as much dignity as she could muster. Climbing the short staircase to the living space she and her mother shared above the shop, she wiped away the angry tears in her eyes and walked into the kitchen. She knew hate was a strong word, but nothing else adequately defined how she felt about her life. It was 1885, she was thirty years old and the world seemed to have passed her by. Unlike her friend Kaye, there'd be no marriage or children for her, at least not unless Tillman grew a spine. For the rest of her life, all she had to look forward to was more of the same. When she wasn't catering to her mother's viperous customers, she was cooking and cleaning for her. It had been that way since Mariah became old enough to handle the stove and push a needle through fabric. According to Bernice, Mariah's father died when she was three years old, and for some unknown reason, Bernice found fault with her daughter no matter the task. Mariah yearned to have the warm and loving relationship Kaye had with her mother, Winnie, but learned at an early age that the sun would rise in the west first. Bernice was mean, caustic, and short-tempered. The only joys in Mariah's life came from the books she borrowed from the local lending library, and the charity work she did alongside the matrons at Mother Bethel, the AME church. Twice a month she and the other women visited the sick, checked on the children in the orphanages, and dispensed food and medicine to those in need. It was satisfying work, and a tradition that had begun during abolition. She dearly enjoyed helping others but wished her own life held more caring and kindness.

By the time her mother entered an hour later, dinner was done, but instead of being offered thanks, Mariah was scolded instead. "How dare you make me a laughingstock!"

Countering that she was the one who'd borne the embarrassing brunt of Julia Porter's sharp tongue would only evoke more railing, so again, she kept her lips sealed.

"You dawdled over that hem as if we have a fully stocked larder and no need to pay bills."

"I'm sorry, Mother."

"I'm sorry, Mother," Bernice mimicked cruelly. "If Mrs. Porter and her friends decide to take their trade elsewhere because you can't pin a hem with reasonable speed, then what? How will I keep this shop open so that I can continue to clothe and house you? It's not as if you have a prospective husband waiting in the wings to take you off my hands."

Mariah wondered if her skin would ever grow thick enough to blunt the razor-sharp cut of her mother's vicious tongue.

Bernice said with disgust, "Go. Eat your supper, clean up in here, then get to work on those sketches. I'll be meeting Mrs. Crandall in the morning."

"Yes, Mother." Growing up, it was not uncommon for her to be sent to her room without supper as punishment for sins real or imagined, so she took the small gift and departed.

Later, upstairs in the attic space that served as her bedroom, she pulled out her sketchbook and pencils. One of her other small joys was designing gowns. Her mother often sold the sketches she created to Mrs. Crandall, the modiste of choice for the city's wealthy White women. Although it was never discussed, Mariah was fairly certain her mother had Mrs. Crandall convinced that Bernice had drawn them all. Her mother did have the decency to give Mariah a small percentage of the sale price, which she immediately socked away in her account at the bank, but she was also certain she wasn't being paid anywhere close to what the sketches were actually being sold for. On more than a few occasions she'd secretly gone over to Mrs. Crandall's shop and seen the readymade gowns based on her sketches displayed on dress forms in the window. The asking prices were jaw-dropping.

It took two hours to finish the three sketches: one of a traveling ensemble with a scalloped hem on the formfitting bodice, the second, a flowing velvet coat fit for the opera or some other fancy affair, and the last, a peignoir that could be included in a bridal trousseau, something she doubted she'd ever have. Done, she massaged her weary eyes and went to stand by the tiny triangle-shaped pane that functioned as her window. Dusk was descending on another day. Somewhere in the city of Philadelphia were women her age, dressing for a night out at the theater with their friends, or putting children to bed, or spending a quiet evening at home with their husbands. Although she knew it wasn't charitable, she often wondered what her life would be like had she been born in another time or place. According to the reverend, everyone was where the Good Lord intended for them to be. To question one's existence was to border on being blasphemous. Yet and still, she'd always felt as if her destiny lay elsewhere. Ever since she was small she often wondered about people in other places and if somewhere in the wide world there was a girl like her standing in a window in London or Cathay or another exotic place peering out just as she was. Turning away from the window, she prepared herself for sleep. Undoubtedly tomorrow would mirror today, but she had to face it none the same.

The next morning, while Bernice was away peddling Mariah's sketches, Tillman paid a visit to the shop. She was sewing the final stitches into the hem of the gown his mother was scheduled to pick up later in the week. At his entrance she set it aside. She supposed she should be pleased to see the only man who'd ever paid her court, but because they both knew his mother would never approve his suit for her hand, her feelings were mixed. "Morning, Tillman."

He was a handsome man who very much resembled his father, a bellman at one of the big hotels downtown. Tillman was a graduate of Howard College and was presently employed as the accountant for the city's year-old Black newspaper, the *Tribune*. Because its editor, Mr. Christopher Perry, couldn't afford to pay him very much, he supplemented his income as a waiter at the same establishment where his father worked. "Morning, Mariah. How are you?"

"I'm well, and you?"

"On my way to the paper, thought I'd come by and sneak a kiss to sweeten my day."

She gave him a leveling look even as she smiled. "No kisses for you until you stand up to your mama."

"Aw, 'Riah, come on. You know I can't afford to do that. At least not until I make enough to be able to survive on my own."

He crossed the distance between them. Taking her by the hands he gently urged her to her feet. "You know you enjoy kissing me just as much."

She was about to respond when her mother came through the door. The glare in her eyes froze them both.

Tillman stammered, "Um, morning, Mrs. Cooper. I—I just stopped in to ask about my mother's gown."

"Is that why you two are holding hands?"

He released hers as if they were suddenly red hot. Mariah's lips tightened.

"Your mother's gown will be delivered on Thursday. Now, I'm sure you have pressing duties, elsewhere. Am I correct?"

He gave her a quick nod and moved to the door. "Good day, ma'am." He had no parting words for Mariah.

In the silence that rose on the heels of his hasty exit, Mariah braced herself for what would follow.

"Why are you encouraging him to go against his mother? Hasn't Mrs. Porter made it quite clear that she finds you and your witch eyes unacceptable? All that man wants is what's between your legs, and until he takes a wife, you'll do." She then warned ominously, "Bring a bastard child into this world, and it and you will be on the street. Do you hear me, girl!"

"Yes, ma'am."

"Now, get to work, and I don't want to see him in my shop again."

"Yes, ma'am." Mariah hated being so weak, but like Tillman she had no choice but to endure. Her bank funds weren't nearly enough to allow her to set out on her own. And even if they were, for all her longings for another life in another place, she didn't know if she had the inner fortitude to just up and leave. Bernice was her mother. The Bible specifically stated she was to honor that bond; so, instead of placing the blame for the visit on Tillman's head, where it rightly belonged, Mariah did as she was told and went back to hemming his mother's gown.

By the end of June, rumor had it that he'd gotten himself engaged to a young woman from Boston. Because his family traveled in different social circles and attended St. Thomas Episcopal instead of Mother Bethel, Mariah had no real way of knowing the truth. She hadn't seen him since the ill-fated visit six weeks ago, nor had his mother stopped by the shop to order any new gowns. She supposed she should be happy for him, but found herself angered by the rumor instead.

Her day was brightened by a visit from her good friend Kathleen Jennings. After sharing an affectionate hug of greeting, they took seats on the shop's stools and Mariah said eagerly, "So tell me everything about the wedding plans."

"We've decided to marry in the fall, and I'd like for you to make my gown."

Mariah's heart leapt excitedly. "I'd be honored and the gown'll be my wedding gift to you."

Her mother came out of the back and the two friends sobered instantaneously.

"Afternoon, Mrs. Cooper."

They both stood.

"Kathleen. You're aware that I don't like Mariah visiting when she's supposed to be working?"

"I understand but I'm here to ask her to make my wedding gown."

"Really? At what price?"

Mariah spoke up. "I want the gown to be my gift to her, so I won't be charging her."

"And you made that decision all on your own, did you?"

Sparks of anger flared to life in Mariah's eyes. "Yes. It's the least I can do to repay her for her friendship all these years."

"Is that friendship going to pay next month's rent?"

"Mother, I—"

"Kathleen," her mother said coolly. "Mariah's very busy. I'll come up with a price and talk to you and your mother about it in a day or so."

"Yes, ma'am." Clearly upset, Kaye gave Mariah's hand a parting squeeze and departed.

Once they were alone, Bernice stated pointedly, "When your name is on the sign outside you can be charitable, but until then nothing goes out of this shop for free."

Mariah was so weary of being walked upon and criticized and verbally flayed, she wanted to scream. Her friendship with Kaye meant everything. They'd known each other since primary school and were the sisters neither had. Growing up, they'd shared dreams and hopes and on those rare occasions Bernice allowed Mariah to visit the Jennings's home and stay overnight, they'd giggled until dawn.

Now, her mother was trying to deny Mariah the one way she knew to repay Kaye for her many years of kindness, and for being one of the few bright spots in her life. As she looked into the brittle face, something told her that if she didn't take a stand there and then, she'd spend the rest of her life with Bernice's foot on her neck until her spirit withered away. "I am going to make Kaye's gown, and it will be at no cost to her. I'll buy the fabric and threads out of my own money."

"Are you deaf now, girl?"

Mariah's temper flared. "No, but she's my only true friend and were it not for me, you'd have no shop! I do most of the sewing, I create the sketches that you sell downtown as your own. I do the deliveries and everything else that makes *your* shop such a success!"

That earned her a slap filled with so much anger and malice, the force of it sent her to the floor.

Staring up into the smug pleasure sparkling in her mother's eyes, Mariah slowly wiped away the blood on her lip. For the first time in her life, she saw the true depths of her mother's loathing. In spite of all the nastiness and beatings she'd endured, she'd never shown her mother anything but respect. She had no answers to why the hatred existed, but in the face of the satisfaction her mother displayed from having delivered the blow it was plain that it was time to leave. Bible or not, she refused to spend another moment living with such unfounded malevolence. Simmering with rage, she stood. Without a word, she snatched up her handbag and marched out the door. Her mother yelled for her to return but Mariah didn't slow her steps. She was hurt, furious, and in need of answers to questions that had plagued her for her entire life. The only person who could possibly enlighten her was her mother's eldest sister, Libby. Getting on the trolley, Mariah ignored the curious looks her bleeding lip garnered and rode silently across town.

Chapter 3

Unlike Mariah and her mother, Libby Brown lived well, thanks to the estates of her three late husbands. Her large house was in the tonier Black area of the city. The maid answered the door and eyed Mariah and her injured lip suspiciously. "May I help you?"

"I'm Mariah Cooper, Mrs. Brown's niece. I wonder if I might speak with her?"

The hard eyes didn't soften. "I'll see if she's receiving. Wait here, please."

A few moments later, Libby appeared, and upon seeing Mariah's lip, exclaimed, "Oh my gracious, Mariah! What happened to you?"

"Mother and I had an argument."

"Come in. Come in." Taking her by the hand, she pulled her into the front parlor. "Sit right there. Willa, get her a cold rag."

Mariah gingerly touched her swollen lip and shook her head in a mixture of anger and wonder that she and her mother had come to such a terrible state. Willa returned and Mariah pressed the cold compress to the injury. It did much to soothe the fiery sting. Rising to her feet, Mariah walked over to the ornate framed mirror hanging on the wall and surveyed the damage. Her bottom lip was split and puffy. She dabbed at the dried blood gently in an effort to clean it up and once again shook her head.

Libby's dark face appeared in the glass behind hers and Mariah saw the empathy her eyes held. "It's going to take that a few days to heal," Libby pointed out quietly. "But we'll keep it cold so the swelling doesn't increase. Would you like to tell me what happened?"

They sat in the parlor and Mariah related the story. When she finished, Libby's lip tightened with disapproval. "Bernice knows how close you and Kaye are. It isn't right for her to deny you such a small thing, especially when you've offered to pay for everything."

Mariah agreed. "She's the only friend I have. May I ask you something?"

"Of course."

"Why does mother hate me so, and please don't tell me it's my imagination because I know it isn't."

The expression on her aunt's face was unfathomable, and after a moment Libby looked off into the distance at something only she could see. The prolonged silence made Mariah think she wouldn't reply, but eventually she did. "You have your father's eyes, Mariah. Every time Bernice looks into them, I'm sure she sees him and remembers her pain."

"From the grief of his death?"

"No," she countered quietly. "The pain of being

abandoned and betrayed. Your father, Arna, didn't pass away, Mariah."

Surprise filled her and her voice. "But I was always told—"

"I know, I know, but that isn't the truth. Your mother received a letter from him right after your third birthday stating he'd be staying on in London with his true wife and children and wouldn't be returning to Philadelphia ever again. He wished you and her a good life, and Godspeed. It was the last she ever heard from him as far as I know."

Mariah felt as if she'd been punched in the stomach. "He was married to someone else?"

"Yes, both before and during the times he spent in Philadelphia with Bernice."

Mariah truly thought she might be ill.

"Your eyes are twins of his. Tiger eyes, he called them. Said he had an ancestor who'd walked as a human by day and a tiger by night as punishment for offending one of his gods."

"Surely no one believed such blarney?"

"Your father was so beautiful, the women he met didn't care whether the tales were blarney or not as long as he favored them with a glance, a smile, or whatever else he might send their way. When he settled his attention on your mother, she was ecstatic."

Mariah found this not only hard to believe but wondered what her father could have seen in such a dried-up shrew of a woman. Her aunt seemed to sense her thoughts. "Your mother was not as she is presently. At that time in her life she was one of the most beautiful women in Philadelphia, of any race or class."

Mariah had difficulty reconciling that claim, too. "What country was he from?"

Libby shrugged. "He said Egypt to some and Bengal to others. I heard him claim to be a Spanish Moor one minute and the son of an African king the next, but he courted Bernice as if she were a queen, married her, and a year later you were born."

While Mariah fought to make sense of the surprising revelations, Libby continued. "Because his work as a seaman took him on voyages all over the world, your mother only saw him twice, maybe three times a year. When he returned he came bearing gifts: cups carved from elephant ivory, floor rugs from Persia, bananas from the Sandwich Islands. The longer he was gone, the more treasures he brought back. Then his letter arrived. She was devastated of course, and then furious at being used so baldly and badly. To save face, she passed around the story that he'd been swept overboard and died at sea. She wore weeds and pretended to mourn even as everything he ever gave her was tossed into the grate and set afire. His betrayal shattered her and is the reason she treats you so horridly."

Now Mariah understood. She could only imagine how devastated and heartbroken her mother must've been, but none of it gave her the right to take out that pain on her daughter. Mariah set that aside for the moment. "May I ask another question?"

Libby nodded.

"Why are the two of you estranged?" As far as she knew Bernice and Libby hadn't spoken in years.

"I was the one who introduced them."

After letting that shocking piece of the puzzle settle in, she reached over and gave Mariah's hand a fond pat. "You'll be my guest until you decide what it is you'd like to do. Or are you anxious to return to Bernice?"

"No."

"Good. In the morning, I'll go over and get your things."

"She's not going to let you take them."

"I am three inches taller and fifty pounds heavier. I doubt there will be a problem." And she winked. "You go upstairs and lie down for a bit. When you're ready, we'll have dinner."

Even though her lip continued to throb, the talk with Libby eased a large portion of her inner tension. She gave her aunt a strong hug, and whispered, "Thank you."

"You're welcome. Now, go on up before I begin to cry. I'm so glad you're here. Life will be better from this moment forward, my niece. I promise."

Upstairs, Mariah made herself comfortable on the bed in the guest room, and while lying there thought back on the shocking tale her aunt divulged. Though she felt sorry for her mother, there was no excusing what she'd forced Mariah to endure: not the whippings she'd received almost daily as a child, nor the verbal ones that replaced them as she got older. She was so tired of it all, from having to walk on eggshells twenty-four hours a day, to being forced to slave for her mother as if she'd been purchased on the auction block. She hadn't asked to be born to a woman who'd been so terribly used, any more than she'd asked for the eyes that reminded Bernice of him so much. She'd often wondered how she'd ever find the inner strength to leave her mother, and now the day's circumstances made the question moot. From that day forward, her mother would have to run the shop alone because she wouldn't be returning. Aunt Libby promised life would be better. Mariah prayed she was right.

The next morning, Libby returned from the shop and presented Mariah with her possessions, including her beloved sketchbook and pencils.

"Did Mother give you a hard time?"

"Of course, and she'll be wearing an eye patch for a few days as a result."

Mariah's heart stopped.

Libby smiled and waved her off. "Nothing to

worry about. Sisters squabble all the time. Now, once we get everything up to your room, I want you to write a note to Kaye and let her know you'll be making her wedding gown. I'll have my houseman Randall take the note to her home."

The request instantaneously erased Mariah's unspoken concerns about the altercation between her mother and her aunt. After Randall hauled the trunks up to her new room, Mariah immediately sat at the mahogany writing desk and penned the note to her friend.

Kaye came calling the next day. They retired to the parlor, where Mariah filled her in on what occurred after she visited the shop yesterday.

"Oh, 'Riah. I'm so sorry and look at your poor lip. If there's anything Mama and I can do to help you, just let us know."

"Thank you. There is one thing I need your assistance with."

"Whatever it is, I'll do my best."

She handed Kaye the three wedding gown sketches she'd drawn up. "I need your assistance in picking out the one you prefer."

Kaye's eyes widened with glee. After a few moments of silently evaluating each one, she gushed softly, "Oh, 'Riah, these are all so lovely."

"You only get one."

Kaye finally decided. "This one."

Mariah nodded approvingly. In terms of design, the choice was the most basic of the three sketches, but with the seed pearls and under-stated headpiece and train, it was easily the most elegant. "If you wouldn't mind, I'd like to take all the measurements now, while you're here." She was ecstatic knowing she'd actually get to give her friend the gift.

"That's fine because the sooner you begin the sewing, the sooner I'll have my beautiful gown."

After the measurements were taken and written down, the two friends spent the remainder of the afternoon having a grand time. They discussed fabric choices, how soon the gown might be done, and Mariah's future plans.

"I've no idea, what I'll do, but I can't stay with Aunt Libby forever, nor will I be returning to my mother."

"You are going to stay in Philadelphia, how-ever?"

"I suppose, but I'm really not certain about that either."

"In the very bottom of your heart, Mariah Cooper, what do you wish for?"

Mariah went silent and thought about the reply. They'd shared dreams their entire lives, so she felt safe in admitting aloud for the first time, "I'd like to own my own shop, but preferably in a place far away."

Disappointment filled Kaye's face.

Mariah called her on the reaction. "You asked for the truth, Kathleen."

"I did, didn't I. I'm sorry. I just can't imagine life away from you is all. Is there anything else?"

There was. "Yes, to meet a man who won't mind my 'Witch Hazel' eyes, and who'll love me just as much as your Carson loves you."

Kaye studied her silently. "Then that is what you shall have," she stated firmly.

Mariah chuckled and rolled her eyes.

"Don't doubt. I'm your best friend and I get to declare such things. You've had a horrid, rotten life up until now, and my love for you as a sister will make all you want yours."

"Then I shall thank you in advance," Mariah answered with a hint of sarcasm.

Kay tossed back with a smile. "What you desire is going to be yours. Just wait and see."

Mariah would take the advice, but she wouldn't hold her breath.

When it came time for Kaye to leave, they shared a strong hug and Mariah whispered, "Thank you for your friendship all these years, Kaye. And for always braving my mother to come and visit, and never once calling me Witch Hazel."

Kaye hugged her tightly. "You're welcome."

They stepped out of the embrace and Kaye admitted, "To be truthful, I always wanted eyes just like yours."

"Are you daft? Why?"

"They're different, exotic-looking. They make you stand out."

"I'd rather have good old normal brown. Thank you very much."

"You have what you have, and you'll find a man who'll love them."

Again, Mariah didn't plan on holding her breath. She walked Kaye to the door, and once her friend was gone, Mariah felt better than she had in a very long time.

For the next few weeks she threw herself into making the wedding gown. To aid her efforts, Aunt Libby gifted her with a brand-spanking-new sewing machine from the Singer Company. There was a machine at her mother's shop, but it was so ancient and in such disrepair, Mariah swore she spent more time repairing it than she did using it to sew. But the new one ran like a dream.

One evening while Mariah sat sewing the seed pearls to the gown's skirt, her aunt sat nearby reading the *Tribune*. "Your Tillman's wedding announcement is here."

"He isn't *my* Tillman," she countered, not looking up.

"Says here the girl is from a very prominent Boston family. Her name's Leola Franklin."

"I hope they'll be happy and I'm sure Mrs. Porter is very pleased."

Libby smiled and turned to the next page. She read silently for a few minutes, then asked, "How would you like to live in California?"

This time she glanced her aunt's way.

"There's an advertisement here. A fine Coloured gentleman is seeking a housekeeper."

"And?"

"You could go work for him and save up enough to get that shop you say you want to open. From everything I've read, California is becoming quite the draw, even for people of the race. Their schools are no longer lawfully segregated and there are people who own quite large parcels of land."

Mariah mulled over the idea but quickly dismissed it. "I'm sure he doesn't want an unmarried woman."

"So, you claim you're a widow. Who would be the wiser? Most women can clean house, but few possess your needle skills. Being able to make him shirts and trousers would put you at the top of the list, I'd be willing to bet."

"But all the way to California, and to lie?"

"You've been saying you want to travel and see other places, so why not California, and lying about being a widow isn't going to send you to Hades, Mariah."

Mariah continued to harbor doubts, but asked, "How do I let him know I'm interested? Is there an address?"

"It says here to wire a Mrs. Yates in Sacramento."

"May I think it over?"

"Of course, but I wouldn't tarry. This says Mrs. Yates will pay for the train ticket, so I'm certain she'll have more women applying for the position than she'll know what to do with."

"Does it say who the gentleman is?"

"No, but maybe it's her father or a brother." Libby shrugged.

That evening as Mariah prepared for bed, she thought about the advertisement. The only thing she knew for sure about California was that it had gold and was thousands of miles away. She didn't particularly like lying, but as her aunt stated, it was just a small one, and she had longed for a new place to start life over, so why not California? Yes, she'd miss Kaye, but she'd be married soon, and their friendship would have to play second fiddle even if Mariah stayed in Philadelphia. In reality, she was a bit afraid of making such a bold move. Having never had to negotiate life on her own, she didn't know if she had what it took to do so. However, the offer seemed to call out to her, and she was at a point where something in that vein was needed. Moving such a long distance wasn't something to take lightly, but she decided to give it a bit more thought and revisit the idea in a few days.

But two days later, her aunt entered the bedroom she'd allowed Mariah to turn into a sewing room and handed Mariah a narrow envelope. "Your train ticket to California."

Stunned, she looked from the ticket to her smiling aunt. "But I haven't sent the telegram."

"I did. I didn't want this opportunity to pass you by."

"Sounds more like you're trying to get rid of me," Mariah countered with amusement.

"Sounds more like having a niece I can train out to visit in California."

"What did you tell Mrs. Yates about me?"

"That you are young and strong, educated, and lost your husband in a carriage accident. I also touted your sewing skills, and called you one of the best needlewomen in the city, which is the truth. I also told her you'd been employed by me for the past two years and are an excellent employee."

Mariah was a bit overwhelmed.

"She has given you thirty days to get your business affairs in order here, and will expect you in Sacramento at the end of next month."

She was even more overwhelmed. "But Kaye's gown."

"I suggest you get it finished because you are on your way to California, dear niece."

Mariah spent the next week putting the finishing touches on the wedding gown. She was glad she'd started it early because once it was done and presented to the bride to be, she had time to whip up a few new serviceable skirts and blouses for herself as well.

On the day before she was due to leave, she gathered her courage and went to pay a call on her mother to say good-bye. If her new life in California worked out the way she hoped, Mariah had no inkling as to when she might return to Philadelphia, if ever.

The familiar tinkle of the bell above the shop's door announced her arrival. Her mother hurried out to greet what she thought would be a customer. Her smile faded at the sight of Mariah. "What do you want?"

"I'm traveling to California in the morning to take a job as a housekeeper, and I've come to say good-bye."

"Then go on with you, you ungrateful bitch."

She spat the last words as if they were fire and they burned Mariah as if they were. Taking in a deep breath while reminding herself this might be the last time they'd ever speak, she said quietly, "Aunt Libby told me the truth about my father— that he didn't die."

"He did die!" she snapped. "He was swept overboard on one of those ships and left me here alone to raise his lazy, witch-eyed git who was more trouble than she was ever worth."

"I'm sorry for your pain, Mother."

"Be sorry for yourself. Go on to California or wherever the hell you're going and don't ever come back here again. You understand?"

"Yes, I do."

For a short moment they stared into each other's eyes. Mariah had no idea what her mother saw reflected in hers but in Bernice's, Mariah saw anger, pain, and what appeared to be grief and loss. "If you ever need—"

"I'll never need anything from you. Now, get out!"

Mariah didn't have to be told twice.

Outside, she climbed back into Libby's carriage and saw the concern lining her aunt's face. Taking a moment to wipe at the tears forming in the corners of her eyes, Mariah whispered, "That certainly went well."

"At least you tried," Libby offered assuringly. "And it's certainly more than she deserved."

Mariah agreed, but still, her heart ached for what might have been.

The next morning, Mariah was accompanied to the train station by Libby and Kaye. Hugs were shared as were tears, but Mariah was admittedly excited about the adventure ahead.

Eyes wet, Kaye stated, "Make sure you write to me just as soon as you can, and thank you so much for my beautiful gown. I do wish you were coming back to stand up with me."

Mariah wished the same but doubted she'd have the money saved to do so, nor did she envision Mrs. Yates allowing her take the time off after only a few months of employment.

Libby said, "Wire me when you arrive, so that I'll know you got there safely."

"I promise."

The train's whistle blew. It was time to depart. She gave the two women who meant so much to her another fierce hug. Having already sent her trunks to the baggage car, she stepped aboard. Through another round of tears, she blew them a kiss and went to find her seat.

Chapter 4

As the whistle sounded and the train slowly pulled out of the station, Mariah was filled with mixed emotions. On one hand, she was embarking on a new life, but on the other, leaving her mother under such acrimonious circumstances continued to resonate with sadness. Would they ever reconcile, or live apart until death? In spite of all the pain and heartache she'd suffered, Mariah tried to remain optimistic, even though she knew her mother held no such feelings.

For the rest of the morning, the train made the trek across the state of Pennsylvania before crossing the border into Ohio. The conductor said the cross-country trip to Sacramento could take as many as five days; what with stops to pick up passengers in places like Chicago, St. Louis, and Denver, the possibilities of inclement weather, engine failures, derailments, and accidents with livestock on the tracks, travel time could be increased to a week. Mariah wasn't looking forward to being stuck in her seat that long, but was grateful the conductor wasn't enforcing Jim Crow, otherwise she might've been forced to pass the time in the end of the train with the cattle or with questionable men with pipes and cigars in the smoking car.

While the train chugged along, she took out her embroidery hoop to keep busy. She also gazed out her window and wondered about the people on the farms and in the towns they passed. Were they content with their lives? Did they have dreams of adventure, too? Were any of them estranged from their parent? She had no answers.

By the time they took on more passengers in Chicago and pulled away from the station, it was full dark. Although Mariah'd had no seat mate upon leaving Philadelphia, she was now joined by a tiny, dark-skinned older woman who got on with a large number of brown shopping bags. She introduced herself. "I'm Mrs. Daisy Stanton. Was in Chicago visiting my cousin."

"I'm Mariah Cooper. Pleased to meet you, Mrs. Stanton."

"Same here. Where are you traveling to?"

"California."

"Ah, the only state in the Union named for a Black woman."

Mariah stilled.

Mrs. Stanton gave her a kind smile. "You look surprised."

"I am. I never heard of such a thing."

"Few outside of the state have. I'm a native of California and taught school there for many years. Live with my daughter in Denver now. I'll tell you all about Queen Calafia in the morning. Too tired right now, so I'll bid you good night, Mariah."

"Good night, ma'am."

A few seconds later, her eyes closed, leaving a very stunned Mariah to try and find sleep as well.

The following morning, true to her word, Daisy told Mariah about the Black queen the state of California was named for.

"She was written about in a book back in the fifteen hundreds titled, *Las sergas de Esplandian*, which in English means, 'The Adventures of Esplandian.' Its stories of Calafia and her island of gold are what many believe first brought the Spanish conquistadores to our shores."

"She wasn't a real woman was she?"

"No, dear, but the world would be less exciting were it not for myths, don't you think?"

Mariah had been given a limited education, and so had no idea how to answer that, but apparently Daisy didn't need a reply, because she launched into the telling with a gusto that kept Mariah riveted for miles. The tales of warfare waged by the queen, her army of Amazon warriors, her battle-trained griffins and fleets of ships, were interspersed with historical truths about the first Spanish explorers, particularly a Black Spaniard by the name of Estabanico. He, along with Cabeza de Vaca wandered from Florida to the Southwest on a seven-year journey that laid the foundation for the explorers that followed them. "I always told my students that Estabanico was the first man of African descent to set foot in America."

After hearing more about Queen Calafia being captured during a battle in Constantinople, Mariah asked, "What happened to her?"

"She converted to Christianity and married a Spanish knight, but she and her army eventually returned to California for more adventures."

Mariah sat back, satisfied. She didn't know what impressed her more: hearing about the Black queen's exciting adventures, or Daisy's knowledge of all things California. Thanks to further stories, Mariah learned about the Black forty-niners, and that both slaves and free men panned for gold; Jim Beckwourth, who discovered a pass through the Sierras that bears his name and who was also a member of the Bear Flag Party; William Leidesdorff, who operated the first steamship in San Francisco Bay and was so wealthy and influential he was appointed American vice consul to Mexico under President Taft; and the fascinating Biddy Mason.

"She came to California as the slave of a Mormon man named Smith," Daisy explained. "And in fifty-five, Mr. Smith decided he wanted to move to Texas and take his slaves with him. Biddy brought suit against him in court and won freedom not only for herself but for many other Mormon slaves as well."

"And after she won her freedom?"

"She worked as a housekeeper and a nurse, and eventually became one of the wealthiest women of any color in the city of Los Angeles. Her efforts to provide schooling for youngsters of our race is still celebrated to this day."

Mariah was very glad Daisy chose to sit next to her. She'd learned a lot. "You must have been a very good schoolteacher."

"I like to think I was."

"Thank you so much."

"You are most welcome."

"I'll miss you when you get off in Denver."

"I'll miss you as well. Not many young people will allow an old hen like me to ramble on for hours about the past."

Mariah didn't think it was rambling at all. "I enjoyed myself."

And when the train reached the Denver station, she and Daisy shared their good-byes and a content Mariah settled in for the rest of the ride to Sacramento.

A weary Mariah stepped off the train in Sacramento after nearly a week of travel, and the wealth of people rushing back and forth caught her by surprise. She knew California was home to a large number of people but she hadn't expected the crowds to rival the ones back East. She saw a few women, but most of the passersby were men, and were of a variety of races. Black, European, Spanish. There were even a few Chinese; the first she'd ever seen, and she did her best not to stare their way like a country girl at her first fair. Myriad conversations assailed her from all sides and were in so many different languages she wondered if the train had somehow deposited her in a foreign country.

It was wonderful. The hustle and bustle and the new surroundings competed with her excitement of being in a new place. Some of the men passing by smiled and tipped their hats. She returned their greeting with polite but terse nods. Libby warned her not to encourage strange men, lest they think her fast.

Instead she trained her attention on the area beside the idling train in an effort to search out the porter she'd tipped in advance to retrieve and deliver her two trunks. Since he had yet to return, she began to worry that he'd simply taken her coin and gone on about his business, but he suddenly appeared pushing a small handcart holding her trunks.

"Here you go miss. Do you want them sent on? What house will you be working in?"

"I'm to be employed by a Mrs. Yates."

"Yates," he echoed. "Don't know a pleasure house run by a Yates."

Pleasure house! It took all Mariah had not to faint right there on the spot. She had such difficulty breathing and her heart pounded so hard in her chest, she was certain everyone in the depot could hear it. The porter had mistaken her for a woman of ill repute! She supposed he'd made the assumption because she was traveling without a companion, but it was 1885. Women were making all kinds of strides toward equality. Surely dressed in her smart gray traveling ensemble she didn't resemble a prostitute! When she finally calmed enough to draw in a steady breath, she told him, "She lives near Guinda. Someone's supposed to meet me here."

"I didn't know the Coloreds up there had a pleasure house."

"I am not a pleasure woman," she gritted out. She'd had just about enough of this conversation.

His face beeted up. "I'm so sorry, miss. Most of the girls traveling alone—I—"

"Thank you for bringing my trunks. I'll manage from here. I don't wish to keep you from your duties any longer."

He left her trunks on the hand truck and beat a hasty retreat. She was happy to see him go. According to the wire she'd received from Mrs. Yates, someone from the household would be meeting her, but Mariah had no idea who it might be, or how she might go about locating the person. Then she heard one of the porters calling her name in the singsong manner used by street vendors selling ice or vegetables. "Mrs. Mariah Cooper. Looking for Mrs. Mariah Cooper."

"Here!" she called and waved her gloved hand so she could be seen in the crowded station.

The porter waved back. Walking beside him was a tall, wide-shouldered man. From the dime novels she often peeked in at the lending library, she knew the brimmed hat on his head was a Stetson. His brown suit had a western cut. The short heels on his fancy black boots increased his already towering height. He had a long commanding stride and an even more ruggedly handsome brown face.

"Are you Mrs. Mariah Cooper?" the giant asked while paying the porter, who took the tip and melted away.

"Yes, I am." In spite of the sea of people flowing around them, Mariah felt alone with the big man and his cool, assessing brown eyes.

"Do you ride?" he asked.

"A horse?"

"Yes, a horse," he replied in a tone that made it sound as if her question had been an ignorant one.

"No."

He didn't bother masking his displeasure, which caused her to point out, "In Philadelphia we ride trolleys, or we walk."

"Can you drive a buggy?"

"No."

Muted impatience showed on his face in response and he didn't bother hiding that either.

"Your name, sir?"

"Logan Yates."

"Thank you."

Logan wasn't sure what to make of this short, terse woman who seemed to question his manners for not introducing himself. She was certainly not the older, spinsterish female he'd expected to be meeting. She was wearing a pert little hat, and dressed in a dove gray traveling dress with a long-sleeved, formfitting bodice that emphasized her nice curves. A thin line of white lace peeked above the high collar and across her wrists. Arresting gold eyes were set in a light brown face that could only be described as beautiful. She certainly didn't look like any housekeeper he'd ever seen. "Welcome to California."

"Thank you."

Prim, he thought, but the feline gold eyes and the ripe mouth, in tandem with the curves, exuded something else entirely. Sensuality wafted from her like the arousing notes of a heady perfume. Shaking himself free from thoughts of what it might be like to slowly open all those buttons marching between her breasts and sample the glory inside, he returned to the matter at hand. "Those your trunks?"

She nodded.

"Then let's head out. Buggy's parked over there."

Pushing the handcart holding her trunks, Logan led her away, all the while thinking she wouldn't be staying. The widow Mariah Cooper was way too citified to take on the job she'd been hired for.

Hell, she couldn't even ride a horse. By his estimation, once she got a gander at the state of his place, she'd be on her way back to the train and to Philadelphia real quick, which suited him just fine.

"I need to send a telegraph to my aunt to let her know I've arrived safely. Is there an office near the station?"

Logan wasn't pleased with her request because it would further delay the long ride back, but from her stance it was obvious she didn't care how he felt. "This way."

Once her business with the telegraph agent was accomplished and her trunks loaded in the bed of the buckboard, he helped her to climb up and was lured by the soft sway of her skirt. That aside, it had been his hope she'd be able to drive the wagon so he could spend the four-hour ride home to Destiny on horseback instead of on his ass on the decidedly uncomfortable seat. Being a horseman, he preferred the familiar comfort of a saddle. Resigned, he cast a longing look at his stallion, Diablo, trailered to the back of the wagon, then took his seat. Glancing her way and receiving an unflinching gold-eyed response, he slapped the reins and guided the team away from the depot.

After leaving the train station they headed east, and soon the land opened up like a banquet for the eyes. There were mountains in the distance, the first Mariah'd ever seen. Living in Philadelphia, with its bevy of buildings, she was unaccustomed to seeing so much open sky and she found it enthralling. She had many questions about the surroundings and where they were heading, but Yates didn't seem to be in a conversational mood, so she settled for enjoying the beautiful scenery.

"Lived in Philadelphia all your life?"

"Yes." That he was actually speaking to her after nearly an hour of silence was pleasing. "And you? Were you born in California?"

"No, Texas. Parents came here to work the mines right after I was born."

"The gold mines?"

"Yes."

Natural curiosity compelled her to ask if they'd struck it rich, but she was too polite and well-mannered for that. Instead she focused her attention on the large birds lazily gliding overhead. Having no experience with wildlife she didn't know what they were, but their winged soaring was fascinating.

"Are there eagles in Philadelphia?" he asked.

"Is that what those are?"

"Yes."

She tracked the flight. "I've no idea. I've never seen one before."

He shook his head.

"Are you always so judgmental?"

He glanced over. "Meaning?"

"Well, first, you were unhappy about my inability to ride a horse or drive a buggy, and now, you seem to be finding fault with my ignorance of eagles."

"You always speak your mind?"

"I do." Or at least, she planned to. She never wanted to be browbeaten or walked on by anyone ever again. A new life called for a new Mariah, and although it might be considered silly to emulate a myth, she wanted to be as formidable as the warrior Queen Calafia.

"A woman out here needs to know how to ride."

"And if she doesn't, is it expected that she learn before she leaves the train station?" Eyebrow raised, she waited for his counter. If he had one he didn't voice it.

Instead, his attention back on the team, he asked, "Your late husband like your feistiness?"

A small wave of panic roiled her insides. "Yes, he did," she lied.

"How long have you been widowed?"

"Almost three years." It occurred to her that maybe she should've worked out the details on her fictional marriage and widowhood beforehand, but she hadn't anticipated being questioned about what is normally considered a private matter, at least back East. She thought it best to change the subject. "Mrs. Yates didn't inform me who'd I'd be employed by."

"Me."

She went weak. He settled his eyes on her just long enough to show dry amusement before concentrating on his driving again. "Mrs. Yates is my *madrastra*, my stepmother."

"I see."

"I have two younger brothers, Andrew and Noah."

"Do they live with you, too?"

"No."

"Are you married?"

He shook his head. "Not looking to either. You planning on marrying again?"

"I doubt I'd meet another man as honorable as my Henry, so no." There, she'd given her mythical husband a name. "How much farther do we have to travel?"

"About three hours."

"That long?"

"Be considerably shorter if you knew how to ride."

Suppressing a snarl, she ignored him in favor of taking in the impressive view and the expansive sky.

They'd been on the road for close to two hours. They'd driven past a few farms and large fenced-in fields, which assured her that although it appeared as if Yates was escorting her to the middle of nowhere, there were other people around. However, she'd yet to see anything resembling a town or an inn. She needed to use the facilities.

Wondering how he might react if she asked that he stop somewhere convenient, she gave him a quick glance.

"Problem?" he asked.

Mariah had no idea how to ask a man about something so personal.

"Thought you always spoke your mind."

Determined not to rise to the bait, she replied calmly, "If you could stop someplace convenient where I might use the facilities, I'd be ever so grateful."

He hauled back on the reins and the two horse team halted. "Trees over there look like a good spot."

Mariah first took in the thick stand of trees he'd indicated, then him. Surely he must've misunderstood her request. However, as she met his unreadable features, it dawned on her that he hadn't misunderstood. He actually expected her to . . . in the trees!

"Not trying to embarrass you or anything," he told her, "but this is the way it is out here in open country. And the longer you wait to decide, the longer it's going to take us to get where we need to be, Mrs. Cooper."

There was something about him that made her think he was enjoying this, and that set her to simmering again. She understood they were in open country, but where she hailed from, people, and especially women, did not use trees. Doing so not only subjected you to public disdain and ridicule, it could also get you hauled before a magistrate and fined.

"Your decision?"

The light of humor in his eyes made her want to sock him right in the nose. "The trees will suffice."

He came around to help her down. Hoping her fiery glare would reduce him to ash, Mariah politely took his hand only to have him swing her down and set her on her feet before him. Surprise warred with her temper, while odd unnamed feelings washed over her from standing close enough to feel his body heat mingle with her own.

He looked down. "I'll wait here."

"I most certainly hope so." Mortified beyond belief, she marched to the trees.

"Keep an eye out for snakes!"

She stopped, stared back and after shooting him a quelling look, resumed her march.

Upon her return, he was leaning leisurely against the wagon. "Better?"

She couldn't believe he'd asked her that. "Don't you know anything about being a gentleman, Mr. Yates?"

"From your squawking you obviously don't think I do, so what did I do wrong, now?"

Before she could reply, he picked her up and held her aloft for an inordinate amount of time before slowly depositing her back on the seat. The warmth of his hands on her waist meandered fleetingly up her spine. Fighting off the effects, or attempting to, she managed to find her wits. "A gentleman never asks a lady something so personal."

"I'm a rancher. Spend my time breaking horses and shoveling manure. Never had time for gentleman's finishing school."

She closed her eyes and counted to ten. How on earth was she going to work for this insufferable man?

"What are you doing?"

"Counting to ten."

He actually chuckled. "Does a gentleman ask why?"

She opened her eyes. "Only if a gentleman wants to see a lady lose her religion and begin speaking in tongues."

He folded his arms and surveyed her with a smile teasing his full lips. "You're pretty plucky for a city woman."

"I'll take that as a compliment. Now, are we going to finish this journey or not?"

"Bossy, too."

"Thank you."

He climbed back up to his seat and without uttering another word, set the team in motion.

Logan grudgingly admitted that he liked her. He rarely ran into women capable of giving back as good as they got. Most seemed content to simper and twitter, especially in his presence. There was no simpering or twittering in this one. Her pluck made him wonder who'd worn the pants in her marriage. No getting around her beauty though— gorgeous as a morning sunrise. With the dearth of eligible women in the area, every man within fifty miles would come calling on her and her feline gold eyes, but it wouldn't matter because he was pretty sure she wouldn't be staying.

Mariah spotted a large gray boulder on the side of the road. It appeared to have writing chiseled into the surface. "What's that?"

"Locals call it Owl Rock."

"What's its purpose?"

"New settlers in the area carve their names into it when they arrive in the county."

She found that to be very interesting. "Can we stop, so I may see it?" To her surprise he did, and walked around to her side of the wagon. Again, his hands found her waist and swung her down. As he set her on her feet, that same smoke life feeling returned. Something about him was attracting her, even though it was the last thing in the world she wanted. "If you'd just offer me your hand, I can get down on my own."

He folded his arms and studied her before saying, "I'll try and remember that."

Breaking away from the invisible hold of his gaze, she walked over to the boulder. It was necessary for her to peer close in order to make out the names: Logan, Henderson, Haskell, and others. Many were coupled with dates, which she assumed were when the people arrived. "Would it be all right if I added my initials?"

"Let's get to the ranch first. I can always bring you back if you decide to stay on."

Mariah thought that was an odd thing for him to say, but she didn't challenge him. Instead she walked with him back to the wagon. He offered her a hand so she could climb back up. She told herself she wasn't affected by the warmth of his grasp, but it was a lie. "Thank you."

"Trying to be a gentleman."

She shook her head but said nothing as they resumed their journey.

"Is there a church in the area?"

"Yes. It's Baptist."

"Do you attend?"

"No."

He'd spoken the word so succinctly, she didn't ask him why.

They were now within hailing distance of the ranch, and Logan thought over how he wanted to proceed. No sense in stopping by Alanza's first. He'd take her by his place, and once she saw the mess inside, she could go to Alanza and cry off. "We'll be coming up on the ranch in a few minutes. I'll take you by my place first. If you decide you don't want to take the job, you can spend the night with my stepmother and I'll get one of the hands to take you back to the train in the morning."

"Why wouldn't I stay?" Her tone was as cool as the golden she-cat eyes.

"Place needs a lot of work. Once you get a good look at it you may not want to take it on."

"I see." Mariah sensed he was attempting to scare her off. He'd already made it clear that he found her unsuitable, but he must have straw for brains if he thought she'd made the long journey across the continent just to run back to Philadelphia. No matter how hard the work proved to be, it would be a cakewalk compared to putting up with him.

Thoughts of their ongoing battle were soon set aside as he guided the team through a set of tall wrought-iron posts that had to have been created by an artisan of great skill. Worked into the pillars were roses, horses, cattle, and elaborate Christian crosses. Emblazoned across the front of the arch over the gate were the large scrolled letters *DESTINO*. She wanted to ask him for an interpretation, but the team propelled the wagon forward.

"Welcome to Destiny."

She assumed that was the English translation of the word on the gate, but before she could ask or acknowledge his welcome, her attention was caught by a large sprawling house ahead. Philadelphia had some grand homes, but this beautiful place surpassed anything she'd ever seen. It was two stories and constructed of stone and wood. On the upper portion were a series of verandahs made of the same fine ironwork as the posts at the entrance. At ground level and set out off to the left was more ironwork encasing a courtyard bursting with colorful flowers and shrubs.

"My stepmother's home," he explained as the wagon rumbled past on the narrow unpaved road. "Her family originally owned this part of the ranch. My father owned the portion I live on. We combined both places when I was young."

"It's very lovely." The courtyard led to a breezeway covered by a long stone roof whose length continued across a series of low-slung connected buildings.

"I've never seen a house built this way."

"Alanza's Spanish."

That surprised her because she just assumed his stepmother would be a woman of the race. They were now past the house, and the land on either side of the road opened up as it had upon leaving the train station. Up ahead, mountains loomed in the distance, but the immediate area was grassland as green as jewels. She saw horses and a small herd of cattle and men on horseback tending to both. She spied orchards and a small group of workers moving among the trees.

"What do you grow in the orchards?"

"Lemons, oranges, a few apples."

"Lemons?"

"Yes. They grow on trees."

She held on to her temper. "I'm aware of that. I've just never seen any before." Near the orchards, was a field of staked, squat, treelike plantings that were also unfamiliar. "And those?"

"Vineyards."

"Grapes?"

"Yes."

She'd seen grapes growing back home, but those vines bore very little resemblance to this California version. Things were certainly different. "How much farther?"

"Just over the next rise."

"This is quite a change from Philadelphia, with all its buildings." The quiet was noticeable as well. No vendors hawking wares or trolleys rumbling over tracks, no streets filled with people and voices. She wondered how long it might take her to get used to the quiet and the slower pace.

A house came into view that she supposed was his. Like his stepmother's, it, too, was made of stone and wood, but it had only one level. The outside appeared tidy enough, so she couldn't imagine what it was about the interior that had him so convinced she wouldn't stay. Near the house were corrals and barns and mounted men moving between them. A small group of men in boots, vests, and hats sat perched on the rungs of one of the corrals. From the loud hoots and yells, she assumed they were engaged in something, but she was too far away to make out what.

He must've seen the questions on her face. "They're breaking horses for sale."

And at that moment, a rider on a horse popped into view. His jumping and twisting mount seemed to be trying to unseat him. Just when she thought the man might stay in the saddle, he was sent flying through the air and her hand flew to her mouth in dismay. He landed on the ground inside the corral. The angry horse charged him, but he scrambled to his feet and cleared the short fence a second later. The other men laughed at his plight while the horse raced around bellowing with rage. Mariah had no idea what to make of it. A glance over at her employer showed his amusement.

"This is how you break a horse?" she asked, her eyes still on the beautiful, angry horse trying to find a way out of the confining corral.

"One of the ways."

The wagon caught the attention of the men and upon seeing her they went still. Mariah felt self-conscious under their quiet regard.

"They'll want to meet you, but we'll wait until later, unless that's ungentlemanly, too."

"Are you always so trying?"

He smiled. "Always."

The men were still watching.

"Back to work," he called over. "You'll meet her later."

He jumped down. When he came around to her side, she said firmly, "Again, I prefer to step down on my own, if you don't mind." She didn't want to be gossiped about before she even crossed his threshold. Nor did she care to be swept up like a sack of flour or worse, his paramour.

He complied. Still cognizant of the men's curious eyes, she followed Yates to the door and inside.

Chapter 5

The unpleasant smell assaulted her first. She'd smelled chicken coops more fragrant, but the acrid order was quickly eclipsed by the sheer size of the unholy mess spread out before her, and for just a moment her knees weakened as she slowly took it all in. Piled-up boots, horse blankets, trousers, union suits, and tin plates competed for space with coils of rope, rain slickers and a multitude of other items so unfamiliar she didn't even know their names, let alone their purpose. The windows and walls were dirty, and she had no idea if the floor was carpeted or bare wood. A pointed look behind her showed Yates standing with his arms folded, his face again unreadable. "I see why you need a housekeeper, but someone with kennel experience might be more appropriate."

He stiffened in response, giving her a modicum of satisfaction. She removed the pins from her hat and took it off, but held on to it because there was no clear space to set it down. "Why is all this in here and not in say, a barn?"

"Bunkhouse burned down a year ago. Barns are full of barn implements, so I had the hands move their gear in here."

"So is the new bunkhouse nearly finished?"

"Haven't had time to start it." Once again, his eyes offered no discernible reaction.

"I see."

Logan figured in about thirty seconds, she'd be hiking up her fancy skirts and hightailing it back to Sacramento. No way was a city woman like her going to tackle such a mess. He watched as she continued her survey.

"How many hands are in your employ?"

"Six, full time." Alanza wasn't going to be pleased when told the housekeeper fled the place like her slips were on fire.

"I'll take the job."

He froze.

"I'd like to get started as soon as possible. May I see the rest of the house?"

It took a few seconds for his brain to move. "What?"

"I said, I'll take the job."

"Why?" This was not going the way he'd assumed.

"I didn't travel all this way just to turn around and go home again, Mr. Yates."

"But." He snapped his mouth shut.

"Your home is a sty, but it can be righted. Now, will you kindly show me around, please."

The determination in her gaze made him contemplate her silently before grudgingly surrendering. "Kitchen's that way."

They waded through the chaos toward the

kitchen. She tripped over a bed frame, and had he not reached out and kept her upright, she would've fallen.

"Thank you," she responded, sounding not at all pleased by the misstep.

For unknown reasons, his irritation rose upon seeing the disapproval on her beautiful face. She was judging him by the chaotic mess, and although she had a right to, he didn't care for it.

The kitchen was no better. A battered armoire leaned against the ancient stove and dilapidated cold box. He seemed to notice for the first time how scarred and beat-up everything was.

"And these holes in the cabinets? Moths?"

He shot her a look. "Gunshots."

"Interesting. Were you under attack?"

"No. Horseplay and whiskey."

"I see. Does that stove work?"

"No." And hadn't in over a year.

She exhaled audibly. "What other duties do you anticipate me handling?"

"Cooking and laundry."

"Then I assume you'll be purchasing a working stove."

"Yes," he replied tightly.

"Good." She made her way over to the cabinets and looked inside at the three chipped plates and two dented metal tumblers. "I take it you've been eating elsewhere."

"Most of the time, yes."

"If I'm to cook for you, we'll need proper china and tableware."

He watched her take in the dirty windows.

"What other rooms do I need to see?"

"Bathing room. Follow me."

He escorted her down a hallway that led to the rear of the house. He decided that not only was she bossy, she was bossy and demanding. Proper china indeed.

Judging by all she'd seen so far, were Mariah a less formidable woman she'd already be making plans to return to Philadelphia as quickly as possible. Cleaning this place and putting it into some semblance of order was going to be an undertaking of Herculean proportions. Inside the bathing room now, she glanced around at the large space with its pedestal sink, water closet and huge claw-foot tub. "You have indoor plumbing."

"Yes."

After her encounter with the trees she was grateful for that boon. "And that door over there leads where?"

"My bedroom."

He appeared to be waiting for some kind of reaction from her but she gave him nothing. She pulled off her gloves. "We'll be sharing this bathing room?"

"For now."

She wasn't happy with that, but seeing as there

was nothing to be done, she set her feelings aside. "Where to next?"

"My study."

As they entered she looked around.

"You seem surprised," he observed.

"I am. The bookcases actually hold books, as opposed to, say, socks and dirty shirts."

It was clear he hadn't appreciated the dig, but she saw no reason for him to be offended by the truth. "And where will my room be? Mrs. Yates said she preferred I live in."

Her room was in the back of the house. It was small and blessedly clear of clutter. The only furnishings were a bed and a chest of drawers. Mariah walked over to a door on the back wall. Easing it open she found it led outside to a small fenced-in courtyard that held a small wooden bench. Pleased by that, she closed it again and surveyed her sparsely furnished room. "Would it be possible to have a sitting chair in here, and a lamp?"

"I'll see what Alanza has in storage."

"Thank you. Now, would you be so kind as to bring in my trunks?"

He left her, and Mariah stepped out into the little courtyard again. By all the cigar butts and cheroot tails littering the ground, she guessed the space was used by him and his men. The area needed cleaning, but once that was accomplished, the bench would provide a nice spot to catch her breath after a long day, or to work on her drawings. The magnificent view of the mountains and the low border of tall pines was breathtaking. She could hear the men over at the corral but she supposed at night there's nothing but echoing silence. Definitely something she would have to get accustomed to.

She heard him return and so stepped back inside. "Thank you. I'd like to begin cleaning up the front parlor first thing in the morning. Will it be possible for you to have everything removed by then?"

"No."

"Why not?"

"I've a ranch to run and we're busy at the moment. You take some time writing up a list of things you think you'll be needing to do whatever it is you plan to do, and the hands and I will begin moving things in a few days."

"I already know what I need, Mr. Yates."

"Then take a few days to get your sea legs under you. I'm sure you're tired from the long train ride."

"Don't you want the house cleared out and cleaned?"

"I do, but on my schedule."

"Ah. And if our schedules don't coincide?"

"We go with mine."

"You're determined to lock horns with me?"

"No, you're determined to lock horns with me,

so rest up for now, and when you're ready we'll visit my stepmother and have some supper."

"Do you lock horns with her, too?"

"Often."

Stalemate.

"Let me know when you're ready, Mrs. Cooper."

As he left her alone, Mariah wondered if there was a cure for male arrogance. Apparently, she'd traded one tyrant for another, but as she'd noted on the ride over, she had no plans to revert to her formerly spineless self. It was quite obvious that Logan Yates was accustomed to throwing his weight around and bowling people over with it. And yes, the train ride had taken a lot out of her, but this house needed immediate attention if for no other reason than to rid it of the smell, which was wafting all the way back to her little room. His assumptions to the contrary, she wasn't afraid of work and she certainly wasn't afraid of him. Filled with determination, she changed out of her traveling ensemble and into one of her older blouses and skirts. Once that was done, she tied on an apron, put on her imaginary Queen Calafia crown and went to wage war on his fouled excuse of a home.

Outside, Logan walked over to the corral. Laying down the law to the bossy widow felt good. She worked for him, not the other way around.

Eli Braden was the first to speak up. "Well?"

"Says she's staying, and wants us to start clearing the parlor. Told her I was too busy at the moment. Maybe in a couple of days."

"She as pretty up close as she looked from here?"

The level gaze that greeted the remark made Eli grin. "Guess the answer's yes."

Logan refused to acknowledge that she was one of the most beautiful women he'd ever seen. The golden eyes and full mouth had already branded themselves in his mind's eye. "Real bossy."

"She'll need that to handle you."

"She's here to clean the place, not order me around."

"You must didn't make that clear enough."

Logan appeared confused by his words, so Eli used his chin to direct his friend to what he was referencing. Logan turned around to see the Widow Cooper dragging a bed frame out the door. He also saw that she'd changed her clothing and was now wearing a sweeping black skirt and a high-necked, long-sleeved blouse that fit snugly over her curves. The wire bed frame was twice her size, and her difficulties in maneuvering it were apparent, but she was persistent and soon had it out on the grass. Wiping her hands on her skirt, she walked determinedly back inside.

"Oh, hell," Logan muttered.

His men didn't bother hiding their amusement.

Out the door she came again, this time, arms

loaded with shirts and denims. She dumped them next to the bed frame and sailed back into the house.

"Once word gets around about her beauty, men will be lined up from here to the Bay to take her off your hands," Eli quipped.

The last thing Logan wanted was his ranch overrun by a bunch of calf-eyed men, but any man loco enough to take her on would regret it, because she was obviously too bossy for her own good, and deaf to boot. Hadn't he just explained that he wanted her to wait for him to decide when the house cleaning would begin?

While he and the hands looked on, she kept up her pace. For the next half hour, the pile of items on the grass grew to include boots, bedding, and other items belonging to him and his men. Finally, she stopped and directed those golden eyes their way. To his surprise, she marched over. Pointedly ignoring Logan, she said, "Gentlemen, my name's Mariah Cooper and I'm the new housekeeper. I'd suggest you come and claim your belongings."

Logan found this cat-eyed woman so unlike any other he'd encountered, he wasn't sure what to do. "And if they don't?" he asked coolly.

She finally looked his way. "Anything still in the pile come morning will be kindling for a bonfire."

Eyes widened.

Logan noticed stripes of what appeared to be

blood on her fingers. He thought about her dragging the metal bed frame. "Did you cut yourself?"

"No."

Bossy and a liar. "Let me see your hands."

"Mr. Yates, I suggest you let me worry about my hands. You should be more concerned with getting the lumber for the new bunkhouse you need to build."

Tamping down his rising temper, he repeated softly and slowly, "Let me see your hands."

Her tightly set face and raised chin challenged him as if she equaled him in both height and weight.

"Show me your hands before I take you over my knee and paddle your fancy little behind."

"You wouldn't dare!"

"Oh, I'd dare," he promised.

The ranch hands eagerly watched the exchange as if the boss and the little lady were acting out a play on the stage.

"Once again, you are no gentleman," she tossed back.

"So you keep reminding me. Show me your hands."

Gold eyes flaring, she presented her blood-stained palms.

He took hold of first one wrist and then the other. "Fool woman. Eli, go and get me something to clean up these cuts."

While he hurried off, she pulled her hands free. "I'm perfectly capable of doing it myself."

"Was it going to be before or after the bonfire?"

Her face said she hadn't cared for that dig.

"You trying to get lockjaw?" he demanded quietly.

Mariah had no idea what lockjaw was, but decided it had to be something he'd made up, until he explained, "You get it from rust in your blood. One of the symptoms is your jaws lock up, which for you might be just the ticket, but many people die from it."

She stared.

The man Eli returned with a small brown pharmacy bottle and some gauze. She reached out to take them only to have Yates take possession of the items first. "Hold out your palms."

"I'm perfectly capable—"

"Yeah, I know. Hold out your hands."

Mariah huffed. Dealing with him was putting her dangerously close to a full blown case of apoplexy, but the challenge in his eyes made her remember his promise to paddle her so-called fancy little behind. That he'd actually carry out the outrageous threat wasn't something she wanted to chance, nor did she want it to be witnessed by his employees, so she thrust out her palms.

He poured a bit of the bottle's liquid content onto a piece of the gauze and to her surprise went about the task gently. But whatever was in the bottle stung more than the cuts themselves. "What is that?"

"Witch hazel."

The irony of that was inescapable, but she held still and let him finish. Eli next handed him a small white tube. The paste inside was gently rubbed on the cuts. Mariah tried to ignore the way her senses fluttered in response to Yates's soft-touched ministrations, and to the dark eyes probing her own.

"Where'd you get all these calluses?" he questioned quietly. The slow slide of his thumb over the toughened skin at the base of her fingers sent her senses into a silent swoon.

"Chopping wood and pumping water since the age of nine."

"For who?"

"My mother. Are you done?" She needed him to release her so she could shake off her disturbing reaction. His touch and nearness were affecting her like no man before, and she didn't know the reason for it or how to douse the odd sensations. He, however, seemed to be still mulling over her reply. She assumed her callused hands didn't jibe with his view of whoever he thought her to be, but she let him think what he wanted because she doubted he'd believe the truth, even if she hit him over the head with it.

He unrolled a length of the gauze, wound it

around her cut palms and tied the ends closed. "Now, stop hauling stuff outside until you heal."

"No. You hired me to do a job, bandaged hands or not."

"I don't know how things are done in Philadelphia, but here, we don't work our women until their hands bleed."

"These little cuts aren't going to make me bleed to death, Mr. Yates. Surely the women here are made of sterner stuff than that."

Logan wondered if she'd ever met an argument she didn't like. The sassy firecracker mouth probably drove her late husband to drink, and it made him wonder if she brought that fire to the marriage bed. He glanced Eli's way and found his partner smiling as if he'd read Logan's mind. "Go back in the house and wait for me. We'll ride over and have dinner with my stepmother in a few minutes."

"Do women usually ask 'how high' whenever you say 'jump,' Mr. Yates?"

He closed his eyes and drew in a deep breath. When he opened them, she was standing there blazing in all her golden, cat-eyed glory. Having had just about enough of her for the moment, he placed his hands on her waist and slowly lifted her up to eye level. "You ever use that mouth for something besides sassing?"

Then he kissed her, and apparently caught her so

off guard, that for just the briefest of moments, she softened, and he tasted the sweetness of her lips. Then her mouth clamped shut like a sprung bear trap, and she went stiff as a board. Thinking he'd bested her, he set her down on her feet. He was feeling pretty superior until she dragged her bandaged hand across her lips like she'd just been kissed by a goat and kicked him hard in his bad knee. Pain spread up his leg and he howled, "Shit!" The explosion of agony had him cursing a blue streak while hopping around like a peg-legged sailor doing a jig.

Eli and the men laughed so hard they almost fell down. She, on the other hand, looking angry enough to spit, spun around and stormed back the way she'd come.

Logan was still cursing, and Eli and the hands were still laughing when she disappeared inside the house.

Mariah was furious. The urge to pace back and forth was thwarted by all the remaining clutter, so she stood there in the middle of the parlor and fumed. How dare he! She wanted to march back outside and kick him again. What an insufferable, arrogant, pigheaded excuse for a man! Any woman in her right mind would throw the job in his face like wet wash and tell him to find someone else, but again, she'd not give him the satisfaction. If he fired her fine, but for now, she was staying, and if she had to kick him from

California to Hades and back again to make that plain, she would.

When she looked up, Eli was standing in the doorway. The grin on his face didn't help her temper. "What?" she demanded.

"Came to help you clear out the parlor. If you got the guts to kick Logan, no telling what you'll do to the rest of us, so thought we'd come give you a hand."

Only then did she see the other men standing behind him. They looked equal parts amused and afraid.

"Thank you," she whispered. She was so grateful, tears stung her eyes. Blinking them back she asked, "And Mr. Yates?"

"Rode off to see Old Man Crane to buy lumber for the new bunkhouse."

And suddenly, sunshine filled Mariah's world. She'd won the first round. She was certain there'd be more battles to come because she and Yates got along like two wet cats in a bag, but she savored her victory and put the ranch hands to work.

Chapter 6

A testy Logan gritted his teeth against the angry throb in his knee as he dismounted and made his way into the office of the lumber mill.

"Why you limping, Logan?" Old Man Crane asked.

"Knee's bothering me."

"The wife's got some liniment up at the house. You want me to fetch you some?"

"No thanks. Just want to put in an order for some board feet so I can get my bunkhouse rebuilt."

"Finally going to get it done, huh? How much you need?"

They spent a few minutes figuring out just how much. Once that was decided and the price agreed upon, they walked back outside and Logan limped over to his stallion with as much dignity as he could.

"You sure you don't want that liniment?"

"Yeah, but thanks again." As he remounted, he fought to keep the ache from showing on his face. "You sure you'll have the lumber ready for me by day after tomorrow?"

"Yep. I'll start running the saw tonight."

"Thanks. I'll send Eli over to haul it back."

"Welcome. Take care of that knee. You get rheumetiz in it and it'll be all she wrote."

Logan nodded, wheeled Diablo around and rode slowly back toward home. Although he was determined not to think about her, his mind was filled with images of the firebrand known as Mariah Cooper. He still found it hard to believe she'd actually kicked him. As he'd noted earlier, most women tittered and batted their eyes when he came around. Not a one ever dragged their hand across their lips after his kiss, or registered their complaint in such a pointed and painfully memorable manner. Admittedly, he'd provoked her, but her provoking him with that sassy, kissable-looking mouth was what set the whole episode in motion to begin with. He had no logical explanation as to why he'd kissed her that way, other than having been driven around the bend by her sassiness. He'd never done anything that insane to a woman before. She was knee-high to a bumblebee and weighed less than his saddle, yet she'd challenged him as if she were one of Queen Calafia's Amazon warriors. Damnedest experience of his life. And now, he was riding back from ordering lumber, something he hadn't even thought about doing when he picked her up at the train station that morning. He didn't want to delve into why he finally put in the order because he was too busy trying to determine when he'd lost control of the situation. One moment, he'd been in charge, and the next . . .

The pain in his knee flared up as if to remind

him just how formidable an opponent she was. And her callused hands? That was a surprise as well. She was a housekeeper, so he hadn't expected her to have the soft unblemished hands of a woman waited upon by servants, as Alanza had before she married his father, but the Cooper woman's hands had been hardened by work—real work, and not just the run-of-the-mill scrubbing of floors or polishing silver. She claimed to have chopped wood and pumped water since an early age. Had there been no men in her family during those years of her life? Had her husband Henry been an invalid, and thus unable to take on the responsibilities usually shouldered by a man? The questions tied to his new housekeeper were stacking up like cords of wood, and he had no answers. What he did know was that he'd underestimated her and he'd be damned if he let it happen again. If she wanted a test of wills, he'd give her one because he refused to be bested by a short whirlwind of a city woman who couldn't even sit a horse.

An hour into clearing the parlor, Mariah was outside adding more items to the pile of belongings when a fancy black coach pulled up. Out stepped a beautiful ivory-skinned woman with shining black hair whose face and attire made Mariah stop and stare. She was wearing a divided black riding skirt, a white ruffle-front blouse with long blowsy sleeves, a short black vest with silver buttons, and fancy black boots also shot through with silver. The hat perched saucily on her sleek pulled-back hair had a flat crown. Mariah thought her look odd but very stylish, and wondered who she might be.

"Hello," the woman called in an accented voice. "I'm Alanza Yates. Are you Mrs. Cooper?"

"Yes, I am."

"Welcome to California. When did you arrive? Why hasn't Logan brought you to the house so we could meet properly?"

Mariah wondered how to explain the volatile afternoon. This was his stepmother after all.

Eli Braden walked out with his arms filled with shovels and dropped them on the pile. "Afternoon, Senora."

"Eli. Where's Logan?"

He glanced at Mariah and started to chuckle. "Kind of a long story. I'll let Mrs. Cooper tell it to you."

Mariah wanted to call out, "Coward!" but kept silent.

Mrs. Yates assessed her silently, until Mariah finally confessed, "In all honesty, your stepson is very hard to get along with, Mrs. Yates."

A small smile played across her lips. "I find that to be true at times, as well. So, what happened? Where is he? You haven't killed him, have you?"

Mariah wasn't sure whether to show how

amusing the last question was or not. "No. He went to purchase lumber for the new bunkhouse."

Surprise filled her face and voice. "The one he's been putting off building for nearly a year?"

"Yes, ma'am."

"What brought that on?"

"Me, I suppose. I kicked him in the knee."

Her eyebrows rose above her widened eyes.

Two of the ranch hands walked out and added more items to the pile. After nodding a greeting to Mrs. Yates and giving Mariah a smile, they returned to the house.

"You kicked Logan in his knee?"

"Yes, ma'am. He kissed me and I took exception to it."

"I see."

"I'm fairly sure he'll fire me when he returns, so if you don't mind, I'd like to get back inside and empty the parlor of as much of the clutter as possible before he does. Thank you so much for my train fare. I'll wire my aunt in the morning for a ticket back to Philadelphia. It's been a pleasure meeting you."

She hurried back inside.

The stunned Alanza watched her go. *She kicked Logan in his knee—for kissing her?* And yet, he hadn't beheaded her or fired her on the spot. Alanza knew nothing about the woman except for the information included in Mrs. Brown's recommendation, but deciding she needed more insight into the beautiful golden-eyed house-keeper, Alanza went into the house to offer her assistance.

When Logan rode up, there were people crawling over his house and property like ants. Men were carrying things outside and loading wagons, and women were washing his windows. He spotted Alanza's buggy and assumed she'd somehow gotten herself involved with the effort. If she'd joined forces with the widow, he'd be cooked goose for sure. Gingerly dismounting, he took a moment to free Diablo of the saddle before slapping the stallion on the rump to send it galloping off toward the stable. He placed the saddle on the ground near the house. Mentally pledging to strangle anyone who tried to move it, he went inside.

Ants outside, beehive inside. Walls were being washed along with the inside panes of the windows. A small stream of people were moving in and out the hall that led to his bedroom carrying myriad items that had once been stacked against the walls. Eli and a man who usually worked in the vineyards were hauling the old stove toward the door.

"Welcome back," Eli tossed out as they passed by. "How's the knee?"

Logan growled.

"She's in the kitchen."

Logan took off in that direction. The parlor was nearly cleared out, and he could actually cross the floor without having to watch his step. Entering the dining room, he was surprised to see the top of his dining table free of the rain slicks and tarps that had covered it for the past year. Also gone were the coils of rope that had once stood in the corners.

In the kitchen, the widow and his stepmother were looking up at his cabinets. What they were planning was beyond him, but he figured he'd find out soon enough.

Alanza noticed him in the doorway and smiled. "Ah, there you are, Logan. Mrs. Cooper and I are trying to decide how many new cupboards you'll need in here."

He met the golden eyes of his housekeeper. "May I speak with you a moment? Privately."

"Certainly."

Logan expected her to show signs of remorse, but instead she raised her small chin in challenge. He noticed Alanza's amused interest, but ignored it and gestured the firecracker toward the kitchen door that led outside to the back porch.

Once they were there, she took up a position with her back to the railing and faced him with folded arms. "I assume you've decided to fire me, so I've already told your stepmother I plan to wire my aunt in the morning for train fare back to Philadelphia."

"You're not getting off that easy."

She looked confused and that pleased him

because he doubted she was caught short very often. "I'm not firing you, but if you want to turn tail and run back to Philadelphia, I'll understand."

For a moment she didn't respond. It was as if she was trying to decide if he was telling her the truth. "You deserved that kick."

"And you deserve to be fired, so let's call it even."

She studied him for a moment longer. "My actions to the contrary, I don't like causing other people pain."

"Could've fooled me."

"Decent women don't like being manhandled."

"Did you storm around like this with your beloved Henry?"

"I didn't have to. He was sweet and kind and understanding."

"Uh-huh."

"You don't believe me?"

"Doesn't matter. How're your hands?"

She showed him her still wrapped palms. "They're fine."

"Have you eaten?"

"Not yet, but your stepmother has invited me to supper."

"Good. If the two of you could kindly shut down this work detail, I'd like to sit in my tub and soak my knee in peace."

She looked down at his knee and for a fraction of a second he did see guilt. Pleased to know she did have a conscience beneath all that sass, he offered an olive branch of his own. "Sorry about manhandling you. I'll use a better approach next time."

Her mouth dropped, but before she could begin railing at him, he left her with a small smile and walked back inside.

Mariah stood alone on the porch. She had to have misheard him. *Next time?* Surely that didn't mean he planned to kiss her again. She swore to herself that if he even looked like he was intent upon that, she'd kick him in both knees and sock him in his nose. What a conceited, egotistical . . . Deciding not to let him get her blood up again, she calmed herself and left the porch to rejoin Mrs. Yates.

"Logan wants us to clear everyone out, so he can soak his knee in peace," Alanza told her.

"I know, he said the same thing to me."

Alanza peered into her face as if searching for a clue as to how the talk on the back porch had gone. "You two didn't argue again, did you?"

"Not really. We decided to call our battle a draw."

"Good, then while he's using the tub, why don't you grab your things and come home with me? I'm sure you'd like to clean up before we eat and you can do it there and not have to wait for him to get done."

"I'd love that."

"If he shows up for dinner, fine, and if he doesn't, that's fine as well."

Mariah was looking forward to ridding herself of the perspiration and grime of the day. "Let me get my clothing and toiletries. I'll let him know I'll be leaving with you."

While Alanza went to speak with the workers, Mariah walked down the now clutter-free, empty hallway and knocked on his bedroom door.

"Come in."

When she entered, she found him standing shirtless. For a moment, she was mesmerized by his sculpted bare shoulders and torso and then immediately turned her back. The heat of embarrassment washed over her cheeks.

"You need something?" he asked, sounding amused.

"I wanted to let you know I'll be going home with Mrs. Yates."

"Okay."

She'd never seen a man's naked chest before and she swore the sight of his rock-hard frame was now permanently etched in her mind. Who knew a man could be so beautifully made?

"Anything else?"

Truthfully, she wanted to feast her eyes on him again, which shocked her even more than the sight of his bare chest. "No."

"Then I'll see you later."

She fled.

After her departure, Logan chuckled. He'd never seen a woman turn her back so quickly. Had she never seen Henry shirtless? As prim as she acted, he tended to think not. Many married couples went to their graves having never seen each other totally nude, and even made love mostly clothed. He on the other hand slept nude and made love the same way. Women like Mrs. Cooper might consider that shocking, but he didn't, and the women who shared his bed didn't either.

Mariah rode the entire way to Alanza's home thinking about Logan, but soon put him aside when she was escorted into the large bathing room. Not only were there two such rooms but both had running hot water.

She stared in wonder at the luxuriously appointed room with its white flocked walls and large tub.

"Logan's house has hot water as well," his step-mother informed her. "There are boilers outside feeding the pipes."

Mariah wondered if she'd died and gone to heaven. There'd been indoor plumbing in the flat she'd shared with her mother back in Philadelphia, but the only way to have hot water was to heat it on the stove first. And there certainly hadn't been a tub. Hip baths had been the order of the day for as long as she'd been alive.

Alanza showed her how to work the spigots and then left her alone.

As much as Mariah longed to lounge in the water for an hour or more, she didn't wish to keep her hostess waiting, so she washed up quickly, dried herself and dressed. Upon leaving, she glanced back at the tub with the hope that sometime in the near future she'd be able to linger for as long as she desired.

After dinner, Mariah and Mrs. Yates sat outside at a table in the courtyard while dusk rolled in. The sun dropping below the mountains was a beautiful sight to behold but she was so tired she was having difficulty keeping her eyes open. Her day had begun that morning on the train and ended with the emptying of her pigheaded employer's home. Dinner had consisted of spicy beans and strips of meat wrapped in what Mrs. Yates called a *tortilla*, and the best lemonade she'd ever had. The wonderful meal in tandem with the work-filled day were threatening to put her asleep in her chair, but she was too polite to excuse herself from her hostess so she could make her way back to her room and bed.

"I believe you will be good for my son," Mrs. Yates was saying. "Other than myself, he's unaccustomed to a woman who'll stand her ground as you did today."

"Hopefully, we'll find a way to get along. I don't wish to spend every day wanting to boil him in oil."

"In spite of all the head butting, Logan is a

decent, honest man. You could work for worse."

Had she the strength, Mariah might've debated that, but the weariness was weighing her down like a thick winter coat.

It must have showed. "You look ready to keel over, Mariah." She suddenly looked up and smiled over Mariah's shoulder. Without turning to see who might be approaching, Mariah somehow knew it was her employer.

"Good evening, Logan," his stepmother said brightly. "Have you eaten?"

He took a seat at the table. He was dressed in blue shirt and denims.

"Yes. I ate with Bonnie inside."

"Good. Mrs. Cooper needs to go to bed."

Mariah glanced his way and saw him as she had in his room without his shirt and she immediately looked elsewhere.

"How are your hands?" he asked.

"Fine." Mariah wanted to be distant and aloof, but it was difficult to do so around a yawn wide enough to stick a mountain into.

"This is why you should've rested up today instead of tackling the house."

"Thank you for pointing that out, Mr. Yates." It was a weak response but she was too tired for another round of verbal fencing with him.

He said to his stepmother, "She needs a lamp and a chair for her room. Do you have anything she can use?"

Mariah was surprised that he'd remembered, and inwardly pleased that he had. She heard them discuss searching a barn, but it was the last thing she remembered. She'd fallen asleep in her chair, thus missing Logan shake his head and utter softly, "Fool woman."

She also missed him gently scooping her up into his arms.

"Take her inside," Alanza said. "She can sleep here tonight."

At first, Alanza thought he might challenge her decision. She studied the determined set of his features and the way he held the young woman against his heart and found both actions quite surprising. Rather than questioning him about it, she stood and led him into the house.

Once he laid her down, Alanza discreetly watched his face as he observed his sleeping housekeeper, and saw an uncharacteristic softness that was also surprising. "You can come back for her in the morning."

He nodded but took a moment to remove her shoes. Alanza covered the fully dressed young woman with a quilt and they both tipped out.

In the hallway, they returned to their earlier conversation concerning furnishings for Mariah's room. "Take whatever you think she can use from the stores, and definitely replace that old mattress." The room used to be the place where the tack was stored.

"Will do."

"How's your knee?"

"Sore."

Although Mariah Cooper had been in her son's life less than a day, Alanza could see that she'd affected him in a *grande* way. Even now he was staring at the closed door as if he could see her sleeping on the other side. She doubted he was even conscious of what he was doing. "Go home and rest your knee. She'll be fine here."

He gave one last look at the door and departed.

Logan was sitting in the dark on his back porch smoking a cheroot and recalling the day. He'd gone to the train station to pick up a woman he figured wouldn't last any longer than the previous women he'd employed, but instead found a golden-eyed virago with more temper than a teased rattler, and as prickly as a desert cactus. In less than twelve hours, she'd called him out on his manners, accused him of being judgmental, given him a kick in the knee worthy of an irate mule, and made him buy lumber for a bunkhouse he'd had no intention of building until he got good and damn ready. And now, she was sleeping in one of Alanza's spare rooms. From the peaceful look on her face, one would never know that with her eyes open, she was hell-bent on making his life, well, hell. He'd gotten a clean house out of the deal, however, and although he hadn't been a party to the decision, he was grudgingly pleased by the outcome. What didn't please him was the idea of having to do battle with her every time she got it into her head to take charge. She was so fiercely determined, not even slicing open her palms on that wire bed frame had slowed her down, but *dios*, she was lovely, and that was the part that seemed to be giving him the most trouble. Were she as dried up and ugly as he'd assumed she'd be, he'd've spent the day growling at her until she quit and fled like the others. However, there was no quit in Mariah Cooper, just a body that drew his eyes, and a mouth he wanted to kiss until spring—neither of which was something he needed to be dwelling upon, considering the steep price he'd already paid. He rubbed his knee. A man with any sense would leave her to her duties as housekeeper and forget about the draw of all that loveliness. Deciding that was the safest road to travel, his reverie was interrupted by Eli Braden stepping up on the porch. "Thought you'd gone home," Logan said suspiciously.

"Nope. Too scared I'd miss something. How's the knee?"

"Knee's fine, and she's sleeping up at Alanza's, so show's over for today."

"Too bad."

Logan reminded himself that Eli was his best friend.

"Couldn't believe she kicked you like that."

"Noticed how funny you thought it was though."

"You have to admit it was."

"Not as funny as that pan of dishwater that was dumped on your head a few months back."

"Let's not talk about that. That suit cost me half a week's pay and it'll never be right again."

"Told you trying to make her jealous was a harebrained idea."

Eli was in love with a woman named Naomi Pearl. She owned a diner on the outskirts of Guinda, and was as much a handful as Mariah Cooper.

"Nobody ever said love was easy," Eli pointed out.

"Uh-huh."

"Did you get the lumber ordered?"

"Yes. Crane says he'll have it ready for us to pick up the day after tomorrow. And don't ask me why I changed my mind. I don't want to talk about it."

But Eli was smiling.

"What?"

"Nothing, just enjoying the show. Regardless of how you feel about her, she worked her fancy little behind off today. Not afraid of work."

Logan agreed. "No, she's not. Not afraid of much else either, apparently." He kept remembering the soft weight of her in his arms while carrying her to bed. For some unknown reason it felt right and he found that oddly disturbing. "I may go see Valencia in a few days."

"Need a female that asks 'how high' when you say 'jump'?"

"Don't you have a house and a bed a few miles from here?"

"I do, and I'm going, but I'll be back first thing in the morning for a ringside seat. Sleep well, my friend."

With that, Eli mounted his horse and galloped off toward his home, leaving Logan alone to contemplate the questions and chaos brought into his life by his golden-eyed housekeeper.

In his dream it was night, the moon was full, the stars twinkled like diamonds in the sky, and Logan was on the seat of the buckboard slowly opening the buttons of Mariah's white blouse. Her lips were parted and swollen from his kisses. He moved his mouth down to the hollow of her bared throat and inhaled her sweet scent while his tongue tasted the soft skin. He felt her tremble and sigh with rising passion. Taking a moment to recapture her lips, he slowly set about coaxing more response while his hands lazily explored her form. More buttons were conquered and he greeted each newly exposed patch of skin with hot flicks of his tongue until nothing stood between his lips and her breasts but the lace-edged top of her shift and the corset beneath. Wanting her with a need as broad as the mountains, he moved the shift and corset aside and freed one dark-tipped beauty. Lowering his head, he savored it lustfully. She crooned in the silence, whispering his name, and when he had his fill, he freed the twin; sucking, licking and biting her gently. Her lilac-scented skin was warm, the sight of her bare breast in the moonlight so arousing he wanted more, so he gently eased her skirt and slips up her thighs. When he touched her in the dark valley that held her treasures she was wet with wanting. He played and parted and teased the tiny nubbin that anchored a woman's delight until she was gasping, twisting, and arching against his hand. He placed her astride him and gently pushed his near bursting erection home. Stroking her with an increasing pace, he filled his hands with her tantalizing hips. Moments later, she cried out her release and he came tumbling after, laid low by an orgasm that made him shout her name to the night. And then he woke up.

Logan sat up panting. Disoriented, he looked around and realized he was in bed and that he'd been dreaming. Dragging his hands down his face, he couldn't believe how erotic the dream had been or how incredibly hard he was. Falling back against the mattress, he quietly cursed her and closed his eyes, but the dream kept replaying itself. Frustrated by his inability to escape the images, he threw back the sheet and got up. Walking out to his back porch, he sat down, but the lust-filled memories continued to tease and taunt. It was his hope that the cool night air would bring him relief, and it did, but it took a while.

Chapter 7

Mariah awakened groggy and confused. Nothing looked familiar—not the room, not the bed, not the room's heavy, ornate furniture or the quilt she was lying beneath. *Where am I?* Puzzled, she peeled the quilt back and sat up. She noticed that she was still dressed in yesterday's skirt and blouse. Then everything came back. Last night. She'd fallen asleep. Concern filled her that she might be in Logan Yates's bedroom, but the draperies and furniture were too feminine in appearance to have been chosen by a man, so she relaxed, though her location remained a mystery. A knock on the closed door sounded. She replied with a wary, "Come in."

Bonnie, Mrs. Yates's housekeeper, entered, carrying a tray of covered dishes. "Good morning, Mrs. Cooper. Brought you something to eat."

Mariah now knew where she was, but was surprised that the plump, red-haired housekeeper was waiting on her as if Mariah was her employer. "Good morning. But you aren't supposed to be bringing me breakfast. I'm help just like you."

"I know that, and so does the senora, but she insisted, and said you are to eat before you return to Mr. Logan's place."

"But—"

"No buts. Bathing room's down the hall." She set the tray on the vanity table and exited.

Mariah fell back on the bed. She doubted Yates would be pleased, knowing his housekeeper was being catered to like quality. She imagined him at home twiddling his thumbs and fuming over her late appearance. Hoping he wouldn't be spoiling for a fight, she left the bed to begin her day.

With her needs taken care of and her breakfast consumed, she managed to find her way down to the front parlor, where Bonnie was sweeping the hardwood floors. "Mr. Logan's outside waiting on you," she said, taking the tray from Mariah's offered hand. "If you need any help at his place, just let me know. Oh, the senora has gone to town. She said she will stop in to see you when she returns."

"Thank you." Girding herself for the day's first encounter, Mariah hurried outside. She found him seated on the bench of the wagon they'd ridden on yesterday. The bed was piled high with something covered beneath a large tied-down tarp. "Good morning. Sorry to keep you waiting, I didn't know you were here until a second ago."

"Morning."

Mariah could see the grumpiness in his face, and even though it probably stemmed from her tardiness, she was determined to be pleasant. It wouldn't do to begin the day arguing. "My apologies for not being at your place this morning.

I don't remember much after you arrived here last evening."

"You fell asleep at the table and Alanza thought it better if you stayed with her, so I carried you up to the room."

"You carried me?"

"You weren't in any condition to make it on your own."

That she'd been asleep in his arms left her somewhat speechless.

"Let's get going."

She went around to the passenger side of the wagon. He slid across the bench and stuck his hand down for her to grab. She glanced at it and then up at him, and since she had no other choice, placed her hand in his. He held on while she found a toehold and climbed aboard. His hand was strong, warm. Once seated, she chose to fuss with her skirts rather than look him in the face, but she couldn't resist for very long. A quick glance showed his tersely set profile. He put the team into motion and drove them away.

It was Mariah's first morning in California and putting aside the distant man beside her, she shivered a bit beneath her shawl in the crisp, chilly air. The sun hadn't fully revealed itself, so the sky still held hints of dawn's gray. She found herself marveling again at the beauty of the mountains now shrouded in a wavering coat of fog. The orchard workers were out and busy, as were the men tending the cattle and horses. Men on horseback rode by and shouted greetings to Logan. A few even called out to her, which she found pleasing. This was to be her home, so it was nice to be acknowledged, even if she was just the housekeeper.

"How're your hands?"

"They sting a bit but Mrs. Yates gave me some plasters yesterday. They're more comfortable than the gauze." Then she ventured to ask, "How's your knee?"

"Still sore, but nothing I can't handle."

He glanced her way. Even though he appeared angry about something, all she could think about was the sight of his bare chest. The few men she'd known back East paled in comparison in both stature and handsomeness. He was as overwhelming as the mountains rising against the horizon.

When they reached his place, he pulled back on the reins and set the brake. "Furniture in the bed's for your room."

Surprised, she looked back at the tarp.

"The hands and I will unload it."

"I can help."

"Don't need you."

She opened her mouth to protest, but he cut her off. "All you get to do is point and tell us where you want things to go. Think you can do that?"

113

Wondering what rocker he'd gotten his tail caught under, she nodded.

"Good. I'll come around and help you down."

But this time he didn't give her a hand. Instead he picked her up and set her on her feet before him. She wanted to chastise him for going against her wishes again, but she was so vividly aware of just how off balance he made her feel, she didn't say anything.

"Problem?" he asked.

"No."

"Good. Go on in. I'll get some help."

She went inside.

Even though Mariah participated in the big cleanup, she was nonetheless amazed by the interior's transformation. Yesterday when she first arrived she hadn't noticed how the parlor flowed so seamlessly into the dining room, or that its windows offered such a spectacular panoramic view. Once the new stove was picked out and delivered, and the carpenter Alanza suggested be hired started and finished the new kitchen cabinets, it would be a comfortable place to live. If and when Yates married, he'd have a home his wife wouldn't be ashamed to call her own. A cloud crossed over her at the thought of another woman living in the house, but she refused to dwell on it.

The furniture the men were bringing refocused her attention. The thin mattress on the bed was replaced by one more substantial. To her delight, the men, Logan, and Eli carried in a bed frame for it to rest upon, and there were even sheets and pillow slips. Added to that was a chest of drawers, lamps, a small wardrobe, a nightstand, and the sitting chair she'd requested.

Once everything was positioned to her satisfaction, she thanked them. In response, they politely touched their hats and left her and Yates in the room alone.

"Do you need anything else?" he asked.

"No. This is far more than I ever expected." She thought back on the tiny little space that served as her bedroom back in Philadelphia. Although this new room was small as well, it felt as large as a cathedral in comparison. "Thank you."

"You're welcome."

She eyed the small undressed window. "Once I save up enough money, I'll buy fabric and make curtains. My aunt promised to send my sewing machine once I arrived here, so I'm hoping it will get here soon."

"Thanks to my brother, the sea captain, Alanza has more fabric than she'll ever use. Have her or Bonnie show you where it's stored. You may be able to find something you like."

"I'll do that. Thank you."

Silence rose and an awkwardness rose in Mariah, too. He was watching her with such intensity, she felt the heat from across the room. "I sew well enough to make you new shirts or trousers if you are in need of any."

"I'll keep that in mind."

"Your mother said I was to speak with you about purchasing a stove, and about hiring the carpenter for the new cabinets."

"I suggest the two of you get together and decide what's needed. Just leave me enough money in the bank to buy feed and pay my hands."

"I wouldn't purchase anything without your approval."

"If Alanza's involved, my approval or disapproval won't matter. Get whatever you think the house needs."

"I'll try and be frugal."

"I appreciate that, and as for the carpenter, decide how many cabinets are needed and I'll talk with Max Rudd. That was who she suggested?"

"Yes." Mariah hadn't expected the conversation to go so smoothly. She'd had visions of them locking horns over not only prices but the necessity of some of the items on the long list of items she thought the house needed. Yet, they hadn't exchanged one cross word, which made her wonder if he'd suffered some sort of brain malady as a result of the kick she'd given him yesterday.

He must have seen some of what she was thinking on her face, because he asked, "What's the matter?"

"Truthfully, I expected us to argue."

"I can be cooperative when it's in my best interest."

"That's good to know, because I'd like for us to get along. I don't expect us to be friends, but being able to deal civilly with each other will go a long way toward making our dealings less acrimonious."

"I agree."

"I have two requests."

"And they are?"

"I'd like to take a tour of the ranch and I'd like you to teach me to ride, or at least drive."

Logan had been grumpy all morning because of the dream he'd had about her last night, and now, her talk of riding instantaneously transported him back. She was again astride him and he had the sweetness of her hardened nipples in his mouth. The reason he was so attracted to her continued to confound him because he didn't even like short women. Yet she had the ability to undo the control he was accustomed to exercising over himself and that left him not only wanting her, but even more irritated. "Have Alanza give you a tour and we'll see about the riding when your hands heal."

"Can't I wear gloves?"

"Did you challenge Henry this way, all day?"

"If we leave my deceased husband out of this maybe we can come to a compromise. You were the one who insisted I needed to learn, and I heartily agree."

He ran his eyes over her gorgeous smart-alecky mouth and thought about the kisses he'd drawn from it last night in his dream.

"If you don't wish to teach me, just say so, and I'll ask Mr. Braden or someone else."

Logan didn't want Eli teaching her anything. "I'm going to ride over and talk to the carpenter. I'll be back later." And he left her. It was either that or risk being injured again.

Mariah was so outdone by his abrupt departure, she wanted to call him back so she could shake him. She'd tried her best to be cooperative, but he seemed intent upon being difficult. "He really needs to stop having vinegar for breakfast," she drawled sarcastically and picked up the sheets to make her bed.

Outside, Logan walked over to the corral where the hands were still breaking the horses. He stood next to Eli and watched for a moment as the big chestnut mare threw her rider again and again. "You and the little lady at it again?" Eli asked.

"How can you tell?"

"Your face looks like a Texas thunderstorm. What happened this time?"

"I don't want to talk about it." Logan refused to reveal that she'd infiltrated his dreams and that he was as randy as an adolescent in a whorehouse as a result. "I'm going to ride over to Max's to talk to him about the bunkhouse build. Keep an eye on things until I get back."

"You want some advice?"

Logan snorted. "From you? No. Not a chance."

Eli laughed.

Logan felt a bit less stormy as he and Diablo reached the road that led to Max's ranch, but the approach of a familiar-looking buggy brought back the clouds. The driver was rancher Jim Deeb, president of the local cattlemen's association. Some of the other ranchers were encouraging Logan to run against him in the upcoming election because not only was Deeb a braggart, but he was also taking money under the table from some of the distributors they all depended upon to move their beef to the markets back East.

As Deeb's buggy neared, Logan hoped the man would drive on by, but of course he didn't.

"Morning Logan."

"Jim."

"I hear you hired a new housekeeper. What's she like?"

"Why?"

"Seeing as how I got one of the biggest spreads in the county, something always needs cleaning. Just wondering if maybe she'd like to work for me, if she's looking for extra money."

"She isn't."

"Hear she's quite a looker, too. High yella and

eyes to match. Val know you got a woman like that living with you?"

"Why do you care?" Deeb reminded Logan of those small yappy dogs women had taken to carrying around. He was half Logan's height yet insisted on challenging him as if he weren't. They'd known each other since childhood and had more than a few fights in their younger years. Deeb invariably lost, but that hadn't deterred him from continuing to be an aggravating son of a bitch. "Felicity know you're trying to hire someone without asking her permission first?" Felicity Deeb was a nice enough woman but rode her husband like a caballero in a horse race.

Deeb took immediate offense. "I don't need her permission."

"You need her permission to piss and we both know it. So how about you drive on and do whatever it is she sent you out for before she comes looking for you."

And while Deeb puffed up angrily and began to sputter, Logan rode away.

Max Rudd had been one of his father's best friends. He was a rancher, horseman, and did carpentry on the side. After Abraham's death, when life became hard for the family Abe left behind, Max did what he could to help. He paid some of the taxes, took Logan and his brothers hunting so there'd be fresh meat to eat, and anything else Alanza needed to ease her burdens. Logan was fairly certain Max was in love with Alanza, but loyalty to his late friend kept him from acting upon it. Alanza was a force of nature; few women could match her tenacity and strength. Were Logan to choose someone to take his father's place in her life, Maxwell Rudd would get his vote because he wouldn't try to change her, or more importantly, tame her.

Logan found him in the barn that served as his wood shop.

"Well, hello there, Logan. How are you?"

"I'm faring."

"Hear you got yourself a new housekeeper."

"Is there anyone who doesn't know?"

Max chuckled. "Small town. Folks have nothing better to do than be in your business. Anything new is news."

Logan agreed but wished the news belonged to someone else.

"How's your brothers?"

"Drew's in Mexico City. Noah's in the Indies according to a letter we received a few weeks back. Both should be here for Alanza's party."

"And she's well?"

"Right as rain."

"Good. Now, did you come to simply chew the fat or you wanting something done?"

He told him about the kitchen cabinets.

Max studied him silently before saying, "That

housekeeper must be something if you're wanting new cabinets."

Logan didn't reply.

"Since you seem to have lockjaw on the subject, guess I need to ride over and see her for myself."

"Let's just say, she and I are bumping heads."

"Got you a woman who doesn't like you ordering her around?"

Logan didn't reply for a second time.

Max's eyes showed his amusement. "Be out there tomorrow, or the day after to take some measurements. Any idea how many cabinets she wants?"

"No."

"Okay. Can't wait to make her acquaintance."

Logan rolled his eyes. "I'll see you at the rancho."

He headed for the barn door. Max's chuckling followed his exit.

Once Mariah had her room in order, she'd decided not to ruin the rest of her day by brooding over her exchange with her employer. It was her plan to walk down to Mrs. Yates's house and ask her to give her a tour. She didn't know if Mrs. Yates was at home or had the time but she wanted to find out.

As she stepped outside, it was impossible not to hear all the noise coming from the horse and the cheering men at the corral, so she walked over to get a closer look. The men were still trying to break the horse. The poor rider kept being thrown out of the saddle and the horse continued to charge angrily.

The men acknowledged her arrival with nods, and Eli walked over.

"Morning again, Mrs. Cooper. Something I can help you with?"

"No, I just came over to take a peek. How long will it take before the horse is tamed?"

The men cheered lustily as the rider again tried to stay in the saddle of the leaping, bucking horse. "Each one's different, but she's particularly hardheaded, so it may take another few days."

"It's a mare?"

The rider was thrown and his comrades greeted the failure with howls of laughter and good-natured ribbing. The man grinned and raced to the fence ahead of the horse's angry charge.

"Yes, ma'am. She's a beauty, isn't she? Soon as she takes to the saddle, she'll be heading for a rancher over near Stockton."

Mariah watched a different man enter the ring and approach the rearing horse.

"Do you have plans for the day, ma'am?"

"I'd like to have Mrs. Yates give me a tour of the ranch."

"If you don't want to walk, I'll drive you down in the wagon."

Mariah had planned to walk the half mile there but a ride suited her just fine.

On the drive, he asked, "So what's it like living in Philadelphia?"

"Compared to here, much louder. More hustle and bustle, too. Where are you from?"

"Houston, Texas."

"You're a long way from home."

"That I am."

"Family?"

"Mother and father. Three brothers. Two sisters."

"Do you miss them?"

"I do. Hoping to go back one day, but for now, I'm enjoying making my own way on my own place."

"Is it nearby?"

"About five miles west. Logan and I are in business together."

"I thought you worked for him."

"He thinks so, too, sometimes, but we're partners. We make a trip to Montana a few times a year to bring back mustangs."

"Do you have a wife, children?"

"Not yet."

"Sounds like you have someone in mind."

"I do, but trying to convince her is like trying to put a saddle on one of those wild horses."

"What's her name?"

"Naomi Pearl."

"Pretty name."

"Be prettier if it was Naomi Braden."

Mariah smiled. "Then I wish you luck."

"Thanks."

When they reached their destination, he offered her a hand to help her down and she thanked him.

He replied, "Anytime."

"May I ask you a question?"

"Sure."

"I'd like to learn to ride, do you think you might have time to teach me?"

He paused. "Not much call for being on horseback in Philadelphia I take it?"

"No. I can neither ride nor drive."

"Let me talk with Logan first. He might think it's his responsibility, and I don't want to step on his toes."

Rather than tell him about the discussion they'd had, she replied simply. "I understand. Thanks again for the ride."

Watching him drive off, Mariah thought, *What a nice man*. Too bad his partner lacked such an easygoing manner.

Chapter 8

When Bonnie let her in, Mariah found that Mrs. Yates had just returned from town. In response to Mariah's request, she smiled. "I'd love to give you a tour."

They set out in Alanza's buggy. Mariah watched the way she handled the reins and wanted to ask if she'd give her driving lessons, but she already felt as if she were overstepping her place by having her conduct the tour. She'd just wait and work it out with Logan.

First off, she was introduced to Mrs. Lupe Gutierrez and her chickens, and told what time was best to come for eggs.

"Early morning, just after the sun gets up is best," Lupe told her.

"I'll remember that."

She also met her husband, Hector, who was Mrs. Yates's driver. He in turn introduced their three young sons: Marco, Eduardo, and Juan. Mariah noticed a small cabin near the coops and wondered if the family lived there.

After she and Mrs. Yates thanked the family and continued their journey, she asked about the little cabin.

"Yes, that is their home. Some of the other employees live on our rancho as well. The father of Mrs. Gutierrez's grandfather worked for my parents. When her Hector lost his job after the railroad was completed, I hired them both. In the old days, rancho owners always took care of the people they employed, and I am carrying on that tradition."

Mariah found that very charitable.

"My Logan complains sometimes, and says I have more workers than there is work to do, but I am responsible for them and their children."

Their next stop was the orchards. Mariah marveled over the trees of oranges and lemons and the glorious scent in the air. "I knew lemons grew on trees but had no idea where."

"Christopher Columbus brought seeds with him on his voyage to Hispaniola, and they were spread by the Spanish who followed him."

"The lemonade last night was the best I've ever tasted."

"Why thank you."

Mariah noticed children stuffing handfuls of leaves from the trees into burlap sacks. "Do you burn the leaves after the fruit's harvested?"

"No, we steep them for tea, it's very good for coughs. We use nearly all parts of the lemon here. We make the tea. We use the oil from the peel on our wood floors, and a halved lemon dipped in a bit of salt makes copper pots gleam like the sun."

Mariah was impressed.

Leaving the orchard behind, Alanza stopped the

wagon for a moment so Mariah could see the grapevines.

"We've only had these vines a few years," she explained. "It will take many more before they bear enough fruit to sell and make a profit."

Mariah assumed grapes grew as easily as apples or pears.

"I would love to have these vines produce like the ones once owned by *La Beate*."

Alanza apparently saw the confusion on Mariah's face. "She was the daughter of one of the old Spanish families. Her true name was Apolinaria Lorenzana."

"She grew grapes?" Mariah asked, still confused.

"Yes, in fact she planted the famous grapevine of Montecito. In her time it was the largest vine in the world, and produced six thousand clusters of fruit in one growing season."

Mariah's jaw dropped. While she picked it up, Alanza told her the story of how Apolinaria turned her life over to teaching and charity after the death of her lover, and that many of the old families thought she should have been made a saint after her death.

"So what does *La Beate* mean?"

"To whom all doors are open and to whom all sorrows are brought."

Mariah found that very moving.

"Come, let me show you the rest of your new home."

They paused to view the field where the vegetables were grown and then moved on to the storage barns. Alanza led her inside one and showed her where the rows and rows of put-up vegetables and fruits were stacked. "Feel free to take what you need when you need it. Everything is replenished at harvest time."

"What does your son like to eat?"

"That is a question you should ask him, but I will tell you that he loves apple pie and large steaks."

Another barn held all the fabrics Logan mentioned and by Mariah's visual estimation, there were enough bolts to supply her mother's dress shop for years. "There's quite a lot here."

"I keep telling Noah not to bring any more home, but I believe he's deaf. I know you sew, so please help yourself to as much of it as you like."

"Do you sell any of it?"

"I do. Some goes to the dressmaker in town, and to others in Sacramento, but the more I sell the more my son seems to bring back."

"May I take a peek?"

"Certainly."

Mariah tore off a tiny corner of the heavy brown paper some of the bolts were wrapped in and found silks and cotton of all colors. There were also serges and fine Egyptian linens. One bolt held mattress ticking and another heavy blue denim.

There had to be at least one hundred different bolts of various kinds and weights. She was in seamstress heaven and couldn't wait for the arrival of her sewing machine.

A further walk through the huge barn revealed farming implements like shovels and hoes. There were saddles and bridles, bed frames, and an old trunk filled with bags of down for pillows and duvets. Upon seeing that, she gave Alanza a questioning look.

"I've no idea where Noah got those, but feel free to use them as well."

Mariah was in a state of wonder. "Why didn't Logan use this barn to store all the items after the bunkhouse burned down?"

"We're on the western edge of the rancho. He deemed this location too far away."

"I see."

"I didn't agree, but arguing with him is useless at times, as you yourself know."

"I do."

She saw Alanza watching her closely so she felt compelled to say, "We had a slight disagreement this morning before he left."

"You're both very strong willed, so you'll need to learn to compromise."

"I know that, but does he?"

Alanza gave her shoulders a quick squeeze. "It will get better, *chica*, but stick to your guns."

As they got back on the wagon and Alanza

picked up the reins, Mariah glanced over. "Logan said you were born here?"

"I was. In fact, the room where you slept last night was mine while growing up. My grandfather's original land grant covered about fifteen thousand acres."

"My goodness."

"Sounds like a lot, but ours was one of the smaller grants. Back then there were families who claimed up to fifty thousand acres. Most raised sheep and cattle, which were sold for tallow and hides. Not until the Americans came did the old families realize the cows could also be sold for the beef."

"Things changed after the Americans came."

"Very much. We lost our land and our way of life. In many ways our decline mirrored the decline the Spanish brought upon the native peoples."

As Mariah listened, Alanza explained how the coastal Indians of California were forced to build the Spanish missions in the early years.

"Many thousands succumbed to disease. Those that did survive were made to give up their tribal language, customs, and beliefs."

"Sounds a bit like slavery."

Alanza eyed her for such a long time, Mariah thought she might have offended her, but she finally said, "I suppose it could be looked at that way."

"I wasn't trying to offend you, Mrs. Yates."

"I understand, dear. I just never thought about it in those terms before. The Jesuits and the monks converted the Indians to Catholics to save their souls."

"I see." But in reality she didn't. Deciding she needed to change the subject, she asked, "I don't know how to cook the dishes that are eaten here. Do you think Bonnie or Mrs. Gutierrez can teach me?"

"Yes they can and I applaud you for wanting to learn. Might help if you spoke a bit of Spanish as well."

"Does Logan speak Spanish?"

"As if he were born in Spain. His brothers speak the language as well."

"Where do your other sons live?"

"Andrew Antonio divides his time between Sacramento and Yerba Buena."

"And that is?"

"What the Americans now call San Francisco."

"Oh."

"My youngest, Noah, is on a sea voyage. They'll all be here later in the summer to help celebrate my birthday. You will like them, and because you've given Logan fits, they'll like you as well."

"I look forward to meeting them."

"Good. Now, let us return to my house and have something to eat and then I'll take you back to Logan's."

After eating, Mariah was taken back to Logan's as promised. She looked up at Alanza seated on the wagon and was glad to have spent the time in her company. "Thank you for showing me around, I appreciate it very much. I know my place, so I'll try not to take up too much of your time in the future."

Alanza waved her off dismissively. "Place or no place, I'm pleased to have another female here."

"Thank you, again."

"You're welcome."

Logan was in his study poring over the ranch's ledgers. Profits from the sale of cattle were down; not enough to negatively impact the family's life, but if the trend continued he would have to seriously consider throwing in with a new distributor who offered more than he was presently receiving through the efforts of Jim Deeb. He glanced around at his study. It was the only room in the house that hadn't been buried beneath the clutter after the bunkhouse fire because he couldn't run the business if he couldn't get to the ledgers and accounts to pay the bills. He wondered if his hellion housekeeper had plans for his study on her long list of improvements. He certainly hoped not, because he liked the space the way it was. He knew where everything was and he had his magazines, like *American Farmer* and *Popular Mechanics* in the bookcase right where he wanted them to be.

According to Eli, she and Alanza were out touring the ranch. Alanza seemed to enjoy her company and that pleased him. On the other hand, no matter how hard he tried, he couldn't rid himself of last night's dream. All day, the moment he let down his guard, remembrances of her bared breasts in the moonlight and the feel of her tight sheath sheltering his flesh would take him over like a *bruja*'s spell. He didn't want to remember the sounds of her whispering his name or the tastes and scents of her, but he did.

"Mr. Yates."

As if by magic she was standing in the doorway, and the spell washed over him once again. "Mrs. Cooper."

"I just wanted to alert you of my return. I didn't mean to disturb you."

"You aren't disturbing me. Eli said you asked him for driving lessons."

"I did. I wish to learn and you seemed to take issue with my asking for a pair of gloves."

"Thanks for the reminder."

"You're welcome."

He tossed her the pair of work gloves he'd picked out for her earlier. "Put those on and let's go."

She went still. "You're really going to teach me?"

"It's either that or have you hound me until Christmas."

"Thank you," she said excitedly.

Logan tried to deny the way her smile made him feel, but lost that battle as well. He stood. "Shall we?"

Mariah soon learned that driving a buggy wasn't as simple as it appeared. Especially when the instructor showed no patience. "If you yell at me one more time, I'm going back inside."

"I'm not yelling."

"Yes, you are," she gritted out.

"Then follow instructions. This isn't that hard!"

"Then be more patient! This is my first lesson, remember."

He exhaled a heavy sigh.

She wanted to sock him.

"If you'd waited until your hands healed you could hold the reins tighter," he pointed out for the hundredth time.

She glared his way but kept her mouth shut. Yes, her hands were a bother, but the bigger problem was her lack of strength. She'd not known horses were so strong. Having chopped wood all her life had absolutely no bearing on the strain burning her arms. In truth, she wanted to surrender the reins, but refused to give him the satisfaction.

The horse seemed patient with her ham-handed attempts to guide him up the road at first, but he must've grown tired of her, because he decided to go back to the barn.

As a result, Logan yelled—and Mariah yanked and pulled back on the reins, trying to regain control and steer, but the horse was stronger and picking up speed.

"You're not listening!"

"That's because you've made me deaf!"

The horse's strides lengthened and the buggy left the road. They were bouncing up and down on the grass. People were stopping to stare. She saw the corrals ahead and knew disaster was imminent. She was doing her best, but no amount of pulling back on the reins halted the flight until Logan reached over, took the reins and quickly brought the episode to a close.

"Are you trying to kill us!"

Mariah wasn't a cursing woman but at that moment she wished she were. She was furious at him and the stupid horse. She hopped down from the buggy and stalked off. She'd never let him give her lessons in anything again. His patience was smaller than a gnat.

Behind her, he demanded to know, "Where are you going?"

"To find ice for my ears!" Her pride was hurt, her arms ached, and she was past tired of him.

"I told you to wait on your hands. Maybe now you see why."

Were she a fire-breathing dragon, she would have burned him like a piece of bacon; instead she snapped, "So should I have simpered, 'My hands hurt, Logan. I don't wish to learn. Please cart me around for the rest of my life!' "

Not waiting for an answer, she resumed walking. She had no inkling as to where she was going, but she had to put some distance between herself and him or explode like Fourth of July fireworks. Arms swinging, her steps measured, her gold eyes blazing, she sailed by the corrals, causing the men, including Eli Braden, to stop what they were doing.

Eli called out, "Are you okay, Mrs. Cooper?"

"I need a battle griffin to fly him away and drop him into the ocean!"

The men shared grins, then turned to look for Logan because they knew he had to be close by. Sure enough, he and the buggy came barreling around the side of the house.

When the buggy reached her, Mariah didn't slow. "Go away!"

"It's not my fault you're so hardheaded."

She wanted to chop down a tree and knock him over the head with it. "Go away before I hurt you, you insufferable man."

He had the nerve to laugh.

Seeing a good-sized rock in her path, she picked it up. Aiming high so she wouldn't hit the horse, she pitched it as hard as she could, and it clunked him right in the center of his forehead.

"Ow!"

Her mouth dropped with surprise—she didn't think she'd actually strike him.

The ranch hands were holding their breath up

until that point, but the stunned look on Logan's face sent them into fits of howling laughter.

"Dammit, woman!" He touched the spot to see if she'd drawn blood. She had.

Mariah was filled with remorse. "I am oh so sorry."

"No, you're not," he snarled.

"I really, truly am. I didn't think it would hit you." She dug her handkerchief out of her skirt pocket and walked over to where he sat fuming. "Here."

He took the offering and pressed it against the slowly rising lump on his brow.

"You make me so mad I can't see," she said.

"You saw well enough to plug me with that rock."

"I've apologized, which is more than I got from you."

"Why should I apologize because you refused to listen?"

Mariah swung on her heel and marched away.

Logan was still sitting in the buggy seat with her handkerchief on his forehead when a mounted Alanza came charging up.

"Is Mariah all right? Someone said she was in a runaway buggy."

"She's fine."

"Where is she?"

He pointed to her retreating back.

"Where's she going?"

138

"Probably to look for something else to assault me with."

"What?" Alanza suddenly appeared to notice the handkerchief. "Why are you holding that handkerchief to your forehead?"

"She hit me with a rock."

Alanza blinked and her lips trembled slightly as if she were suppressing a smile.

"Go ahead and laugh. I'll probably think it's funny, too, someday."

"What happened?"

So he told her.

"You know," she said once he finished telling his side, "you really don't have much patience and you probably did yell."

"You're my *madrastra*. You're supposed to take my side."

"Did you apologize?"

"For what?"

"For being impatient, arrogant, high-handed and probably insufferable, knowing how you are."

His jaw tightened. "No."

"It was her first lesson, Logan."

"Every time we're together for more than a minute, we argue. First the kick and now a rock."

"Do you want to fire her?"

"No."

Their eyes met.

Alanza said, "Let her cool off, and then go to

her and see if you can't get past this. Her beauty and fire are already the talk of Guinda."

Logan knew that to be true from his encounters earlier in the day.

She added, "I ran into Reverend Dennis in town this morning and even he asked about her. Wanted to know if she was churchgoing."

"And you told him?"

"Truthfully, I didn't know."

Reverend Paul Dennis had been seeking a suitable wife since coming to Guinda a year ago. Logan was sure once he got a look at Mariah, he'd put her at the top of his list. Logan had his mistress Valencia, so he told himself that it didn't matter if men wanted to court his rock-chugging housekeeper, but it did and he refused to contemplate why.

"Do you have any ice at home?" he asked.

"I believe we do."

"Good. I'll follow you over and get some before my forehead starts resembling the Sierra foothills."

Chapter 9

Mariah didn't slow until she reached the river-bank. Spying a bench, she stripped off her gloves and sat. She was certain Logan would dismiss her this time. His pigheaded personality brought out the worst in her. Never in life had she kicked anyone or thrown rocks, but all she could envision was more of the same if she stayed in his employ. She looked down at her hands. The plasters kept the cuts from opening again in response to holding the reins but they were sore as the dickens. Once she returned to the house, she'd give them a good soaking in soapy hot water, but she couldn't think of anything she might use to cure her of reacting the way she had to Logan. How he could claim he hadn't yelled when he'd been loud enough to break windowpanes back East was beyond her, and he'd given no credence at all to it having been her first driving lesson. Surely he hadn't expected her to handle the reins perfectly right off the bat, but apparently he had. She stood and walked closer to the water. On the other side, she saw a deer and a fawn stop their drinking and look over at her warily. They were too far away for her to bother so they resumed their drinking before bounding back into the cover provided by the trees. Logan was so busy crowing about being right about her hands that he'd given her absolutely no credit for not letting that be a deterrent or an excuse, which is what the old Mariah might have done. Crossing the country to take the job as his housekeeper had emboldened her in ways that made her feel stronger and more confident about who she was. The old Mariah would never have gotten behind those reins. She admitted to feeling more than a bit of trepidation at the prospect of having to control the large horse, but she hadn't let her fears sway her. She was proud of herself, even if her employer wasn't.

Taking a slow stroll down the bank, she wondered if she should quit her position and seek employment elsewhere. Surely she'd be able to find another with someone she didn't want to assault. The more she thought about it, the better that solution seemed to be. The sounds of an approaching rider interrupted her reverie. It was Logan on his beautiful black horse. The sight of him brought back her rising attraction, even as the memories of their last encounter threatened to reignite the nearly extinguished embers of her anger.

With the stallion reined to a walk, he approached. When he came to a stop behind where she was standing, she had nothing to say to him except, "I'll look for another position first thing in the morning."

"I didn't come to fire you."

"It doesn't matter. We don't get along, so to save my sanity and yours, I'll move on."

"To where?"

She shrugged. "I don't know, but this isn't working and we both know it."

Logan looked up at the sky for a moment, then found himself admiring the strong lines of her back and the delicate shells of her ears made visible by her pulled-back hair. He hadn't anticipated this, and as a result was unsure of what to say or do. In spite of the volatile last two days, he didn't want her to walk out of his life. And for the first time in his thirty-seven years, Logan knew he had to eat crow. "I should've remembered it was your first time holding reins, and given you credit for wanting to learn, even with your injured hands."

She turned with surprise written all over her face. Her eyes brushed the plaster centered on his forehead. "I am sorry for injuring you."

"You did warn me."

She dropped her eyes and he saw the small smile. "From now on, I'll do my best to be more of a gentleman if you'll holster your weapons. Your temper's becoming legendary around here."

"Never knew I had one until I met you."

"That's hard to believe."

"I used to be meek as a church mouse."

"You?"

She nodded. "Me."

She looked off into the distance as if thinking. He saw a cloud pass over her features and so asked gently, "What's the matter?"

"Just thinking about that other me."

"What do you mean?"

She turned back to the water and the silence of the trees and mountains rose around them. For a moment, he thought she might not answer, but she finally said in a quiet tone, "My first memories are of my mother berating me. I was beaten, slapped, and called worthless my entire life. I came to California to escape that and her."

Logan froze.

She glanced over her shoulder at him. "And never once did I talk back, or question or do anything but be obedient."

"Things didn't change after your marriage?"

"There was no marriage, Logan. I lied about being a widow so I could get the position and flee."

He had no idea why he felt so elated but he began chuckling softly.

"What's wrong?"

"Nothing. Just you."

"So, now you really have ample grounds to dismiss me."

"But I won't, and I'll keep your secret if you decide to stay on."

"Thank you."

He saw her then in a whole new light. Not many

women would leave the safety of their homes and set out across the country to seek out a new life, not knowing what they'd find on the other side. Yet she had, and turned herself from church mouse into a very formidable woman. He wanted to know more about her relationship with her mother, but decided to defer it for now. Just hearing what he had and that she was as prim and as innocent as she appeared was enough for him to digest for the moment. "Would you like to ride back to the house with me?"

"No, I think I'll walk if you don't mind."

"That's fine."

He turned Diablo.

"Logan."

"Yes."

"Thank you, again."

"My pleasure." Filled with thoughts of her, he rode away.

Watching him depart, Mariah certainly hadn't planned to tell him about her mother or the truth about her marital state, but it felt right, and she felt better inside as well.

On the walk back, she let the beautiful scenery remind her why coming to California had been such a grand idea. It was a gorgeous day, a mirror of the one before and she wondered if the weather was always so glorious. Up above, birds soared beneath the fat white clouds. She saw more deer and a fat rabbit who ran from her as if its tail was on fire. Next, she came upon a stand of wild-flowers that took her breath away. She'd seen them on her way to the river, but at the time had been too upset to stop. Now, she paused to pick a few, and inhaling their fragrance made her smile.

As she moved on, she wished Kaye were with her to experience all she'd seen and hoped she and Carson were doing well. She held the same hope for her Aunt Libby. Had it not been for her and her copy of the *Tribune*, Mariah might still be in Philadelphia trying to figure out her future. Her mother crossed her mind. Did Bernice care about how Mariah might be faring? It was impossible to know. Since leaving the dress shop on that awful day, she'd prayed for her mother every night and vowed to continue to do so.

Her journey brought her back within sight of the house and corrals, and as she passed the ranch hands hauling away the burnt wood from the old bunkhouse, Eli walked over to her and asked, "Did Logan find you?"

"Yes, he did."

"You plan to let him live?"

"I do."

"Good. He can be a pain in the rear sometimes, but me and folks around here like him a lot, so I'm glad you two worked things out."

"So am I."

Inside the house, Logan quickly packed enough

clothes for a few days, then went into the bathing room to grab his shaving kit. That the rock-throwing Mariah Cooper wasn't a widow but in reality an innocent infused him with muted delight. Virgins usually made him run for the hills, but the idea of being the first to initiate the hellion into the realm of pleasure made the challenge of doing so that much more enticing—thus he had to go. It was his hope that visiting Valencia would counteract Mariah's steadily tightening spell because it made no damn sense for him to be this damn hard over a woman he'd met two days ago.

Mariah took her flowers into the kitchen to put them in water and realized there was nothing suitable for the purpose except one of the dented metal tumblers. Hoping its owner wouldn't mind, she took one down, filled it with a few inches of water, and set the short-stemmed beauties inside. Smiling, she turned and the sight of Logan standing in the doorway brought her up short. The intensity in his eyes made her heart race so swiftly it took her a moment to remember she knew how to speak. "Um, you look very nice," she said, referencing his brown suit.

"I have some business I need to take care of. Be back the day after tomorrow."

Because he'd not said anything about this earlier, she found his declaration surprising, but he wasn't legally bound to discuss his comings and goings with her beforehand, so she replied, "Have a safe trip."

"If you need anything, see Alanza or Eli."

"I will." For a moment, he looked as if he might have more to say, but he abruptly turned on his heel and left her. Wondering why the exchange felt so strange, she shook her head and left by the back door to place her flowers in her room.

When Logan entered Stewart's, the town's general store, the sight of Valencia behind the counter made him relax. With her there'd be no kicking, throwing rocks, or arguing. She glanced up and gave him a smile. She didn't offer more of a greeting because of the female customer she was helping with a perfume purchase. Rather than interrupt, he walked over to where the store's catalogs were kept, hoping he'd find a suitable stove for his home.

The store was a landmark and had been in operation for as long as he could remember. It was established by Val's father, Jeremiah Stewart, during the heyday of the forty-niners. He'd come west with a group of free Black men from back East, and like most who'd flocked to California, he and his friends knew nothing about the rigors of mining. They did know hard work, however, and as a result became very wealthy. Jeremiah took his earnings and opened a store to supply other miners with the goods and tools they needed, and because they paid in gold he became even more wealthy. When the mining panned out and settlers moved in, he began selling things they needed, like farm implements and dry goods. He died five years ago, leaving the enterprise to his wife, Ida, and daughter Valencia Rose.

The store was busy and Val was still helping customers, so after writing down the order numbers for a stove, an icebox he liked, and a few other items, he nodded a greeting to some of the customers he knew. He crossed to the newspaper stand and picked up the latest issue of the *Daily Alta California*, one of the San Francisco papers. Leafing through, he paused to read an article on the Congress of Berlin awarding Africa's Congo to Belgium, and Nigeria to England, when a familiar feminine voice said, "You know I charge two pennies for reading my newspapers without buying."

It was Val.

Pleased, he set the paper back on the stack. "How are you?"

"I'm fine. Sorry it took me so long to greet you. Been a busy day."

"I see that. Can I steal you away long enough for a piece of pie?"

"Sure can. Let me tell Curtis I'm leaving for a little while." Curtis Adams was one of her two clerks.

Once that was done, they started up the walk.

"So, anything new?" he asked.

"Mama's been feeling poorly, so I'm leaving tomorrow afternoon to go see her."

Her mother lived in San Francisco with a sister. "Nothing serious, I hope?"

"I don't think so, but I won't know for sure until I get there."

Of course Logan didn't like hearing that her mother wasn't well, but he was disappointed that they wouldn't be able to spend more than a night together. "Sorry to hear that. Was hoping to take you shopping."

She stuck her hand in the crook of his arm and leaned close. "You are so sweet. Maybe some other time."

They entered the small diner run by Naomi Pearl. The place was crowded as always and they were greeted by the beautiful chocolate-skinned owner.

"Afternoon, Val. Logan. What can I get you?"

"Pie," Val answered.

"Get yourselves a seat and I'll be back directly."

Naomi's diner, Pearl's, was yet another landmark. It was founded by her parents, Wesley and Anna, who began life as slaves in Panama. When Colombia abolished slavery in the Isthmus in 1852, they, like many of their freed countrymen, came north to seek their fortunes in the Mother Lode counties of California. They were both cooks, and because good cooks were in such high demand by the miners, they set steep prices for their services as they traveled from claim to claim. According to legend, Anna's pies alone brought in enough gold for the couple to live on quite comfortably. They'd recently returned to Panama to enter the hotel business. Naomi, born in the States, opted to stay.

She arrived a few moments later and set down two still warm pieces of her famous apple pie. "Enjoy," she told them and left to tend to her other customers.

"Eli still sweet on her?" Val asked.

Logan nodded. "Yes."

"Poor fellow."

"Why's that?"

"She isn't the most even-tempered woman around. Any man after her heart would need the patience of a saint."

He immediately thought of Mariah Cooper. "Whereas you?"

"Are of sound temper and mind, and undoubtedly a fine catch," she offered up teasingly.

He raised a forkful of pie in agreement. "Yes, you are."

But she had no plans to marry. Due to the laws governing wives and their rights to hold property, she worried that a husband might gain control of her business and assets.

"What happened to your forehead?"

Logan froze. "What do you mean?"

"You've a plaster on it, Logan."

He touched the spot. "Misjudged the height of a branch while I was riding," he lied. "It's nothing."

He watched her study it for a bit longer before returning to her pie. He didn't like lying to her, but the last thing he wanted was to discuss or be reminded of his run-in with his housekeeper.

"I hear Alanza found you a housekeeper."

He froze again and swallowed the pie in his throat. "Yes, a woman from back East. Widow named Cooper."

"Word is she's very lovely."

He wouldn't look at her. "I suppose, but she was hired to clean and cook, nothing more. Alanza said Reverend Dennis asked after her, so maybe he'll find her to his liking since he's looking for a wife."

"Quite possible. Do you think the two might do well together?"

"I've no idea."

"Well, we can only hope. He's a nice man and deserves to find someone who's nice as well."

Logan doubted the reverend would know what to do with such a headstrong woman, but he kept that to himself. "How about dinner after you're done for the day?"

"I'd like that. Been a while since we've seen each other. I've missed you."

"Missed you, too." He'd been in San Francisco for two weeks previous for a horse auction. He'd returned to the ranch only a day before the arrival of the spellbinding Mariah Cooper.

"How about I cook us a nice meal at my place so we won't be disturbed."

"Great idea. Do me a favor."

"Sure."

"Will you order the things on this list for me?" He handed over the numbers he'd written down.

She took a moment to read it over. "I know the numbers by heart and this is a pretty fancy stove, Logan. Very expensive, too."

"I know but I don't have one in the house."

"China, too?" she asked looking up from the paper with surprise.

"Nothing proper to eat off, either."

"Never known you to care about these types of things before."

"Blame it on the housekeeper."

She studied him for such a long moment he almost squirmed, but she finally refolded the paper and stuck it into the pocket of her skirt. "Do you want everything shipped here or to the house?"

"The house, please."

"Okay. Consider it done. I'll wire the store in San Francisco. Should take no more than a week."

"Thanks."

Mariah was in her room basking in the afterglow of her long soak in Logan's tub when she heard the door pull. She hurried to answer it and found Alanza Yates on the porch holding what appeared to be a napkin covered plate. As she held the door open to let her enter, Alanza said, "Logan stopped by on his way out and said to make sure you have dinner."

"Mrs. Yates, you keep acting as if you're the help instead of me."

"You don't have a stove. Should I let you starve?"

"No, ma'am," Mariah replied with amusement. "I do appreciate your kindness."

"That's better. You and Logan are better as well."

Mariah took the plate from her hand. "Yes. He promises to be more patient, and I promised to holster my weapons."

"Good. When he gets back from his *concubina*, maybe he can show you how fine a man he really is."

Mariah could pretty much guess from the sound of the Spanish word what it translated to in English, but just to be sure, she asked, "And that word means?"

"Mistress. Paramour."

"I see."

Alanza shrugged. "You may as well know what he's about. Her name is Valencia Stewart. She owns the general store in town, and although she is very lovely and cultured, I prefer he marry someone else."

"And the reason being?"

"No *caliente*."

"Which means?"

"Heat. They've know each other for years, but for me, she lacks the passion and toughness Logan will need in a wife."

Mariah wondered if Alanza had a candidate in mind that she did prefer, but was too polite to ask.

Alanza moved back to the door. "Enjoy your dinner and your evening. How are your hands?"

"Still a bit sore from the reins, and my arms are weary from the strain, but I'll be fine."

"All right. I will see you tomorrow."

"Thank you."

Alone again, Mariah took her food out to the bench of her little courtyard and ate the meal of rice, beans, and *tortillas* filled with spicy beef. So Logan had a mistress. She supposed with his looks and wealth she shouldn't be surprised, but she hadn't expected to have the fact revealed to her by his stepmother. Alanza, with her fancy Spanish riding clothes and plain way of speaking, was a decidedly unconventional woman. Then again, she'd have to be, in order to run a ranch and raise three sons without the benefit of a husband.

Mariah turned her attention back to her plate and told herself that Logan having a mistress meant nothing to her, but a small voice inside shouted, *"Liar!"*

Logan was seated on the edge of Valencia's bed with his head in his hands. She knelt behind him and stroked his back gently. "It's nothing to be ashamed of, Logan. Maybe you're coming down with something."

He was both embarrassed and angry. He'd never had this happen before. Never.

"I'm sure things will be right in a little while."

He'd heard about this happening to other men, but he was Logan Yates and in his prime, not a doddering old fossil who took his teeth out at night, and needed a horn for hearing. What type of man takes his mistress to bed only to be unable to . . . perform. He'd be mortified if he wasn't so furious. As it stood, he was grateful for the darkness because he couldn't look Valencia in the face.

She came and sat beside him. "I've been wanting to talk with you about something and I suppose now is as good a time as any."

"What is it?"

"I'm leaving town."

"I know. You told me about your mother."

"That isn't what I mean. I'm leaving California."

"To go where?"

"Boston."

"For how long?"

"Hopefully forever. I'm going there to marry."

Logan stilled. "What?"

"I'm getting married."

"To whom?"

"His name is Daniel Roberts."

Logan dragged his hands across his face.

"I met him last year in San Francisco. He was there visiting. We've been corresponding ever since."

"He doesn't know about us, I take it?"

"No," she replied quietly. "He believes I'm a widow living with Mother."

He sighed aloud. He'd been hit by rocks, turned inside out by dreams of a woman he swore he didn't even like, and now? He wondered if this day could get any worse.

"He's asked me to marry him, and I said yes."

Logan sat silent.

"It's not like you've ever made me an offer," she pointed out crossly.

"Because you told me you didn't want to marry."

"Every girl wants to get married, Logan. If I'd told you that in the beginning you'd've jumped on Diablo and never come near me again."

She was correct. He had no desire to marry. As he'd explained to Alanza, he was content with his ranch and horses, and because Val expressed a similar contentment with her own life, she'd been the perfect choice for his mistress. Angry and yes, hurt, he stood and gathered his clothes from the chair near the bed. "Then I hope you'll be happy, Val. I truly do."

Ten minutes later, he was riding home. He felt the need to blame someone. He blamed Val for not being truthful and playing him for a fool. He blamed himself for thinking life was supposed to function the way he wanted it to, and he blamed Mariah Cooper for being so bewitching he couldn't make love to another woman.

The night was warm and Mariah's small room was hot. Tossing and turning, she kicked aside the sheet, hoping that would bring her some relief. It didn't. Before going to bed, she'd tried to open the lone window but it was sealed shut because of the many layers of paint on the jamb. Now, with no breeze to cool the air, she was sweltering. Getting up, she sat on the edge of her mattress and sighed resignedly. Moonlight streamed in through the curtainless window, filling the room. Guided by it, she dug through the drawers of her dresser until she found another nightgown to replace the damp, twisted one she was wearing. That accomplished, she padded over to the door that led outside and opened it. The night air drifted in, bathing her humid face and skin, bringing with it the relief she'd been seeking. She stepped out onto the wooden walk that connected her room to the kitchen's back door, and looked up at the giant moon. The surface was dappled with shadows. Against the night sky, it looked close enough to reach out and touch. She couldn't remember ever seeing such a beautiful moon in all her years growing up back East, and was once again glad she'd made the decision to change the circumstances of her life. The faint scent of sweet smoke drifted to her nose. Puzzled, she turned, and the sight of Logan Yates seated on the bench in the dark stole her breath. The smoke flowed from the cheroot in his hand. Although the night masked his features, she felt the potent power in his eyes as if it were full day.

"Evening," he said quietly.

Willing herself to breathe, Mariah nodded and replied, "Evening. I—didn't know you were back."

"Change of plans."

She fought to master the trembles suddenly racking her skin, and felt the need to explain why she was outside in her thin nightgown. "My—room was hot. I came out to get some air." And because she couldn't seem to master wits either, added inanely, "I—couldn't get the window open."

"I'll look at it in the morning."

What Logan really wanted to look at was her bent over his arm with the nightgown undone and her breasts lit by the moon. He noted that although his body refused to rise to the occasion with Val, he was instantaneously erect the moment Mariah Cooper stepped into view. He realized he had two choices—either pursue her and hope a taste of her loveliness would finally cure his desire, or continue to deny his need and thus make himself insane. "You should probably go back inside, Mariah, because if I stand, I'm going to eat you up."

Mariah's knees turned to water. The heat in his voice flowed up from her thighs, tightened her breasts and whispered over her lips until they parted of their own accord. Over her pounding heart, she once again forced herself to breathe. No man had ever whispered such a thing to her before, and she sensed he meant each and every word. Rather than attempt to fight a battle she had no weapons against, she responded shakily, "Good night," and fled like a hare before a wolf.

In the dark, a small smile crossed Logan's lips.

A shaken Mariah crawled back into bed. Lying there, she willed herself to calm and revisited his warning. Why on earth had he said that? According to Alanza he'd gone to visit his mistress, so shouldn't he be reserving such talk for her? *Change of plans.* Had he not gone? There were no answers, but the overpowering force of his warning continued to haunt her, mainly because she'd never experienced anything like it before. The potent remembrance resonated inside again, and only in the dark would she admit that parts of herself were curious and that her body had been left restless and awakened in a strange new way.

She turned over to get away from her racing thoughts. Was he still outside? Had he said what he had just to vex her in retaliation for the battles they'd been having? She didn't put it past him, but there'd been something in his tone and manner that made her think something more serious was afoot. She just wished she knew what.

Chapter 10

After her fretful night, Mariah was grateful for the pink rays of dawn because it meant she could get up. The window would definitely have to be fixed; she didn't want to spend another night tossing and turning. In truth, the heat hadn't been the only deterrent to a restful sleep, but she refused to dwell on it. Whatever last night meant would eventually be revealed. The only question remaining was did she have the confidence to handle the outcome? and she answered herself with a rousing yes.

A sharp rap on her hallway door made her glance up. "Yes?"

"Are you awake?"

Logan. She leapt from the bed and quickly dragged on her robe to hide her nightgown. "Yes."

"Just want to let you know that the bathing room is all yours."

"Thank you."

"I'm going to Lupe's to get some eggs so I can cook breakfast."

"That's supposed to be my job."

Silence held for a few seconds. When the door opened, she drew back with surprise and dragged the belt of her robe tighter.

He studied her from the doorway with a look of amusement and part exasperation. "Do you get up every morning spoiling for an argument?"

"Of course not."

"Good morning by the way."

She nodded. "Good morning."

"Do you know how to cook over an open fire?"

"No, but I'm willing to learn."

"So if I promise to teach you, is it okay for me to cook today so we don't starve?"

Her smile peeked out. "I'm sorry, I just want to earn my salary."

"You'll get your chance. I ordered your stove yesterday and an icebox."

"You did?" She was elated by the news all the while terribly uncomfortable standing there talking with him in her nightgown.

"What's the matter?"

"You shouldn't be in my room when I'm in my nightclothes."

"Another one of those gentleman rules?"

"Yes."

"Sorry." But he didn't leave and the longer he stayed the more her nervousness was replaced by that strange awakening.

"Should I apologize for what I said to you last night?" he asked quietly.

Mariah's heart pounded. The conversation was so unlike any she'd had before, she had no idea how to respond.

In a tone equally as soft he confessed, "Not sure what I'm supposed to do about you, Mariah."

Trembling, she asked, "What do you mean?"

"You've kicked me, thrown rocks at me, and all I want to do is slide you into my arms and kiss you until the mountains turn to dust."

She was going to faint—she just knew she was going to faint.

"And you're an innocent, too, so that complicates matters, but my attraction's rising, and I think yours is, too."

He was right, though well-raised women weren't supposed to acknowledge such things. "Are you telling me all this just to vex me?"

"No, *querida*. It's to keep myself talking so I don't come over there and kiss you the way I want to."

The sensuality in his eyes and low-toned voice turned her insides into warmed lazy streams of response. She didn't know what *querida* translated to, but the parts of herself now attuned to him wanted to be named so again.

And then he walked over to where she stood shaking.

"I lost," he whispered and ran a finger down her cheek. He was standing so close that the heat of his big body penetrated the thin fabric of her nightclothes to her skin as if she had on nothing at all.

"Have you ever been kissed?" He lowered his

mouth to hers and pressed a slow series of opening kisses against her lips that stole her reason.

"Once, maybe twice . . ."

He continued to tease her lips lightly, brushing the sealed corners until they parted from the coaxing. "I want to love you in a field of wildflowers beneath the sun and breeze, then take you again outside in the moonlight, but I can't . . ."

She moaned and her legs turned to sand. His strong arm gently braced her back and pulled her in flush against him. The contact sent them both soaring. She'd never felt so boneless; he'd never tasted a mouth so sweet. She wanted to remain unmoved, he was determined she would be, so her lips parted to allow the heated delving of his tongue.

Someone whispered, "Oh my Lord . . ." and when Mariah realized the words were hers, she backed away, breathless and dazzled.

Logan gazed down at her passion-lidded eyes and traced a finger over her kiss-swollen lips. She made such an alluring picture, all he wanted to do was tip her back on the bed and spend the rest of the day making hot carnal love and whispering *querida*, but he needed to leave. He'd already lost one battle with himself. If he lost the one he was fighting now, she would end up on the bed. "I'll get the eggs and meet you out back."

Treating her to a soft kiss of parting, he exited

and the shaken Mariah dropped to the edge of the bed and fell back against the mattress. *Goodness!* she thought over her racing heart. The few kisses she'd shared with Tillman had never left her pulsing or throbbing so scandalously. Kaye shared with Mariah the details of the marriage-bed talk Kaye'd been given by her mother, and it was the only lesson Mariah had ever received on man-and-woman things. According to Winnie, all a woman need do was lie there and think about the next day's household chores, and that *it* would be over quickly. Mariah knew that kisses could lead to *it,* but Kaye hadn't mentioned anything about throbbing or wildflower meadows. She suddenly felt as ignorant as a squirrel in a classroom. How in the world was she going to face him for the rest of the day? Would the throbbing in her blood soon cease? Lord, she hoped so, because at the moment, all she wanted was to call him back and ask him to kiss her again. Shocked at the direction of her thoughts, she sat up and grabbed her things. Maybe by the time she took care of her needs in the washroom, her body would return to its normal state and she'd be able to remember that he had a mistress.

When Logan rode up, the Gutierrez boys were seated on the grass under their olive tree eating breakfast. Offering them a wave he continued on to the coop, where he found Lupe and Alanza talking.

"Morning ladies."

They both offered him greetings in return.

"Lupe, I need about a half dozen eggs, please."

"Certainly. Is Senora Cooper cooking breakfast this morning?"

"No I am. She doesn't know how to cook over an open fire, at least not yet." Logan knew he'd be recalling the sound of her breathless, *oh my lord* for the rest of his days.

Alanza asked, "Have you ordered the new stove?"

"Yes. Should be here in a week or so."

Lupe said, "I'll go and get your eggs."

"*Gracias.*"

She departed leaving him and Alanza alone.

"I didn't expect to see you so early," she said. "Is Valencia well?"

His lips thinned for a moment. "She's so well she's heading back east to marry."

"Marry? To whom?" Alanza looked stunned.

He shrugged. "A man she met in Yerba Buena last year and corresponded with since."

"Oh, Logan, I am so sorry."

He waved her off. "Water under the bridge now." He hadn't loved her but he had cared and thought she'd cared for him in return. Obviously, he'd been wrong.

"You and Mariah are well?"

"Yes."

"You aren't turning your eye to her now are you?"

"I don't seem to be having much choice. Dreamt about her."

"Logan. Dios! She hasn't even been here three days. You haven't seduced her already have you?"

"No."

"But you're thinking about it, I can tell."

Whenever Alanza got upset or exasperated she slipped back into her native Spanish and did so then. "I should never have allowed you and your brothers to go to Mexico City with Francisco. The three of you have been cocky and arrogant as stallions ever since."

Her fussing made him smile at her with tender amusement. He'd been sixteen years old the first time he was allowed to go and traveling with her cousin Francisco had been an eye-opener. For a month, he was entertained by some of the finest courtesans in the city. Everything Logan knew about pleasing a woman could be directly attributed to Francisco's patronage. When Drew and Noah became old enough, they, too, began spending summers with him. Sadly, five years ago, he was laid to rest as a result of a duel over the ruining of the eldest daughter of a wealthy Mexican Don. Alanza might regret allowing her sons those visits, but Logan would be grateful for the rest of his life. "What are your plans for the day?"

Still giving him the evil eye, she replied, "I'm going over to the Wiyot *rancheria* to help with the preparations for Green Feather's Brush Dance."

Green Feather was his goddaughter and a young woman in the Wiyot tribe. The Brush Dance was being performed in honor of her leaving home to attend Hampton Institute in Virginia. "Do they need my help with anything?"

"Can you ride over and talk to her sometime today. She's getting a small case of cold feet and Sweet Water's worried she may back out and not go."

Sweet Water was her mother. "Sure."

"Thank you, and do me another favor?"

"And that is?"

"Leave Mariah alone unless you plan to make her your *eposa*."

Since he doubted taking his housekeeper as his wife would be an outcome, he said nothing.

Lupe's return saved him from more motherly directives. He took the basket she'd placed the eggs in, and after giving the silent Alanza a parting peck on the cheek, he rode off. On the way back to his place, he stopped in to see Bonnie, who gave him bacon, a few steaks, and the last of the morning's biscuits. Loaded up, he finally headed home.

When Mariah joined him outside, he had a small fire going in a pit bordered by stones. Above the flames was a piece of metal upon which sat two black skillets similar to the ones she'd used back home to fry chicken. One skillet held thick slabs of fragrant-smelling bacon and the other a very large steak.

"What do you usually eat in the mornings?" he asked, turning the bacon over with a long-handled fork.

Grateful he hadn't referenced their kissing, she replied readily, "A couple pieces of toast and tea."

He shook his head. "Not enough to keep a tadpole alive. It's a wonder you haven't blown away."

"It suits me." She took a look at all he had been cooking, and at the bowl holding what appeared to be the yolks of at least a half dozen eggs. "I see you eat much more."

"Yes, I do. Man has to keep up his strength."

His eyes moved over her and her stomach fluttered as if there were tiny wings inside. To distract herself, she studied the height of the flames and how the skillets were placed in hopes of duplicating the setup tomorrow morning. "What are your plans after breakfast?"

"Soon as we're done here, Eli and I will ride the perimeter."

"And that is?"

"The ranch's borders. Need to make sure the fences are intact so our cattle won't stray, and those that aren't ours stay out."

"Is that a big problem—other people's animals?"

"It can be when you own the largest stand of fresh water and the most grass like we do. Got a neighbor who thinks he should be able to graze his herds on Yates land because he doesn't have enough of his own."

She looked out at the ranch's vast grassland. "Seems like you have enough to share."

"We don't."

His tone made her sense she'd hit a nerve.

He went on to explain. "When I was growing up, there were no fences, but when the settlers moved in they squawked about the herds moving over their land, so the government made us put up fences. Now that most of the water and best grass is fenced in, they're squawking again about wanting access. They can't have it both ways."

Mariah guessed she understood his point.

Logan was just about to explain more but he paused at the sight of Reverend Paul Dennis walking in their direction. *Dammit.* He genuinely liked the man, but he hadn't planned on sharing Mariah's company.

"Morning, Logan."

"Reverend. What brings you out so early this morning?" The way the man's eyes kept straying to Mariah, Logan was pretty sure he knew the answer.

"I came to discuss a need for the school but who might this lovely lady be?"

"Mrs. Mariah Cooper. Reverend Paul Dennis. She's my new housekeeper."

"Good morning, Mrs. Cooper. I'm pleased to meet you."

"As am I."

He appeared to be so awestruck by her, you'd've thought he was a miner who'd just found a fist-sized nugget in his pan. Logan wondered how he'd react if he knew she kicked like a mule and threw rocks.

"In speaking with Senora Yates, she said you are a widow?"

"I am."

"My condolences on your loss."

"Thank you," she replied.

Logan noticed that she made it a point not to look his way, but he'd promised to keep her secret and he would.

"Are you a churchgoing woman?" the reverend asked.

"I am. Attended Mother Bethel in Philadelphia my entire life."

"Ah, one of the most famous houses of worship in the nation. Bethel's role during abolition is the stuff of legend."

"Yes it is."

Logan removed the bacon from the skillet and set it on a tin plate. He hoped Dennis didn't want to be fed, too.

"Have you had breakfast this morning, Reverend?" she asked.

Logan went still and gave her a look, which she ignored.

"Yes, I have, thanks."

Before Logan could exhale his relief and begin an attempt to hurry Dennis on his way, Eli rode up. "Morning. I could smell that bacon a mile out."

"Go away. This isn't for you." The other hands were out working the horses. He hoped they didn't come looking for handouts, too.

Again, Logan was ignored. "Morning, Mrs. Cooper. Reverend. You step in a bear trap this morning, Logan? See how he treats me?" he asked Mariah.

"I do. Would you like some breakfast?"

Wondering if she planned to feed everyone around, Logan poured some of the milk he'd gotten from Bonnie into the bowl of eggs and beat them with a fork. "Don't encourage him. He's like a mongrel. Feed him once and you'll never get rid of him." He poured the eggs into the hot skillet.

Eli's eyes radiated humor through the lenses of his spectacles. "I've eaten already, but just for that, I want some of that bacon." And bold as day walked over and snagged two pieces.

Reverend Dennis was still so focused on Mariah, Logan swore if he and Eli hadn't been present, the man would've already tossed her over his shoulder and beat a hasty path back to his buggy. "Our services begin at ten, Mrs. Cooper. I'm always looking to increase the congregation, so if you need a way to church, I'd be honored to drive you."

Before she could respond, Logan offered up a response of his own. "If she wants to go, I'll take her, and bring her back."

The reverend stared as if seeing the Second Coming. Eli choked on his bacon and began coughing violently. Logan ignored them both along with the surprise in Mariah's eyes.

The stunned-looking reverend asked, "You'll bring her—to church?"

"Yes."

Eli was still coughing and viewing Logan as if he'd never seen him before. What went unsaid was that although Logan generously paid for most of the church's construction costs seven years ago, he'd yet to set foot inside.

Logan asked Reverend Dennis, "Is there a problem?"

"Um, no," and he glanced back and forth between Logan and Mariah.

Eli did the same, and shook his head.

Logan held the reverend's eyes. "You said you had another reason for stopping by."

"Um yes, I did. Miss Carmichael's taken a higher-paying position and has given her notice." He stopped for a moment to explain to Mariah. "She's our schoolteacher."

"I see, thank you."

He continued, "I know how busy you are, Logan, but I was hoping you'd volunteer to be on the committee to find her replacement."

"Sure. Just let me know when and where you want to start."

"Wonderful. You're always a blessing."

Logan enjoyed doing positive work, but now, he wanted the reverend to go on about his day, preferably taking Eli with him, so that he could eat breakfast with Mariah—alone.

Dennis must've seen that in his face. "Well, I've a lot to do today so I'll get going." But first, he turned to Mariah. "Mrs. Cooper, it's been a pleasure making your acquaintance."

"Same here, sir."

"I'll see you and Logan in church on Sunday."

"Looking forward to it."

His next words were directed squarely at Logan. "As am I."

Logan kept his face void of expression. "Thanks for stopping by."

"You bet." Eyeing Mariah one last time, he walked away.

Mariah asked, "Is he as nice as he seems?"

Logan concentrated on handing her a plate and sitting down with his own. He left the answering to Eli.

"Yes, he is. Does a lot to raise the race, and, he's looking for a wife."

"Is he?"

Logan watched her turn and view the departing reverend with what appeared to be interest. He was so taken aback, he accidently knocked over his plate. The eggs, steak, bacon, and biscuits stared up at him from the dirt. He growled and speared Eli with a look that was met with all the innocence of an angel.

"Oh no," Mariah responded disappointedly. "And after all your work." She had her plate safely in hand. "Here, take some of mine, I'll never be able to eat all this."

Thoroughly disgusted, he declined. "Quite all right. I'll grab something later. I need to get to work. Let's go, Eli."

Barely hiding his mirth, Eli walked to his horse and mounted up, while Logan struck out for the stable to get Diablo.

As they rode off, Logan saw Mariah seated in the grass, happily eating her breakfast—alone.

Chapter 11

Logan looked at the cut in the fence and angrily scanned the surrounding foothills as if searching for the perpetrators.

"Wiley, again?" Eli asked while visually surveying the area, too.

"More than likely. He's the only one around dumb enough not to care what we think about him trespassing."

Arnell Wiley had been a pain in the ass since moving into the area a year ago. He ran a dairy operation, and why he'd purchased land with sparse grass and no water showed how little he knew about the business. Word was he'd been a store clerk back in Kansas and came to California to start over. He was as pretentious as he was irritating.

"You going to talk to him again?"

"Yeah. I have to ride over and see Green Feather, so I'll swing by his place when I'm done there."

"I'll put a crew of night riders together to keep an eye on things out here."

"Good." Logan surveyed the tracks left by the cows. "Looks like he had the whole herd in here."

Where they stood was less than a mile from the river that meandered through Yates land. "I don't want to see a man go broke, but we offered him a

177

reasonable price for his right to water and he rejected it."

Eli countered sarcastically, "Why pay when you can steal it."

Logan sighed angrily and looked at the way the fence had been peeled back to allow the herd inside. "I'll get this repaired later." One more thing to add to his list of duties for the day, when all he wanted was to be at home with Mariah. "Oh, and thanks for making me drop my breakfast."

"Had nothing to do with it. Did enjoy the look on your face though."

Logan rolled his eyes.

They mounted their horses and Eli asked, "You really going to church on Sunday?"

"Yes." The smile on the face of his friend made Logan ask, "What?"

Eli shrugged. "Remember that roan stallion a few years back? The one that tried to keep us from roping his mare?"

"I do." The stallion had put the mare behind him and reared and charged for quite a while, trying to protect the female.

"You reminded me of him this morning."

"I'll see you later." Tightening Diablo's reins, Logan rode away.

After finishing breakfast, Mariah gathered up the dishes and skillets and took everything into the house so she could wash them in the battered metal sink. That there was hot water coming out of the spigots continued to amaze her. She made a mental note to ask Logan where the boiler was located, and what she needed to do to ensure she had hot water when needed. Only then did it occur to her that she had no idea where he kept the soap, but it didn't matter: there was a wealth of buckets and brushes and other cleaning items left on the back porch after the clutter detail. A quick search turned up a small pail of flaked soap. She chiseled some out with a spoon, dropped the globs into the water, and used her hand to swish it around until it began to foam.

While she washed the dishes, she set her passionate encounter with Logan aside for a moment and thought back on Reverend Dennis's visit. He was a decidedly handsome man: tall, dark, and although lacking the mountainlike stature of Logan and Eli, he'd impressed her with his kind and courteous manner. That he was interested in her was plain. In fact, he seemed unable to stop taking peeks at her and that made her smile. Eli said the man was looking for a wife, and from Mariah's initial impression a girl could do worse. Scrubbing the plates, she wondered what it might be like to be married to a preacher. Back in Philadelphia, her pastor's wife held a special place in the hearts of the congregation. She was well respected and known for her quiet, calm nature. Mariah couldn't remember her ever raising her voice in anger, and was certain she'd never kicked or thrown rocks at her husband. Those thoughts brought her mind back to Logan. Why in the world had he offered to take her to church when, on the ride from the train station, she distinctly remembered him saying he didn't attend church? Was she correct in assuming it had to do with the reverend's invitation? If that was the case, she couldn't for the life of her understand why he'd care. One would think he was jealous, but Mariah knew better. Did he think she'd let the reverend kiss her the way she'd let him? Even though Reverend Dennis appeared quite taken by her, he hadn't given her any reason to think he'd do something so ungentlemanly, or would speak to her as scandalously as Logan had. Would his kisses leave her breathless and throbbing? Remembrance rose on the heels of that, along with being called *querida* in a tone of voice that made her senses bloom again. Deciding she didn't need to be thinking about any of this, she focused her thoughts on more tangible concerns, like, How would the congregation view her?

Being a housekeeper, she wasn't expecting to have any status in the community, but she hoped they'd be kind and not whisper behind their hands about her odd-colored eyes. Growing up, in addition to being cruelly named Witch Hazel, she'd also suffered slings and arrows about her light-colored skin. "Straw Hag," some of her classmates called her derisively, along with "uppity" and "light bright—damn near white," even though she wasn't close to being pale enough to pass herself off as anything other than a woman of the race. Her mother seemed to have issues with her coloring as well, which only added to Mariah's low opinion of her looks. Although she wasn't the only bright-skinned child among her peers, she had drawn the cruelest remarks. Her mother explained the cause as "those ugly gold eyes of yours." Thinking of her mother, she wondered again how she might be faring, then went back to the dishes.

Once she was done, she put everything away in the battered cupboards and decided to do some housecleaning. At home, she had begun her day by removing the day-old ashes from the stove and refilling it with new kindling so it could be lit for the breakfast meal, but because there was no stove, she instead went through the house and gathered the glass chimneys from all the lamps and set them in a sink of fresh, soapy dishwater. They needed washing in order to rid them of the soot and grime caused by the kerosene used to light them.

When they were all clean and sparkling, she spent a few moments trimming all the lamp wicks with a pair of sharp scissors before replacing the chimneys.

Kerosene was foul smelling and once the house had furniture and curtains, she'd have to wash the drapes weekly and wipe down the furniture daily to rid them of the smoke, soot, and fumes.

Since all the windows were clean and the clutter removed, she decided to take up the rugs and give them a sound beating. After that, she'd scrub the floors.

Alanza placed the flowers she was carrying at the base of her husband's headstone and stepped back. Today was his birthday and although her grief had run its course, she still missed him very much. The family cemetery was on the far north end of the ranch and held the remains of her grandparents and parents. When her time came, her grave would be there, too. She visited his resting place often—to talk, to reminisce, to vent, but mostly to think back on the day Max Rudd and the others brought his lifeless body home. She'd been so devastated by the sight, she'd wanted to join him in death, but knew she had to remain stoic for the sake of her equally devastated sons. Only after they'd been put to bed did she ride out to riverbank, and there in the darkness she'd keened and rocked herself until sunrise. During those first few months of widowhood, men wanting to marry her circled like vultures, but she was so afraid they wanted the land more than they did her and her sons, she sent them away. Armed with a headstrong determination to make the business pay, she vowed to go it alone, but as she'd noted earlier, she didn't know anything about doing it properly and eventually paid the ultimate price for that ignorance. The business floundered, and in spite of her clawing and scratching and praying, their way of life plummeted so far that there came a day when she had nothing to feed her children. Her father, who'd refused to help even when Abraham was alive, had passed away a few years earlier, and her mother soon after. Her only other family was her father's brother residing in Yerba Buena. Pride and the remembrance of the shame she'd brought down on her parents kept her from asking for his assistance earlier, but after looking into the hollow eyes of her starving sons, she swallowed that pride, put them in a wagon and drove to Yerba Buena. Once there, she dropped to her knees before her uncle and begged.

Alanza looked into the distance at the mountains and remembered that day as the most humbling experience of her life. She who'd been born to money and privilege had nothing, and by God's grace her uncle was moved. He helped her to her feet and showed her a copy of her father's will leaving his rancho and accumulated wealth to her second son, his first blood grandson, Andrew Antonio. Her uncle then sent her home under the escort of fifteen of his *vaqueros*, who were to assist her and the then fourteen-year-old Logan with everything they needed to make the ranch a success. She cried grateful tears the entire way.

The sound of an approaching rider interrupted her reverie. She turned to see Max Rudd on his signature palomino stallion. He'd been a great help both before and after her visit to her uncle, and was as generous and kind to her as his friend Abraham had been. Max was only a few years older than she—handsome, too, if she were being truthful. However, after Abe's death, she'd vowed to never turn her heart to another man—not after the disastrous results from her first flirtation with what she thought to be love. She did enjoy his companionship, because outside of her sons, he knew her best.

"Good morning, Max."

He swung easily out of the saddle and approached. "Morning, Lanz. Bonnie told me you were up here."

"It's Abe's birthday."

He nodded knowingly. "Miss him."

"As do I."

For a moment they eyed the headstone in silence. The day after he brought Abe's body home, he'd dug the grave and stood beside her and the boys while the priest read the words. Those deeds alone endeared him to her for a lifetime.

"He'd be proud of you," Max voiced. "His sons are fine, upstanding men, and you've turned this spread into something to behold."

"You were a big help with both." She looked back down at the headstone and silently sent Abe her regards and love.

Max waited soundlessly at her side.

"I'm ready now." She placed her hand in the crook of his arm and together they walked back to the horses.

"Did Logan talk to you about the cabinetry?" she asked.

"He did. I brought my tapes with me to do some measuring, but I'm more interested in meeting this new housekeeper. Figure she must be quite a pistol if he's having cabinets made."

"Mariah's more like a Colt. She's a widow from Philadelphia and got that house of his cleaned out the very first day she arrived."

"Do you like her?"

"Immensely."

"And Logan?"

"Good question. I think he likes her more than he's willing to admit at the moment. She's been giving him fits."

"Good for her. It's about time he met a woman who didn't melt in his mouth."

Alanza wholeheartedly agreed. "She's also a very beautiful young woman. I imagine the men will be lining up to court her very soon."

"How'll Logan handle that, do you think?"

She shrugged. "With Valencia no longer in the picture, we'll see."

"What do you mean?"

She told him about Valencia's upcoming marriage.

"That must've been a kick in the head for him."

"I'm sure it was, but you know Logan, the last thing he'll show is his feelings. He called it water under the bridge." Of her three sons, Logan was sometimes the easiest to figure out, but also the hardest when it came to discerning how he felt inside. She thought it might be because he was alone a lot after his mother died in childbirth and had only himself to confide in. Abe did what he could with his raising, but he had a ranch to run and horses to wrangle, neither of which were conducive to raising an infant, so Logan spent his early years with a variety of wet nurses and women Abe paid to keep an eye on him until he was old enough to be at the ranch alone. When Alanza first met him he was only six, but he could already cook and ride with the confidence of a boy twice his age.

When they reached Logan's house, Mariah was outside beating rugs. Stopping at their approach, she called out cheerily, "Morning, Mrs. Yates."

"Morning. I see you're busy."

She wiped away the perspiration on her brow. "Just earning my keep."

"This is Max Rudd. He's a wonderful carpenter and a great friend. He'll be making the new kitchen cabinets. Max. Mariah Copper."

"Pleased to meet you, Mr. Rudd."

"Same here. Welcome to California."

He and Alanza dismounted. "Is Logan around?"

"No. He and Eli went to ride the perimeter. Would you like to come in? I'd offer you refreshments but there aren't any. I'll make up for it next time."

"Don't worry about it. Let's go look at the kitchen."

Inside, he surveyed the job to be done. "Made these cabinets myself, Mrs. Cooper, a long time ago." He ran his finger over the bullet holes and turned questioning eyes her way.

"Apparently, whiskey was involved."

He chuckled and shook his head. While Alanza and Mariah looked on, he spent a few minutes measuring and writing down his calculations on a piece of paper. "Be a while before they're done. Anything else you need beside the cabinets and counters?"

"Would it be too much trouble to ask for a couple of breadboards?"

"No trouble at all. Anything else?"

"Not that I can think of. How about you, Mrs. Yates?"

Alanza shook her head. "I can't think of anything either."

"Then I'll head over to the mill, pick out some wood and get started."

Mariah thanked him and the three left the kitchen. In the parlor, he stopped and stared around. "Lanza said you whipped this place into shape your very first day."

"I had to. It was quite the mess and smelled even worse."

Alanza added, "And he's starting on the bunk-house as well, thanks to Mariah."

"Really? Are you one of those conjure women, Mrs. Cooper?"

Amusement lit her gold eyes. "No. Just trying to be as stubborn as he is."

"Well, keep it up."

"Thank you, and thank you for stopping by."

"My pleasure."

Outside he and Alanza walked to their mounts. "Thanks Max."

"You're welcome. So, he's going to rebuild the bunkhouse, too?"

She nodded.

"Have you started picking out names for your grandkids yet?"

She exploded with laughter. "Only you would be able to read my mind."

For a moment their eyes held and Alanza sensed everything she felt for him rise to the surface. As if reading her thoughts, he said knowingly, "One day soon, you and I are going to talk."

"About what?"

He mounted up. "We both know you're way smarter than that, so no sense in you playing dumb all of a sudden."

"I've no idea what you're talking about."

He gave her a lazy grin and reined his horse around. "Keep pretending then. See you, Lanz." And he rode away.

Chapter 12

Still simmering over not getting any breakfast, and the trespassing Arnell Wiley and his cows, Logan shook it all off and rode to the *rancheria* where his fifteen-year-old goddaughter Green Feather lived with her parents. She was the pride of her people, teachers, and the surrounding community. She was also his pride and joy, and that she might not attend Hampton was disappointing. She and her family were members of the Wiyot tribe, Indians who once inhabited the California coast. With the arrival of the Spanish, followed by the influx of the multitudes drawn to the area by the gold strike, the way of life for the state's native tribes was irrevocably changed. None more so than the Wiyot. In 1860, a man named Hank Larrabee, who'd often boasted of having murdered Indian children in the past, entered the Wiyot village while the men were away and massacred most of the women and children. The few that survived moved in with neighboring Mattole and Yurok tribes and now lived on *rancherias*, small plots given to some of the tribes as compensation for the confiscation of their ancestral lands. On the *rancherias*, they set their own laws and were allowed to govern themselves without interference from the legislators in Sacramento. Logan wasn't sure how dead set she was on not attending, or if talking to her would make a difference, but he'd grown up with her father and knew the struggles their people faced in the years since the massacre. When Reverend Dennis first floated the idea of her enrolling, Logan offered to provide the funds for her clothing, train fare, and other essentials, because her success could be the way to a better life for her, her parents, and the tribe.

Her father stepped out of the house as Logan dismounted and greeted him with a smile that mirrored their many years of friendship. "How are you, Logan?"

"Doing well, Walks. And you?" His tribal name was Walks Like Mountain, but in the White world he was called Enoch Redwood.

"Sweet Water has me running from sunup to sundown getting ready for the Brush Dance. I'm honored to be Green Feather's father but I may not survive this."

He nodded understandingly. Sweet Water's Christian name was Lucy. Many tribal members were given White names after the massacre in hopes it might deter bigots like Larrabee from targeting them again. As it stood, the hate formerly directed at Blacks and Indians had now turned to the Chinese, but hate was hate, and Logan didn't want it touching anyone.

"So, has she really changed her mind?"

He shrugged. "Says she has. Sweet, course, is having none of it and refuses to let her back out, but Feather's my only daughter and has always had my heart, so I'm willing to let her make up her own mind."

"Even if you don't agree?"

"Even if I don't agree, which is why my Sweet Water sent for you."

"So where's Feather now?"

"Out back. She and her mother just had another argument, so Sweet's gone up the road to visit her sister to cool off, and Feather's outside doing the same."

Feather's Christian name was Louisa. She and her mother were both strong-minded individuals. Logan had played the role of peacemaker before. "Wish me luck."

"You know I do. Are you coming to the Brush Dance tomorrow night?"

"Wouldn't miss it for the world."

Logan found his goddaughter behind the house seated on a large boulder. Her black eyes were red rimmed and teary and she had a wadded-up handkerchief in her hand. At the sight of him, she stood and her watery smile filled Logan's heart.

"Hi, Uncle Logan."

"Hi, Feather. How are you?"

"Been better. Mama sent for you?"

He nodded.

She flounced back down on the boulder and sighed dramatically. "I'm fifteen. You'd think she'd let me make up my own mind."

He sat beside her. "So, give me your side."

"I don't wish to go to Hampton anymore. I'm very grateful to Reverend Dennis for all his help, but I want to stay at home."

"And your reason?"

She shrugged. "I just do."

"You know I'll need a better reason than that, so try and explain it to me if you can."

"I just don't want to go."

"Are you afraid?"

"Of course not."

"I would be."

She turned to him. "But why?"

"Long way from home. New place, new people. I'd probably be scared to death." *Had Mariah been afraid?*

She looked away.

"I'd wonder whether my mates would like me, or if they thought I was strange. Whole long list of worries. But then, you've always been brave— except that time you ran away because you didn't want to start school. How old were you? Five? Six?"

She didn't reply.

"You weren't even big enough to see the top of the dining table but you had your mind made up, and told us you weren't going to school because

192

your parents and your brothers would be lonely without you. Do you remember that?"

"I do," came her softly spoken reply.

He placed his arms around her shoulders and pulled her close. "So, now. Tell me what's really going on inside."

She didn't say anything at first, but then she looked up into his face and water filled her eyes. "I'm so scared," she whispered. "For all the reasons you just said. It's so far away, and I won't know anyone, and I'll miss you and Mama and Papa. What if I don't have the right clothes, or say the wrong things, or turn out not to be smart enough? Please don't make me go."

He gave her a squeeze and kissed her forehead. "It's okay to be scared. As for smarts, you'll win that race hands down. I don't know anyone around here who's smarter than you. And don't worry about your clothing. I know a lady who just moved here from back East. She's a seamstress, and she'll help us make sure you'll be the best dressed young lady that school has ever enrolled."

She pulled back. "Really?"

"Truly. She's my new housekeeper. I'll talk to her when I get home. And remember, you have a pretty wealthy godfather as well, who'll send you spending money and train fare so you can travel home in the summers, and for Christmas. Personally, I think you'll be the envy of every girl there."

"I don't know," she said doubtfully. "Maybe I should just stay here and marry Carlos."

He stiffened. "Who's Carlos?"

"I met him at Grandmother's birthday celebration a few weeks back. He's a Yurok. He asked me to marry him."

"Just like that?"

"Yes."

"Feather?" he asked in an incredulous tone.

"What? He seems nice, and his parents know my family."

"So, you're going to give up an opportunity to advance your schooling to marry a boy you don't even know? Come on, now, girl. What's happened to your intelligence? Does your father know about him?"

"No."

"Good thing." Logan couldn't believe what he was hearing. "Marrying some boy at the drop of the hat should scare you a lot more than going away to Hampton."

"But—"

"No buts. You're clutching at straws and we both know it."

She sighed resignedly. "I know."

For the next few minutes, she didn't say anything, but he could tell by her contemplative face and the unseeing way she stared off that she was thinking deeply. She finally glanced over. "You really think I'll be okay there?"

"I don't think. I know."

She studied him for a silent second. "You're a very good godfather."

"Think so?"

She nodded a response. "You always help me get past the big things that make me afraid. Like the time I ran away, and you all found me, and I said, I was still never going to school. Mama and Papa were fussing, but you looked at me and said, 'Well, if you want your brother to grow up and be smarter, fine, don't go to school.' I was floored."

They both chuckled.

"And the time I didn't want to learn to swim because I was afraid of the water. You took me somewhere, I've no idea where we were, but we sat on the bank and watched otters. Seemed like we were there all day watching them playing in the water like silly children, and by the time we left I wanted to learn. I let Papa teach me the very next day."

"I'm surprised you remember that. You couldn't've been older than four summers."

"But I do. Sitting on the bank and eating sand-wiches and drinking lemonade and watching the otters play is probably my first real memory of you."

Logan's heart swelled.

She finally smiled. "Thanks, Uncle Logan."

"So what about Hampton?"

"I guess I'm going to go. I'm still scared but talking to you made it okay. Thank you."

"You're welcome."

"Are you coming to my dance?"

"Of course."

"Will you bring your housekeeper so I may meet her?"

"I'll ask her if she wants to come. She might enjoy meeting everyone."

He looked into the dark eyes of the young woman who once fit into the crook of his arm, and spoke from his heart. "You're going to go far in life, Feather. Farther than anyone in your tribe has ever gone before, so go to Virginia and kick some tail, for yourself, your parents, and your ancestors who never got this chance, okay?"

Tears flowed down her cheeks. "I will."

They shared a tight hug and he whispered thickly, "Good girl."

Riding home, he felt good. He decided not to stop by and curse at Arnell about his trespassing because he didn't want to ruin his mood, but because it was his father's birthday, he stopped at the cemetery.

At the grave he took off his hat and stood solemnly. He knew the flowers at the base of the headstone were Alanza's tribute. When his father died, Logan thought the world had come to an end. He remembered how much he'd wanted to cry but the death left him as the man on the place, so he'd held tightly to Alanza's hand and watched Max and the other pallbearers lower the casket in the ground. Abraham Yates had never been overly affectionate, but he had been kind and fair. "Miss you, Pa."

Because Logan's mother died giving birth, he'd never known her. He'd known his father well enough to know that he'd miss the old wrangler for the rest of his life. Placing his hand atop the big cross-shaped headstone, he squeezed it, lingered for a few moments more, and then walked back to his mount.

He turned Diablo out into the pasture, then went to find Eli. He was leaning on the fence of the corral watching one of the hands ride the mare. "She finally came around?"

"Yep. I'll send her on to Stockton in another day or so, just to make sure she's really ready for the saddle."

"Sounds good. Do me a favor and get somebody out to repair that fence. Decided I've got something else I want to do."

"Figured as much. Sent two men up soon as I got back here."

Logan smiled. "You think you know me pretty well, do you?"

"Almost as well as you know me. Try not to get kicked or hit with rocks this time."

Logan laughed and walked over to the house.

As he entered the door, she yelled, "Stop!"

He froze. She was in the parlor on her knees

197

with a brush in her hand. "I'm scrubbing floors. Doorway's still wet."

The sleeves of her blouse were rolled up, and she'd undone a few of the buttons he longed to conquer to cool herself while she worked. There was perspiration on her brow and a rug beneath her knees to cushion her positioning. He'd never seen such a comely scrubwoman. "I'll go around to the kitchen door."

"Thank you." She went back to her scrubbing.

Entering the house again, he was struck by the smell of lemon pervading the air. It was a far nicer scent than the one that had greeted him when the house was in shambles. Maybe having a housekeeper wasn't such a bad idea after all, especially one he was having trouble keeping his hands off of. He cut through the dining room and stood at the edge of the parlor and found her still on her knees. "Smells much better in here."

"Yes, it does."

"Have you eaten since breakfast?"

"No."

"Neither have I. Are you almost done?"

"No. I still have the hallway, the washroom, and your bedroom to do."

He liked the idea of her being on her knees in his bedroom but not scrubbing the floor. "Can I distract you with the offer of food?"

"I really wanted to get as much of this done as possible today."

"You can come back to it later. No sense in dropping from starvation."

"May I remind you that there's no food here?"

"I have a plan."

"Why does that concern me?"

"Could be you have a suspicious nature."

"Could be I have a right to when it comes to you."

He enjoyed bantering with her and wanted it to continue but it wouldn't if she spent the day doing chores. "You wound me, madam. I'm simply offering you sustenance, nothing more. So, how about I dump that bucket while you change into something a bit more dry." As it stood, the front of her blouse was wet, and he could plainly see the outlines of her corset beneath, which brought back the dream of her breasts in the moonlight.

"I am slightly sopped. All right, I'll bite, but I'll dump the bucket. It's what I'm being paid for."

"Must you challenge everything?"

"Yes, I must. I think women agree with you far more than is healthy."

He studied her with a smile. "Will you ever give me quarter?"

"No, because you'd run over me like a team of horses."

"And you won't allow that."

She shook her head. "Not you, or anyone else for that matter."

Determination momentarily hardened her

features and he was reminded of her admission that she'd been mistreated before coming west. He was admittedly taken by her beauty but the small shows of strength were equally intriguing. "All right. You take care of the buckets. I'll hitch up the wagon and meet you out front."

"Are we going to eat with your stepmother?"

"No."

"Then where?"

"It's a surprise."

"Surprise," she echoed doubtfully.

"Only way I know to keep you off balance." That and kissing her, he reminded himself.

"And you believe that to be a good thing, I take it."

"Give the lady a cigar."

She rolled her eyes. "All right. I'll meet you in a moment." But she was smiling, so he left her with his mood still high.

Mariah dumped the dirty water into the yard behind the house and set the bucket and brush back on the porch. After drying her hands, she walked the short distance to her room and entered via its courtyard door. She had no idea what Logan was up to now, but housework did have her stomach longing to be fed, so she changed her blouse and skirt, took a brush to her hair and went to meet him.

As promised, he was waiting beside the buggy.

"Ready?" he asked.

She nodded. She half expected him to lift her onto the seat, but he surprised her by simply offering her his hand in assistance. The warm contact sent heat wafting up her arm, and her heart pounded in reaction, but she refused to look his way lest he see it in her face. Once she was settled, he came around and took his seat behind the reins.

"So, where are we going?"

"Told you it was a surprise, so just relax."

"That makes me worry."

"Figure it would."

He drove them away.

Chapter 13

They set out toward the river, passing the corrals and the outbuildings on the way. All day long, she'd thrown herself into the household chores as a way to keep from thinking about this morning's potent kiss, but now, without that to distract her, coupled with his presence on the seat beside her, the memory rose and refused to leave. She wondered if she'd be immune to his kiss the next time—the way one became immune to, say, the mumps. She was so out of her element, she wished Kaye was near so she could ask her if Carson's kisses moved her in the same breathtaking manner.

"Penny for your thoughts."

"Just thinking about my friend Kathleen and wondering how she's faring."

"How long have you known her?"

"Since primary school. She's been a true friend since the first day we met."

"And how'd you meet?"

So she told him about Liam Anderson and Kate's father and Mrs. Ainsley's dress. She left out the part about the whipping she'd received. The unfair punishment had left her bitter for weeks, not that that mattered to her mother. Once again, she wondered how she might be faring, but pushed the thoughts away.

"So whatever happened to Anderson?"

She shrugged. "I heard rumors that he wound up in a reformatory but no idea if they were true or not. I was just happy to never lay eyes on him again. I don't imagine you were picked on in school."

"Nope. Had a few fights though, but never picked on anyone. Alanza would've taken a buggy whip to my hide." He looked her way. "Do you want to continue your driving lessons?"

"I do, but not with you."

"Why not?"

"Because you have no patience and frankly, you're terrible at it."

"Mariah?"

"It's the truth, Logan. You are. I'm not trying to hurt your feelings, but to keep peace in the land, I should have someone else teach me, okay?"

"Okay, but you really know how to wound a man."

She thought he kissed far better than he gave driving instructions, but she kept that to herself. His head was big enough as it was.

A short while later, they arrived at the riverbank. It was the same area she'd stomped off to yesterday after pelting him with the rock. She looked over questioningly. "What's to eat here?"

"Fish, soon as I catch a couple."

"How might I help?"

"By peeling some potatoes, and not throwing rocks."

She dropped her head to hide her smile. "You have a deal."

He came around to help her down, and this time, he swung her down very slowly before setting her on her feet. The heat of his hands on her waist made her think about his kisses yet again and he was standing near enough to flare her senses to life. Not wanting to succumb, she backed out of his hold. Hoping to sound nonchalant, she asked, "What kind of fish are in the water?"

"Bass, mostly."

"Do you fish here often?"

"Often enough. You ever been fishing?"

"No." She found herself staring at the shape of his mouth and lips. Catching herself, she snapped her eyes back up to his and saw him smile.

"Let me get my pole and gear out of the wagon."

While he fished, Mariah peeled the four potatoes, and did what she could to offset his effects. Nothing worked—not thinking about scrubbing floors, or washing lamp chimneys or beating rugs. Every thought centered on him— from the shape of his mouth and the feel of it mastering hers, to the remembrances of his hard chest against her breasts, to the whispered word, *querida*. She glanced over at him standing on the bank. He was as bold in stature and ways as the wild, untamed surroundings. Were he on the streets of Philadelphia men would scurry out of his path and women would flock to him like birds to corn. Growing up, she had no idea men like him existed. In her world, the opposite gender was represented by gently raised men like Tillman and Kaye's father. Granted, Tillman had no spine, but had he proposed marriage, she would've said yes because he was the type of man well brought up women were supposed to be drawn to. Yet, she found herself drawn to Logan Yates and it made no sense. He had a mistress, which told her he viewed her as just another female amusement. When it came to kissing and the rest, she might be a babe in the woods, but she took pride in herself and wanted a man who viewed her as more than just someone to dally with.

It didn't take him long to snag a few fat fish, which he promptly scaled, gutted, seasoned, and set in a frying pan over a fire he built in a nearby fire ring. A second pan held the potatoes. When everything was done, he produced two tin plates and tableware. She found the hot fish succulent and the potatoes excellently seasoned.

"This is very good. You cook well."

"Thanks. Started cooking when I was around six or seven."

"That's about the age I began to sew."

"Did you enjoy it?"

"No, not at first, but I didn't have a choice. As I mentioned yesterday, she was a very strict task-master."

"The two of you didn't get along very well, I take it?"

"No." Mariah thought back on her joyless childhood. In her mother's household, there'd been no time for play. As soon as she came home from school, there was sewing to be done or household chores needing attention. As she grew older, she'd been forbidden things like socials at the church and parties given by friends. She'd never even celebrated her own birthday, but she didn't reveal any of that to him.

"Do you want to talk about it?"

"No." It still hurt to talk about how much her mother didn't love her, and she didn't know him well enough to trust him with such a painful truth. "Maybe someday."

"Sometimes demons are best conquered when shared."

The gently spoken words caught her off guard. His face mirrored his voice, but she still refused to reply.

"Okay. I won't press you."

"Thank you." That he'd respected her wishes caused her to wonder about the man beneath all the arrogance and bluster. Who was he really? Needing to change the topic of conversation because he'd occupied her mind far too much already, she told him about Mr. Rudd's visit. "He said the cabinets will be ready in a short while." She'd noticed the way Mr. Rudd's eyes kept lingering on Alanza during his visit and wondered if the two were sweet on each other. She didn't ask Logan about that however, because it wasn't any of her business.

"You mentioned you ordered a stove and some other things. That sofa in the parlor is on its last legs. It needs to be replaced as well."

"Ordered one of those, too." He then proceeded to tell her about all the items he'd ordered, and she found herself speechless. "You picked out china? What's it look like?"

He shrugged. "It's white."

"Did someone at the store help you choose it?"

"No. I looked through the catalog and found things that resembled the ones Alanza had and put them on the list."

His explanation went a little ways in allaying her fears about his choices. She supposed she'd just have to wait and see what everything looked like when the items arrived.

They finished off their fish and potatoes, and Mariah wondered how such simple fare could leave her feeling so sated and stuffed. Now, she could return to work on a full stomach. "Thank you for the meal, I should really get back to my chores."

"Not yet. Have a favor to ask first." Logan appreciated her strong work ethic, but for a man who'd never had a problem holding a woman's attention, she was giving him a small fit. "My goddaughter will be attending Hampton Institute in a few months, and I'm wondering if you could sew her up a few of those dresses like the one you had on at the train station. She's worried her clothes won't be fine enough."

"You have a goddaughter?"

"I do. Does that surprise you?"

"Why, yes. What's her name?"

"Green Feather. She's Wiyot Indian. Christian name's Louisa." The wonder on her face pleased him.

"How many ensembles do you think she'll be needing?"

"I've no idea, which is why I thought I'd ask for your help."

"I wasn't aware that Indians were allowed to advance their education. She must be quite the young woman."

"She is. Reverend Dennis made her enrollment possible. According to him, Hampton has been accepting Indian students since seventy-eight."

"I'd be honored to lend a hand. When may I meet her?"

"Her family's holding a Brush Dance tomorrow evening to bless her success. She specifically asked me to bring you along so the two of you could meet. Would you like to go?"

Because she'd never attended social gatherings back in Philadelphia, Mariah's first instinct was to decline. Reminding herself that she was no longer in Philadelphia propelled her to accept. "I'd love to attend, but what is a Brush Dance exactly?"

"It originated with the Yurok people as a dance to heal a sick child or to bestow a blessing on a child. Now, some of the tribes have them to celebrate special events, and Feather going off to Hampton is very special. When I was young, the dance would start on a Wednesday and end at sunrise on Sundays, but because many in the tribes have to work jobs to provide for their families now, the dance begins at the end of the day on Friday."

"Is it like a dance, dance?"

"No. No reels or waltzing. This is tribal dancing and only the members are allowed in the circle, but there will be singers and food though. Would you still like to go?"

"I would."

"Then we'll ride over together tomorrow evening. We'll probably be out fairly late."

"That's okay."

For a moment, the silence of the countryside rose between them and as it stretched, his call on her senses grew so intensely she thought it might be best to end this interlude and get back to the distracting drudgery of scrubbing floors. "I—I should get back to my chores."

"Is my company so boring that you prefer housework?"

The humor in his tone made her drop her gaze

and smile. "I'm being paid to work, remember?"

"Suppose I offer to pay for your companionship?"

"Then I'd have to change my title from housekeeper to mistress, and I hear you already have one of those."

"And if I told you she tossed me over for a wedding ring?"

"I'd say, bravo for her."

"You're a hard woman, Mariah Cooper."

"Thank you." Mariah had never spoken so boldly to a man before, but something told her that boldness would be needed to keep herself from falling into his arms the way half the female population of California was probably wont to do.

"I'd like to kiss you again."

She decided that he was far more bold than she. "No more kisses, thank you very much."

He closed the distance between them and she felt the dizziness creeping over her again. "Are you thanking me for the kiss?"

"You know that isn't what I meant."

"No?"

"No."

He reached out and traced a whisper-light finger over her lips. Her eyes closed in trembling response. "Hard not to kiss a mouth as sweet-looking as this . . ."

Putting action to words, he touched his lips to

hers and kissed her as lightly as he'd touched her. "Very hard . . ."

"Not fair . . ." she whispered. The bones in her body were melting away.

"All's fair in passion, *querida*."

That word again. That pervasive heat again, and then he was kissing her in earnest and she surrendered, because in spite of all the reasons she wanted to deny him, she couldn't deny herself the feel of being in his arms, or the desire unfurling inside.

"Open your mouth. Let me taste you."

She complied, and he slipped the fiery tip of his tongue inside, playing, coaxing, seducing her there on the riverbank while the wind rustled the trees and the sun warmed her gently. His hands roaming slowly over the back of her blouse singed the skin beneath. His lips slid over the outer rim of her ear and then her jaw before dropping to set fire to the thin strip of flesh above her lacy high collar. Her head fell back and his tongue teased the spot beneath her chin while a pulse began to beat in the secret place between her thighs. Her mind told her being kissed by him was a terrible idea, but it no longer ruled the day. Ruling now were her senses, and a body enjoying learning what it meant to be a woman in the arms of a man.

And because of that, she didn't protest when he moved the palm of his hand over the tip of her breast. As the nipple swelled and she crooned, he looked down into her eyes while transferring the bold caress to the twin. The blaze in his eyes matched the blaze coursing through her blood and she couldn't look away.

Still berrying her nipples expertly, he leaned down and bit them gently through her clothing, which increased the pulsing beat between her thighs to such a spiraling crescendo that she flew apart, shuddering, shaking, and crying out, "Oh!"

Logan knew an orgasm when he heard one, but wasn't sure she did, so he held her against him gently while her body rode the waves of completion. "I have you, *querida*."

Still in the throes, she moaned, "Oh my."

Her sweet convulsing made him want her even more, but he sensed this first lesson was about all she could handle for the moment. Now that she'd been initiated into desire there'd be more to come.

When the trembling finally ceased, he kissed her brow and raised her chin. "That's never happened to you before?" he asked gently.

She gave a hasty shake of her head.

His smile was indulgent. "It's your body's way of releasing pleasure."

"So it's normal?"

"Yes."

"I thought I was having a fit of some kind. And don't you dare laugh."

"I wouldn't think of it." He wondered how long he'd be able to hold off taking her in earnest. His blood was still on fire. "Come. Sit with me a moment, so we can talk." He took her hand and led her the short distance to the bench. He sat, and as she moved to sit beside him, he lifted her onto his lap. When she began to protest he teasingly warned, "Either sit still or I'll make you orgasm again, this time with your corset around your waist."

Her eyes popped wide and he found her reaction so endearing, he pulled her close, kissed the top of her hair and smiled above her head to hide his amusement.

Mariah realized that being kissed again hadn't rendered her immune; if anything she'd fallen deeper into the mire. Her breasts were practically singing and the orgasm continued to resonate inside. Her ability to remain unmoved was being undermined by a body that seemed to be in cahoots with him because it wanted more. Her traitorous body notwithstanding, what she really wanted she doubted he'd be willing to give. "Are you pursuing me simply because you no longer have a mistress? I'm not a girl in a gin house, Logan."

"I'm pursuing you because I seem to have no choice."

"Meaning?"

"I've never dreamt about a woman before."

"You dreamt of me?"

"I did. First night you were here. I was making love to you on the seat of the wagon under the moonlight. It was so vivid, I can still taste you."

The fire in his eyes singed her so fiercely, she

had to look away, but he gently turned her back and said, "And since then, every time I see you, it's all I've been able to think about."

The wonder in his voice was pleasing, but not enough to keep her from asking what she needed to know. "And when you tire of me? Then what? You move on to someone else?"

This time, he looked away and it gave her pause. Was he uncertain about his answer or simply avoiding one? Either way, she'd made up her mind. "We can't do this again, Logan. I'm thirty years of age. In society's eyes, I'm far past the age of marrying, but I want to be a wife and mother. Dallying with you may jeopardize that, so thank you for the kisses and all the rest, but you'll have to take your kisses elsewhere, because I'm looking for a man who will commit to me and be faithful. It would be unfair to have such expectations of you, knowing who you are."

"And who am I?"

"Someone who prefers a mistress to a wife."

The way the lines of his face hardened made her wonder if she were the first woman to ever refuse his advances. "Please don't take it personally, but I have expectations, and now, because of you I'll go to the marriage bed more aware."

The way his eyes narrowed at her made her suppress her smile. "Have you never been turned down before?"

"Not to my recollection."

"Then I'm honored to be the first." He didn't appear to be pleased by her jest so she tried to cushion the blow and confessed, "I adore your kisses, but you should save them for someone more worldly, or at least someone who won't mind being another notch on your bedpost."

Logan was so outdone he wasn't sure if he should laugh or be outraged. She was actually telling him to take his kisses elsewhere. No, he had no plans to offer marriage. He liked his life the way it was and finding a woman who agreed with those boundaries had never been a problem, but now? The golden-eyed temptress on his lap was refusing to play along, and because he'd never encountered such a situation before, he had no idea how to proceed. Glowering inwardly, he reminded himself that expectations were the main reason he avoided innocents. This was not working out the way he'd planned.

"So, can we go back to the house now?" Maria asked. "I really want to finish those chores."

"Certainly. Let's not allow my desire for you keep you from doing your duty."

"Don't be angry. At least you know where I stand."

When his features didn't soften, she leaned in and kissed him softly on his cheek. "You'll find another mistress, don't worry." And with that, she left his lap and made her way back to the wagon.

She felt good.

Logan didn't.

Chapter 14

When Logan joined Mariah on the wagon seat, his still-tight features made her view him with silent amusement. She never would've expected a man of his size and sweep to pout like a little boy denied his favorite sweet, but that was the impression he gave. In a way it was endearing, but not enough to make her alter her stance. Yes, his kisses did things to her she never could have imagined; even now her body smoldered with scandalous remembrances. However, she refused to play mistress when there might be a man somewhere who'd like her to be his wife. She wanted to be valued and loved, two things sorely missing from her life, and she didn't think it ludicrous or wrong for a woman her age to have such dreams.

As the slow, bumpy ride across the open grassland began, she took a few quick peeks over his way, which were so pointedly ignored, she chuckled softly.

"Something funny?" he asked upon finally meeting her eyes.

"Just you. I've never witnessed a full-grown man pout before."

He glared, but she wasn't intimidated. Instead she turned her head and pretended interest in a patch of wildflowers to mask her smile.

He didn't utter another word for the duration of the journey and upon their arrival at the house, she saw Alanza step down from the porch and approach the wagon. "Ah, there you are. Mariah, I've a telegram for you."

Her ensemble today was a divided black leather skirt that ended mid-calf over tall black boots. Her short jacket, made of embroidered black felt, was worn over a frilly long-sleeved white blouse. Covering her hair was another stylish Spanish hat that tied below her chin.

Mariah's silent driver halted the team and came around to help her down. Face set gravely, he swung her down slowly, his eyes holding hers the entire time, then set her on her feet. "Thank you," she said.

His dark gaze held her captive for a few heart-beats longer before he turned away and climbed back up to his seat. "I'll be repairing fences if anyone needs me." And he drove off.

Softly chuckling, Mariah took the telegram from Alanza's hand.

"What's wrong with him?"

But Mariah was reading: *Glad you have arrived. Crates and sewing machine en route. Bernice terribly angry. You have my love. Aunt Libby.*

Mariah was pleased to hear from her aunt, and to know that her belongings were on the way. Reading about her mother, however, brought on a sigh of frustration and sadness.

"Everything all right?" Alanza inquired gently.

Mariah looked into her kind eyes and wondered if it would be right to talk with her about the life she'd left behind. "Just my mother."

"Is she ill?"

"No. She's angry at me."

"May I ask why?"

Mariah wondered how to explain her mother Bernice. "I'll simply say, nothing about me pleases her."

"If you need someone to talk to—"

Mariah cut her off gently, "Thank you, but you're my employer. I would never be so presumptuous."

Alanza waved her off. "We are all family here and sometimes it helps to share a burden."

Mariah noted how closely the words mimicked Logan's, which made her wonder if he'd learned them from her.

"When I was growing up, the old Spanish families always took care of one another. They opened their homes to travelers whether they were friends or strangers. If someone visiting needed financial assistance, they were given what was called guest silver."

Seeing Mariah's confusion she explained that a pile of silver covered by a cloth was left in the bedroom of the traveler with the understanding that the boon was not to be counted until after the traveler left.

Mariah had never heard of such a thing.

"My parents once told me the story of an American named Deen who needed money for a business venture. He'd married into the famous Ortega family and decided to go to Los Angeles to see if he could borrow the funds. When the family's priest heard of his plight, he sent Mr. Deen a caro filled with silver."

"What's a caro?"

"A basket that resembles a tube. It holds about four gallons."

"He gave him four gallons of silver."

"Yes, along with a reminder to always come to the priest if he needed help. The families and the church were very wealthy in those days."

"Do people still give guest silver?"

She shook her head. "The Americans were so abusive of the tradition it passed away. I tell you this to let you know that being of help is who I was raised to be. It's in my blood, so to speak, so come to me if you need to."

"I will." And Mariah meant it.

"Now, tell me what's wrong with my son. You two fighting again?"

Another sigh. "When are we not?"

"Is it a serious matter?"

"He apparently thinks it is. You have to promise me you won't tell him we spoke."

"I promise."

"He's pouting because I told him to take his kisses elsewhere, if I may be so bold."

A stunned Alanza began laughing and took Mariah's hands in hers. "You, my dear, are a woman after my heart. I would love to call you friend."

That took her by surprise. "You can't be friends with a housekeeper."

"As if your station matters, and this is my ranch after all. I already told you I've been waiting for someone who matched me in spirit. I would've loved to have been a fly on the wall to witness his reaction. Take his kisses elsewhere." She laughed again. "I'm sure he's never had a woman tell him that. Good for you!"

It was an unexpected reaction, to say the least.

Alanza seemed to read her mind. "Did you expect me to chastise you for telling him what he's been needing to hear? Women raise their skirts for him far too easily. Andrew Antonio is the same way."

The bold description made Mariah blink with surprise, but Alanza didn't seem to notice and steamrolled on. "Arrogant stallions, the both of them. I love all my sons with each beat of my heart, but prayed they'd find a woman who'd put them through their paces, and you are the answer to at least one of those prayers."

Mariah didn't know what to say.

Alanza placed her hands on Mariah's cheeks and gave her a big kiss on her brow. "That is for you, *amiga*. I wish I'd hired you to be a companion to me instead of his housekeeper. We'd do well together, you and I."

Alanza's tone turned serious. "I've spent my entire life on this rancho, and for the last twenty years, I've been the only woman. The girls I grew up with have married and moved away. All my aunts and female cousins are in Mexico. Bonnie and Lupe help fill the void, but they have husbands and families. Having sons and land are things to be thankful for, but I miss having another woman to talk with."

Mariah thought about Kaye and the void in her own heart. "I left a very good friend behind in Philadelphia and I miss her dearly."

"So you understand?"

"I do." It never occurred to her that she would be offered friendship by a woman society would call her better, but it felt right, and Mariah looked forward to having someone to turn to who cared.

"I'd be honored to be considered a friend." She wondered if now might be the time to tell her the truth about her so called widowhood. Logan promised to keep her secret, but she wanted Alanza to know as well so that there would be no lies between them. "I've a confession to make."

"And that is?"

"I'd lied about being a widow so that I'd be considered for the position."

"Does Logan know?"

"Yes. He's promised not to tell anyone."

"Then you can place his promise next to mine. I'm glad you lied. Had you not, you wouldn't be here."

Mariah was so thankful for this unconventional woman.

"And now that that's settled, you are to take your suppers with me and Bonnie until Logan gets a stove."

"You've very kind. Hopefully I won't have to impose for long." She then told her about Logan's request for clothing for his goddaughter. "My sewing machine should be here soon and once it is, I can take her measurements and start making the patterns."

"You make your own patterns?"

"Yes."

"What kinds?"

Mariah told her about her sketches of gowns and nightwear, day dresses and the rest, and how her mother often sold her work to the well-to-do dressmakers in Philadelphia.

"My goodness. I knew you were an excellent needlewoman, but I had no idea you could do so much. Would you sew for me as well?"

"I would love to. One of my dreams is to open my own shop."

"And your other dreams?"

Mariah hesitated, but then remembered they were embarking on a friendship, so she told her what was in her heart. "To marry. Which is why I won't allow Logan to dally with me."

"You're very wise. I'd like him to marry, too, so I can have the grandchildren I've always desired, but he says he's content with his life the way it is. I applaud you for not giving in to him, especially now that I know you've never married."

Mariah was glad her stance met with her approval. "I know I'm considered too old, but I want children to love in the way my mother never loved me."

Alanza stilled. "Your mother doesn't love you?"

"No," she responded quietly.

Alanza searched her eyes questioningly. The concern made Mariah drop the last few barriers. "Come sit with me on the porch and I'll tell you why I came to California."

While Alanza listened, Mariah told her the story about her parents, her mother's betrayal and the joyless life she had growing up because of her mother's pain. Once the story was told, Alanza shook her head sadly. "You poor dear. How could a mother be so cruel?"

Mariah had no answers.

"Know this. There will be no cruelty here—only affection and caring. I know I haven't known you for very long, but from what I do know, had I been blessed with a daughter, I would have wanted her to be like you. You work hard, you're clever, and you have a strong sense of what you want to do with your life. A mother couldn't ask for more of a girl child."

The words made Mariah's heart swell. Never once had her mother said anything close to Alanza's assessment.

"I named the rancho Destiny because every episode in my life is tied to this place. Maybe that will be true for you as well."

Mariah thought about that. Would she find her destiny here?

"So what are your plans for the rest of the afternoon?" Alanza asked.

"I want to finish scrubbing the floors."

"Then I will leave you to that. Don't forget about dinner later."

"I won't, and thank you for lending an ear."

"My pleasure."

"One last question."

"Sure."

"What does *querida* mean?"

"Sweetheart."

Mariah sighed, and a smiling Alanza left for home.

Had Logan known Alanza and Mariah were making a friendship pact, he would've been scared indeed, but he was too busy taking his bad mood out on the fence he was repairing. He stretched the barbed wire across the hole as if he wanted to strangle something with it. The sound of riders made him turn. Approaching were Eli and Logan's brother, Drew. Between the two of them he was sure his day would only get worse, so he went back to his task.

"Look who I found at the train station," Eli called as they approached.

"Can he be returned?"

Drew dismounted with the ease of a vaquero. "Did you get your tail caught beneath a rocker, surly brother of mine?"

"He's sweet on a woman who kicked him in the knee and pelted him in the forehead with a rock."

Logan glared at Eli, while Drew laughingly asked, "What? I take it this isn't Val."

"New housekeeper," Eli replied.

"Would you two go the hell away so I can get this done?"

Drew cracked, "Glad to see you, too, brother. I thought I'd come in early for Mama's birthday celebration. Maybe stay a week or two after."

Logan ignored him.

"But I might spend the rest of the summer here after hearing this."

Logan paused what he was doing. "If you're going to harass me, at least have the decency to help."

Eli dismounted and dug two pairs of gloves out of his saddlebag. He tossed Drew a pair and the three went to work.

Once they were done, they sat and passed around Logan's canteen of water.

"So," Drew said taking the canteen. "Tell me about this rock-throwing woman."

"Nothing to tell."

The always helpful Eli related, "He's taking her to church on Sunday."

Drew choked on the water in his throat, to which Eli responded, "Funny, I had the same reaction."

"Church?" Drew asked in a strangled voice.

Logan pounded him on the back much harder than necessary, but didn't offer a verbal reply.

Drew shot him a hard look on the heels of the too-hard pounding. "Does the reverend know you're coming?"

Logan remained silent. The last thing he needed was more ribbing.

"You never go to church. I, at least, go on Easter Sunday."

Eli added, "Reverend Dennis offered to escort her, but Logan said he'd take her instead."

Logan turned to his partner and best friend. "So are you the town crier now?"

"Just giving Drew the lay of the land."

"Well, stop it."

Drew asked Eli, "How long has she been here?"

"Three, four days."

Drew stood and started walking back to his mount.

"Where are you going?" Logan yelled, getting to his feet.

"Any woman who has you turned inside out in less than a week is one I want to meet. And I'm betting she won't throw rocks at me!" He swung up into the saddle and galloped away.

"Dammit!" Logan slammed his hat to the ground. Shooting an evil eye at the smiling Eli, he snatched up the Stetson and rode out after his brother. He had no idea what Drew intended, but he'd seen his brother dazzle more than a few women with his courtly Spanish manners and distinguished law degree. Mariah hadn't been moved by his own legendary charms and he doubted she'd be by Drew's either, but he'd be damned if she'd pick his brother over him.

With her mare reined to a walk, Alanza started toward home. Mariah's story was still on her mind. She found the mother's treatment unconscionable and could only imagine how heartbreaking it must have been growing up unloved and not understanding why. Alanza had grown up adored by her parents, especially her mother. Not until her willful ways broke their hearts had she ever been punished. Yet Mariah had been browbeaten and switched over circumstances she'd had no hand in. No wonder she'd fled. And to move all the way to California to start a new life in a place she'd never seen amongst total strangers spoke to her determination and her dreams. In spite of her age, Alanza found nothing wrong with her wanting to be a wife and a mother, and no doubt any child she bore would be loved immeasurably. In Alanza's perfect world, Logan would eschew his unmarried ways and choose Mariah as his bride. And if not, she'd find her new *amiga* someone worthy and be content with that.

Thoughts of worthy men brought back to mind her morning encounter with Max Rudd. Whatever was she going to do with him? Pretending to be ignorant of his intentions hadn't fooled him, and admittedly, she did have feelings for him but she was afraid. She could break horses, brand cattle, and do everything else on the rancho needing to be done, but when it came to affairs of her heart, she knew no more than she'd known at the age of fifteen.

She'd almost reached home when she saw a rider galloping hard in the direction of Logan's place. *Andrew?* Right on the heels of his mount was an equally hard-riding Logan. Whatever are they doing, and how long had Drew been home? Were the two men still adolescents, she'd guess that her middle son had done something to raise the ire of her eldest, and that Logan was set on wringing his brother's neck, but they were past that age, or were they? Shaking her head, she turned her mare around and galloped back toward Logan's house.

Mariah stepped out on the back porch to dump the bucket holding the water she'd used to scrub the hallway floors, but was brought up short by the sight of Logan and a man unknown to her wrestling in the muddy grass. Curses filled the air, fists were flying, and they were rolling back and forth apparently intent upon beating the tar out of one another. She was momentarily distracted by the arrival of Alanza, who began calling their names and yelling angrily at them in rapid Spanish. From that, Mariah discerned that the unknown man was Logan's brother Andrew. What or who started the fight was yet to be explained, and neither of them were paying their mother one bit of attention. As the battle continued, and the two combatants rolled closer to where Mariah stood, she was again momentarily distracted, this time by the arrival of the mounted Eli, who looked on, chuckling. When the brothers crashed into the wooden walkway only a few feet away from where Mariah was standing and broke off a section of the dilapidated wood, she'd had enough. Hoisting the bucket, she threw the dirty water at them with as much force as she could muster. The fisticuffs immediately ceased. As they stared up at her, stunned and dripping wet, she tossed the bucket at them for good measure, turned on her heel and went back inside, which made her miss Eli almost tumble out of his saddle with laughter.

Logan glanced over at the shock frozen on his brother's face and began laughing. With his long black hair plastered to his face and head, Drew resembled a drowned rat. Drew apparently didn't think Logan looked any better and began laughing as well. Soon, they were both howling and Logan admitted it felt good. He'd been needing to work off his temper since being told to take his kisses elsewhere. He had a split lip, a bloody nose, and Lord knew what else, but he didn't care. It had been years since he and Drew had gone full tilt, and their fight was the perfect way to welcome him home.

Alanza was still raging in her native Spanish. Calling them an embarrassment and comparing them to lunatics in an asylum, she was so worked up, they tried to take the upbraiding like straight-faced, chastised children, but failed miserably and burst into laughter again, which made her so furious, she mounted, dragged her mare's head around and rode off.

As they watched her disappear, Drew said, "We owe Mama an apology."

"I know."

"Your rock thrower is quite a beauty."

"That she is."

"Not as docile as I like, so I'll cede her to you."

"As if she'd've preferred you."

"She may have."

"And there's a diamond mine in the middle of the Pacific."

They shared a smile reflecting a lifetime of brotherly affection.

"So," Drew asked pushing his wet hair out of his eyes. "Are you coming down to Mama's for dinner?"

"You sure she'll feed us?"

They both turned to Eli, and Logan asked, "You staying for dinner?"

"No. Think I'm going to go home and see if I can't figure out how to sell tickets to all this madness. I might get rich."

More laughter.

"Okay, you do that and we'll see you tomorrow."

"First thing. Welcome home, Drew."

"Thanks, Eli."

Logan and Drew shook hands and shared a brotherly embrace. "I'll see you later."

Drew rode off. Logan was unsure of what type of reception he was in for, but went inside.

Chapter 15

Mariah decided she'd have to do laundry soon because she was down to the last of her clean garments. As she changed out of the clothes she'd worn to do the scrubbing, she shook her head at the row between Logan and his brother. She'd never seen anything like it before in her life and wondered if the fighting was something they did routinely. She had no answer but decided it was a very odd way to welcome someone home.

"Mariah?"

It was Logan at her door.

She stepped over and opened it. "Yes." He was a mess. His clothes were muddied, his lip split and puffy, and a black eye was forming.

"I'm going to get cleaned up so we can ride down to Alanza's for dinner."

"Are you sure she'll feed you after that performance?"

He grinned. "Drew and I were wondering the same thing. We're hoping she'll have calmed down by the time we arrive."

"Do you two fight like that often?"

"We did growing up, but rarely now that we're grown."

Mariah wanted to ask why they were fighting,

but in truth, didn't really want to know. "It was an interesting way to be introduced."

"I figured it was. Alanza used to break up our fights with her buggy whip, so your scrub water was novel if nothing else."

"And your youngest brother, does he participate in these free-for-alls, too?"

"Sometimes, but most times not. Being the baby, picking on him really got us whipped. Hope we didn't scare you."

"No."

"Good. Brothers can be volatile sometimes but we do care deeply for each other, even if our actions appear otherwise."

"I did wonder." She'd always wanted a brother or sister and hoped the Yates men were aware of how blessed they were to have both the companionship and love.

"Once I'm done cleaning up, there should be enough water left for you to take a bath, too." After the wild and woolly day, a bath sounded heavenly. "Thank you but I want to take a long soak, so I'll take it after dinner."

Neither seemed to know what to say next and as the silence lengthened, the familiar inability to control the cadence of her heartbeat stole over her again. Why this man? an inner voice asked. Why was she so attuned to a man she knew to be wrong for her, no matter where she turned? Yet, as their gazes held, all she could think about was that morning's kiss, their time together on the riverbank and what he'd made her feel. Not even his facial injuries dampened the responses of her senses.

"Looking at me that way makes me want to kiss you again."

She dropped her eyes and took a small step backward. "Go get cleaned up. Let me know when you're ready to leave for your mother's."

"But I'm not going to kiss you again until you ask."

"Since I won't be asking, I hope you aren't holding your breath."

Sounding amused, he replied, "We'll see," and exited her room, leaving her alone with thoughts of a man she had no business thinking about.

She had a wonderful time at dinner. The meal was conducted outside in the flower-filled court-yard, and in honor of Andrew's homecoming, there were thick steaks done on the grill, ash-baked yams, and to drink, a fruit-infused wine called *sangria*. Her experience with spirits was as limited as it was with men, so she only allowed herself one small glass.

But initially, being at the family's table and being waited upon by Alanza's servants left her feeling very awkward.

The ever intuitive Alanza must have sensed something because she looked down the beauti-fully set table and said to her, "You've been invited to share this meal with us, Mariah. Everyone who has ever worked for us has been invited to do the same more times than I can count, so enjoy yourself."

So she did.

Although she'd convinced herself no man could be more handsome than Logan, Andrew was. He had his mother's straight black hair and dark eyes. His skin tone was somewhere between her ivory and Logan's brown. She'd likened Logan's features to having been hewn by a mountain god, but Andrew Antonio's, even with his busted lip, bruised jaw, and black eye, bore the hands of the gods of Mexico and Spain. If a man could be called beautiful, he was that and the playful mischief in his eyes probably brought women to their knees wherever he went.

The talk at the table was of his work as a lawyer, his travels throughout the state, and the relatives he'd recently visited in Los Angeles and Mexico City. At first, the conversation was conducted in Spanish, which she knew to be a normal occurrence for their family, so she did her best not to look or feel left out. Logan noticed, however, and apologized. "Sorry, Mariah. We forget you don't speak Spanish."

Alanza apologized as well, but added, "Logan and I will teach you. English is the second language here."

After that she was able to follow the conversation, although Alanza tended to slip back and forth between the two languages. Mariah wasn't offended, though. It was her home after all.

The talk then moved to the upcoming annual celebration of Alanza's birthday, and from the descriptions of all it would entail, she got the sense that it was a pretty big to-do.

"I just hope Noah gets here in time," Alanza said.

Logan reassured her. "You worry every year, and every year he comes. He'll be here."

Andrew added, "And if not, we'll find him, and sink his ship so he'll never miss the day again. Simple."

His mother raised her glass to him in toast. Afterward, she asked, "Andrew, when you saw the aunts, in Los Angeles, did they say whether they were coming?"

"Yes, they did."

"Good."

After the dinner, Bonnie served them a delicious fruit flan. Mariah'd never had the dish before. It was akin to a custard, only fancier. Alanza explained that it was a traditional Spanish dessert and Mariah looked forward to having more in the future.

Soon, it was time for her and Logan to say their good-byes.

Andrew bowed gallantly over her hand and kissed it gently. "Welcome to Destiny, lovely lady.

Any woman who pelts my brother with rocks holds a special place in my heart."

Beside her she saw Logan roll his eyes. "Thank you."

Alanza wished them a good evening and Mariah and Logan drove back to his house. On the way, she said with a smile, "I feel like I'm glowing inside."

Logan chuckled. "It's the sangria."

"Can't be. I only had a small portion."

"Alanza's wines are pretty potent."

"Well, I feel wonderful." She was silent for a moment, then said, "Your brother's very handsome."

Logan's lips thinned. "You think so."

"I do, not as handsome as you, but he's very good-looking. Charming, too."

That made him feel better.

She asked, "Do you really think I'm tipsy?"

"I do."

"Have you ever kissed a tipsy woman?"

"On occasion."

"Well, don't kiss me, because I probably won't want to stop."

"I'll keep that in mind." He wished he had a way to preserve the conversation so he could show it to her in the morning and watch her scandalized reaction. Instead, he planned to just enjoy the moment. Taking advantage of her was out of the question. When the time came for them to make love, he wanted her to be in her right mind, because in spite of her protestations to the contrary, the time would come.

They reached the house. He set the brake. "Stay put until I come around and help you down. Don't want you to fall and hurt yourself."

"Your mother and I have decided to be friends."

"That's a scary bit of news."

"You think so?"

"Yes."

He went around to her side, swept her up into his arms and carried her toward the house.

"Why are you carrying me?"

"Felt like it."

"The last time you carried me I was asleep."

"I remember." He sat down on the porch and kept her on his lap. He was surprised when she didn't fuss. He thought maybe prescribing a wee bit of sangria for her on a daily basis might be just what the doctor ordered. With her head lying on his chest, she seemed so content he ached from the sweetness. Clearing his throat of the emotion he said, "So, you and Alanza are going to be friends?"

"We both need one. She's terribly lonely."

He never thought about his stepmother needing companionship. She ran the ranch and the people connected to it with such efficiency, it hadn't occurred to him that she might not be content. "Then I thank you for wanting to be her friend."

"She's very nice, Logan."

He loved hearing his name on her lips.

"I told her all about why I came to California and she listened and didn't judge. She even agreed that all the beatings and whippings I received from my mother had nothing to do with me."

Before he could respond, she revealed to him everything she'd told Alanza about her life in Philadelphia but hadn't revealed to him on the riverbank. For Logan, a motherless child who'd been loved by Alanza from the moment they'd met, her story both angered him and broke his heart. No wonder she was so tough. Having to endure what she had must have been hard for her, especially when she was young.

She glanced up. "Do you believe in destiny?"

"It depends."

"Alanza thinks I'll find my destiny here."

"She could be right."

"I think I'd like that destiny to be with you, but you won't marry me, so I'll have to look for someone else."

He went still. On one hand, the sangria-fueled confession confirmed that she was attracted to him and that made him feel good, but the idea of her being curled up contentedly on another man's lap didn't sit well at all.

He glanced down and saw that her eyes were closed. "Mariah?"

She was asleep. He took a moment to savor the softness in her face and the perfectness of her positioned against him. It came to him that he could sit with her in just this way forever, but he'd have to marry her in order to do so, his inner voice reminded him sagely. He wasn't sure what to do about that, but not wanting to let her go, he sat with her sleeping against him until darkness fell, the moon rose, and the owls called across the distance. Only then did he carry her to her room and gently place her atop her bed. While the moonlight streamed through the window and bathed her with its glow, he gazed down on her while she slept unaware. Her words echoed: *I think I'd like that destiny to be with you, but you won't marry me, so I'll have to look for someone else . . .*

Moved, he bent and kissed her softly on the cheek. "Rest well, *querida*." He exited and left her sleeping in the moonlight.

After climbing into his own bed, Logan thought about Mariah and what he'd learned about her: one, it only took a thimble full of *sangria* to make her tipsy, and two, she'd endured years of beatings at the hand of her mother for something that hadn't been her fault. The anger from that revelation continued to resonate. Who would treat a child so harshly in order to gain revenge? He applauded her decision to strike out on her own because it freed her from her mother's clutches and brought her to Destiny, and to him. Hearing that she and Alanza were pledging to be friends was pleasing. In spite of their disparate societal stations, he was certain they'd get along because they seemed to be cut from the same cloth. Separately they were trouble enough; united they'd likely give him fits.

Once again her words echoed in his head. Logan never considered marriage because he'd felt no need to have a woman 'til death did them part. Was he really ready to alter that stance because of a woman he'd met three days ago? That didn't make much sense to him, but then his feelings for her didn't either. Rather than lie awake all night while the inner debate raged back and forth, he turned over and went to sleep.

Mariah awakened the following morning and upon finding herself fully dressed in the clothes she'd worn to dinner, she sighed. Had she fallen asleep again? She assumed Logan was responsible for putting her to bed. She was grateful for that, but decided she really needed to not let it happen again. Her last memories were of the sangria, and sharing conversation with him on the ride from Alanza's place, but she had no idea what they discussed. She'd heard that too much drink could cause one to feel badly the morning after, but in her case, outside of a little stuffiness in her head, she felt fine.

Getting up, she looked out her window. The sky was filled with the pinks and grays of dawn. She paused a moment to listen for sounds of Logan moving around in the house but heard nothing. She'd dearly wanted that bath last night and wondered if it would be possible for her to take one before the day started. Tonight she'd be going to the celebration for his goddaughter and it would be nice to be fully clean.

As if summoned, he knocked on her door. "Mariah? Are you awake?"

Since she was already dressed, she bade him enter.

"Morning," he said. The black eye was in full bloom.

"You look like half a raccoon."

He chuckled. "Why thank you. How are you feeling?"

"I'm well. Thank you for putting me to bed again."

"My pleasure."

"Did I fall asleep because of the wine?"

"More than likely. You were a bit tipsy."

"I didn't embarrass myself or say anything untoward, did I?"

"No."

But there was a twinkling in his good eye that gave her pause. "Please don't lie. If I said something or did something I should apologize to your mother for I'd like to know."

"You didn't say anything that you wouldn't've said otherwise—well, maybe."

She went still. "What do you mean?"

"You told me about your life back in Philadelphia with your mother, and—"

"And?"

"That you thought you'd like me to be a part of your destiny."

"I did not!"

He nodded. "Yeah, you did."

She forced her mind to recall any parts of last night that would corroborate his words, but the effort failed. That he looked so pleased didn't help matters. "We didn't—do anything, did we?" If he'd made love to her, she'd know, wouldn't she?

"No, but you did ask that I not kiss you because you wouldn't want to stop."

Her eyes went wide as plates. This was decidedly not what she'd expected to hear. She grabbed hold of herself. "It was the wine. I hope you didn't take me seriously."

"Sometimes, spirits allow you to say things you wouldn't say under normal circumstances."

"I agree, because I would never have said such a thing had I been in my right mind."

"I'm talking about truthful things."

"You aren't in my destiny and we both know why, so let's discuss something else."

"No sense being angry. You asked me what you said and I told you."

"And I thank you. Now, would it be possible for me to have my bath this evening before we go to your goddaughter's dance?"

"Sure."

She could tell he was amused by her reaction to his revelations, but she was not.

"You want breakfast? I'm on my way over to Lupe's to get eggs."

"Yes. Thank you," she said stiffly.

"I'll see you when I get back."

Once alone, she let out an audible sigh and decided she wouldn't think about last night or anything connected to it. She'd told him to keep his kisses to himself and now she needed to put some distance between them to make certain he knew she was serious. For the past three days, she'd been reacting to him like a silly moon-struck young girl. She hadn't come all the way to California for this. She was his housekeeper; nothing more, and the sooner she began acting like it, the sooner he'd move on to someone else. The scenario was bothersome, but she reminded herself it didn't matter because he wasn't for her.

He returned accompanied by his brother Andrew and Eli Braden. That pleased her in the sense that she wouldn't be his whole focus and he wouldn't be hers. Once the food was ready, she took her plate. "Thank you. I'll eat inside and let you three visit."

"Not necessary," he told her. "We won't be discussing anything you can't be a party to."

"I understand and I appreciate that, but my place is inside. Gentlemen, if you'll excuse me," and she walked to the door that led into her room and went in.

Logan watched the door close and turned back to his brother and Eli with confusion on his face.

"What'd you do?" Andrew asked. "I was looking forward to breakfast with your beauty."

Eli raised his fork. "So was I."

"I didn't do anything that I'm aware of."

Andrew countered, "You must've done something. She acted as if she'd never met us before, let alone you."

Logan's confusion continued and for a moment, he replayed their earlier encounter but that held no answers for him either. He certainly wasn't going to go to her door and beg for her company, but for the life of him he couldn't come up with a reason for her cool exit. Deciding to let her have her way, he sat and ate. His plan for the day centered around replacing the roof on the henhouse, so after breakfast, while Drew and Eli went to the mill to get the lumber for the bunkhouse and the shingles needed for the henhouse roof, he went inside.

He found her eyeing his windows.

She turned. "Do you have any butcher paper on the ranch?"

That was also confusing. "Why butcher paper?"

"I need it to make patterns for your curtains. I'll also be needing them for your goddaughter's dresses. I suppose I can use newsprint if I must."

"Um. I'm sure there's probably butcher paper over at the smokehouse. May I ask a question?"

"Of course."

"What's wrong?"

"With what?"

"With you, Mariah."

She went back to eyeing the windows. "I don't have my tapes, so I'm attempting to do the measurements by eye."

"That isn't what I meant."

"What did you mean?"

"Why'd you leave? We were looking forward to you having breakfast with us."

"I'm your housekeeper, Logan, and it's better if I conduct myself as such."

"Better for whom?"

"Me."

He understood now. "So, you're punishing me for not offering you marriage."

As if amused, she shook her head. "No, Logan, I'm not. I'm simply here to do a job and that's all. My place is not to have breakfast with you."

"So are you still going to attend the dance tonight?"

"Yes, but as your employee—not as the woman on your arm."

His lips tightened. He wanted to argue but had no position from which to do so. She'd already confessed to wanting his kisses, yet seemed determined to deny it and give what he desired to another man.

"Anything else?" she asked.

"No."

"Then I'll go on with my day and let you get on with yours. I'll ask Bonnie about the paper."

"Fine." Not happy with being dismissed, he turned on his heel and walked out.

Hearing the door slam, she shook her head and went back to what she'd been doing.

Chapter 16

Mariah walked down to Alanza's and got not only a large quantity of butcher paper from Bonnie, but the housekeeper also had a measuring tape and a pair of sharp scissors she could borrow. Alanza came in while they were talking and offered to drive Mariah home so she wouldn't have to lug everything back on foot.

While they rode, Mariah told her of the decision she'd made concerning Logan. "I'm his house-keeper and that's all."

"And his reaction?"

"More pouting, I'm afraid."

"He isn't used to being denied, but he'll get over it."

"I certainly hope so." She watched the expert way Alanza handled the reins for the team of horses pulling the wagon. "I've a favor to ask."

"And it is?"

"Asking Logan to teach me to drive turned into a disaster, do you think you might be able to find the time to teach me?"

"Of course. How about now?"

She stopped the wagon, they switched places and Mariah began. It went reasonably well. Not being yelled at by the instructor went a long way in helping Mariah relax and an hour later she was actually able to guide the buggy to the house. The onlooking ranch hands applauded.

But again, her arms ached from the strain.

"You'll get stronger," Alanza promised.

A weary Mariah hoped so. "My arms feel like they're made of lead."

"Get you a nice long soak in the tub and you'll be right as rain."

"Soon as Logan returns. I don't know how to heat the water."

"That isn't a problem. I can show you."

When they walked around to the back of the house, Mariah could see the activity going on with a gang of men on the far side of the corrals. The air rang with the sounds of hammering.

"Looks like they're finally starting on the bunk-house," Alanza noted.

They could hear someone yelling.

"Logan," they said in unison.

"He's not pleased about something," Alanza added.

Mariah didn't give his bellowing a second thought. All she wanted was a long soak in the tub.

Alanza showed her the boiler and how to put water in the short, squat metal receptacle and light the coals beneath so that the coils connected to it would transfer the heated water to the large storage tank.

"Give it an hour or so and you should have enough for your bath. And toss in a handful of bath salts. That always makes me feel better."

"I don't have any," Mariah confessed while eyeing the contraption and willing the water to heat quickly. "We didn't have a tub back home, and even if we had, mother wouldn't have allowed me to spend money on something so frivolous."

"Everyone is entitled to a little frivolity in their lives. So get some soon."

Mariah liked that idea. "I'll see if I can spare the coins."

"If you can't, have Logan buy them."

"That wouldn't be right."

"Maybe, but have him make the purchase anyway."

The look on Mariah's face made her sigh with amused frustration. "You aren't going to do it, are you?"

"No. Maybe once I am paid and have ample funds of my own." She didn't want to be beholden to Logan or anyone else for something as trivial as bath salts. As soon as she was paid she'd consider adding the frivolity Alanza thought everyone needed, but not until then.

"All right. I'll not fuss."

Alanza stayed for a few minutes longer to make sure Mariah knew the workings of her heater and that she planned to attend the Brush Dance that evening.

Mariah had a question. "Do I need to wear something fancy?"

"No. A nice blouse and skirt should do."

"Okay. Thank you."

And with that Alanza waved good-bye and drove home.

An hour later, holding a fresh bar of Cashmere Bouquet soap in her hand, Mariah stepped gingerly into the large tub. Immersing herself slowly, she smiled with pleasure. The warm water felt like liquid silk. It was immodest to be nude, so she had on her thinnest shift, which plastered itself to her body as soon as the water touched it. "Oh, this is wonderful," she gushed aloud. She knew it was silly to be talking to herself, but it was so glorious, she didn't care. Before coming to California, she'd only taken a few baths in her lifetime, but she made herself a promise to take one as regularly as her schedule allowed from then on.

Logan was in a sour mood most of the day. With the help of Eli, Andrew and the ranch hands, the roof of the henhouse was repaired and the beams laid out for the new bunkhouse, but not without a lot of fussing and cussing on his part. By the end of the day, everyone was so sick of him and his temper they hoped that whatever was going on between him and the housekeeper got fixed so that when they reconvened for work on Monday, they could do so without wanting to hit him over the head with a piece of lumber.

As he entered the house, he saw the folded white

butcher paper on the dining-room table, but Mariah was nowhere to be found. Thinking about her raised his ire again. How dare she be immune to his charms. Did she not know his reputation with the ladies? He supposed she did, which was the reason she refused to surrender. Entering his bedroom, he rid himself of his dirty shirt, tossed it on the floor, and walked over to the door to the washing room. Snatching it open, he stepped in and heard her screech, "Get out!"

Stunned by the sight of her cringing in his tub, he ran his shocked eyes over her delectable form.

"Out!" she demanded, while trying to hide herself behind the washcloth and failing miserably, much to his delight. "Are you deaf?"

He thought he might be, but he was glad he hadn't been struck blind. He turned his back, but the sight of her dark nipples against the wet shift was permanently imprinted on his memory. "Didn't expect to find you in here."

"Get out of here, Logan Yates."

"Got my back turned."

"Out!"

"I see you found some paper for your patterns."

"I'm not discussing anything with you. Leave me."

He quickly tried to come up with something to say that would allow him to stay. Even with his back turned, he could still see her. "Water hot enough?"

"This isn't funny! Can you be a gentleman at least once?"

"If I wasn't I wouldn't have my back turned."

He heard her angry sigh and that made him smile. "All right. I'm going. Nice seeing you."

He closed the door just in time to block a flying hairbrush aimed at his head. Once on the other side, he called, "If you need someone to wash your back, just yell!"

A snarl was her only reply.

They drove to the dance in his buggy. She had nothing to say during the drive but Logan admired the nice white blouse and dark green skirt she was wearing. The blouse was high necked as usual with a bit more lace around the collar and wrists. Once again, he fantasized on slowly opening all the little pearl-sized buttons and his quickened desire weighed in with a silent amen. He could still see her in the tub though, which gave rise to another fantasy: one that involved her, him, and a tub of steamy hot water. Deciding he needed to send his thoughts elsewhere, he glanced her way and saw the tight set of her face and chin. "I didn't know you were in the tub, Mariah."

"I don't want to talk about it."

But he didn't have to talk about it. The remembrance was as clear as the road ahead.

The air was filled with the sounds of drumming and voices when they arrived at Green Feather's home a short time later. There were a number of buggies and wagons parked in the field near the home and a stream of people walking toward the festivities. Logan parked, then came around and handed her down. Her displeasure with him hadn't lifted and he found her reaction amusing. He looked forward to whatever the evening had in store.

Mariah was first introduced to the guest of honor and her parents. "Thank you for the invitation," she said to them. Walks was as large as the redwood tree the family had taken as their surname. His wife, Sweet Water, was a slim, gorgeous woman with beautiful dark hair and eyes. Their daughter Green Feather had her mother's slim figure and the facial features of both handsome parents. "Congratulations on your accomplishment," Mariah said to her.

The young woman smiled. "Thank you. I'm admiring your blouse. Did you make it yourself?"

"Feather!" her mother snapped. "Don't be so rude."

Mariah waved her off. "It's okay. The answer is yes. Would you like one of your own?"

"I'd love one. Uncle Logan says you're a great seamstress, and that you might make some things for me to take to school."

"I'd love to help with your wardrobe."

So for a moment, they talked about her and her mother coming out to the ranch to discuss the types of garments needed, and so Mariah could take Feather's measurements. Her mother had tears in her eyes.

"Thank you, Mrs. Cooper."

"You're very welcome."

The happy Feather gave her godfather a big hug. "Thank you for bringing her, Uncle Logan."

"You're welcome."

Mariah was admittedly moved by the display. The affection bestowed on him seemed quite genuine and caused her to try and reconcile the Logan she thought she knew with the man Feather obviously cared about so deeply.

Feather's father said, "I hope you enjoy the dance and our hospitality, Mrs. Cooper."

"I'm sure I will. It's been a pleasure meeting you."

Feather and her parents moved off to see to their other guests.

"They're quite nice," she said to Logan as they moved into the crowd of guests.

"They are. If I had a daughter I'd want her to be like Feather."

Considering his stance on marriage, Mariah was surprised to hear him say anything related to children.

For the next little while, he introduced her around. She met so many people she was certain she'd never remember all the names, but they greeted her with smiles and kindness and that pleased her.

"Let's find Alanza. I'll leave you with her so that no one will think you're here on my arm."

She caught the sarcasm but chose to ignore it. "Thank you."

They found his stepmother and Andrew a short while later, and with a bow, Logan faded into the crowd.

Andrew watched his brother's departure and said to Mariah, "He's never met a woman like you."

To which his mother replied, "And may you meet one just like her."

He laughed. "And on that note, I think I will join my brother in exile."

After he departed, Alanza said to Mariah, "Come. I see some people I want you to meet."

Mariah spent the rest of the evening under Alanza's wing. As night rolled in and fires were lit to help illuminate the gathering, they stopped at the food tables. Mariah ate fish and chicken and fruit and vegetables and cake until her corset threatened to pop. They then drifted over to watch the tribal dancing and listen to the singers. The dancers were inside a circle lined with stones. Unlike the feathers and paint she was accustomed to seeing on the plains Indians like the Sioux and Cheyenne in the newspapers at home, they were plainly dressed. A few of the women were wearing long skirts made of grass, but most of the men were in plain everyday attire of denims and shirts.

The songs were sung in the tribal tongue to the beat of the drums. The voices sounded very foreign to her ears at first, but the more she listened, the more familiar the intonation became, and she found it pleasing.

While she watched the dancers make their way around the circle in time to the drums' slow cadence, some of the female guests came up and asked her about her sewing. The word had apparently gotten around about her needle skills and they, too, wanted fittings and garments made. Mariah had no idea how or where she'd be able to accommodate them but Alanza promised to find her a space on the ranch and encouraged her to take on the work, so she did.

She and Alanza were talking about where she might set up her sewing operation when Reverend Paul Dennis walked up.

"Good evening, Mrs. Cooper. Mrs. Yates."

They both greeted him.

"Are you having a good time?" he asked Mariah.

"I am. We don't have anything like this in Philadelphia, I assure you."

She thought he had a nice smile.

Alanza said, "I see someone I need to speak with. Reverend, will you watch over her for a moment?"

"I'd be honored."

She departed and he looked around. "How about we take a seat over there."

By the light of the fires, Mariah saw the bench he indicated. It was set back from the crowd but not so much that people would talk. "I'd enjoy that."

She found she liked him immensely. He was from Dayton, Ohio, and a graduate of Wilberforce College, which was affiliated with the African Methodist Episcopal church. He had two younger sisters, and had been in California just under a year. He talked about his work with the local school, and his dreams of making his church a center of the community. He told her how proud he was of Feather and his hopes that she would enjoy Hampton and go far in life. He then stopped. "I'm sorry, I've been going on and on about me and my work. How about I keep quiet for a few moments and let you speak."

Yes, she liked him very much.

"Tell me a bit about yourself."

So, she told him about her life in Philadelphia, carefully skirting the uglier parts. She also told him about wanting to open her own seamstress shop.

"Did your late husband support your dream?"

Mariah went still, and lied, "Yes, of course. Why do you ask?"

"Because some men think a woman's only work should be in the home."

"And you?"

"I used to think that way, but coming here and

meeting women like Mrs. Yates and Miss Pearl over at the diner made me question that stance."

"May I ask why?" Mariah had no plans to be with someone who'd deny her a chance to make her own way in life, no matter how nice he seemed. If she'd wanted to do nothing but housework, she would've stayed in Philadelphia with her mother.

"They impressed me not only with their Christian outlooks but with their devotion to their life and the people around them. I doubt they'd be such forces of nature were they confined to the role of a wife as it's presently defined."

Mariah applauded his thinking.

"So," he continued. "That being said, would it be very forward of me to ask if I may call on you?"

She was moved by his very respectful approach. "No, it wouldn't be. To be truthful, I'd enjoy getting to know you better."

Over in the dark, on the other side of the dancers, Logan stood watching Mariah and Paul Dennis. Beside him, Andrew quipped, "I think you may have some competition."

Logan ignored him.

"A girl can't go wrong with a preacher man. Or at least so I'm told."

Logan's glower was hidden by the shadows.

"Are you really going to let him waltz off with the prize?"

"Would you shut the hell up."

Alanza appeared out of the darkness on Logan's other side. "They make a nice couple, don't they?"

Since he couldn't tell her to shut the hell up, too, he said nothing.

She added, "The reverend's looking for a wife, and Mariah's looking for a husband. Possibly a match made in heaven, don't you think, Logan?" Not waiting for him to reply, she left his side as silently as she'd come.

"At least you know whose side Mama's championing."

The darkness couldn't hide the malevolent look he shot his sibling, who responded with, "Shutting the hell up."

Logan released a frustrated breath. He swore Mariah was intent upon driving him insane—not to mention Alanza. Their friendship was giving him the fit he'd envisioned. He wanted to go over there and punch the reverend in the nose for even speaking with Mariah, who now appeared to be laughing at whatever the man was sharing with her. Beating the tar out of a man of the cloth would undoubtedly get Logan his own room in hell, so he stood there and fumed.

Eli walked up holding a plate loaded down with food. "The good reverend and Mariah seem to be having a nice time."

Logan shot him the same look he'd given his brother a moment before, then very calmly flipped the plate out of Eli's hand and strode away.

"Hey!"

Andrew laughed until he cried.

Logan had no idea what to do about Mariah, but she and Dennis had been talking close to an hour. Time was up. Approaching, he said to Dennis, "There's a man looking for you, Paul. Tall, handlebars. Wants to make a donation to the church. I think he might be leaving, but he wanted to speak with you beforehand."

"Really? Who is he?"

"Never met him before, but he said he knew you." Logan wondered about the penalty for lying to a reverend, but decided it had to be less severe than beating one to a pulp.

"Okay." He stood hastily. "Mariah, my apologies for rushing off this way, but donations are the church's lifeblood."

"Quite all right, Paul. I understand."

Paul! Mariah! Logan didn't like hearing that they were now on a first-name basis.

"I will see you Sunday evening?" he said to her.

"Yes. I'm looking forward to it."

"And Logan, thanks for finding me. I'll see you in church." After offering Mariah a respectful nod, he hurried away.

Logan asked her, "What's happening Sunday evening? Is there a program at the church?"

"No, we're having dinner."

"Excuse me?"

"Dinner. You know. Sharing food."

"Why?"

"Because he graciously extended the invitation and I accepted."

He wondered if he'd ever become accustomed to how often she rendered him speechless. He finally found his tongue. "Dinner. Really?"

"He's very nice."

Some people walked by, and Logan nodded a greeting but he remained focused on Mariah and the way the firelight played over her beautiful face. "Are you ready to head back?"

"I believe so, but I'd like to thank Feather and her parents for their hospitality before we go."

He agreed, and once that was accomplished he handed her into the buggy and drove them away.

"I had a good time, Logan. Thanks for bringing me."

"You're welcome." He couldn't shake his irritation over her having dinner with Paul Dennis.

"Now," she asked, "did you lie to Paul about the man wanting to donate to the church?"

He froze and hazarded a glance her way. "And if I did?"

She fell back against the seat. "I knew it! Logan, how could you?"

He tried to come to his own defense. "You were sitting with him for nearly an hour."

"And?"

"That was long enough."

"Are you my father now?"

He didn't reply.

"You are not to meddle in my life, anymore. Do you hear me?"

His irritation fled in response to the joy he felt getting her all riled up. "Then I'm guessing you won't let me draw us a hot bath so I can make love to you like I wanted to this afternoon."

Mariah's breath left her in a whoosh. "No," she managed to say.

"You sure?"

"No."

"No, you're not sure?"

"I mean, no, you can't, and yes, I'm sure."

"You sound confused, *querida*."

"And stop calling me that."

His chuckle was soft as the night surrounding them. "Remember that dream I told you I had about us."

She did, and so, didn't respond.

"It was a night just like this one. Moon was fat in the sky. Weather was warm."

He looked over.

She hung on to her silence.

"Cat got your tongue."

"Do you plan to bedevil me all the way back?"

"I enjoy bedeviling you, but what I'd rather do is ease you onto my lap and kiss you the way we did in my dream."

"And suppose I'm not interested?"

"There is that, but I think you are."

"You are such an arrogant—I can't believe your hats fit your head."

He laughed. "And you'll never have this much fun with Paul Dennis."

"He's a nice man," she protested.

"True, but you need passion, *querida*, and you won't get that from him. He'll probably only make love to you in bed, at night, in the dark."

"And what's wrong with that?"

"Where'd you have your first orgasm?"

As the passionate encounter on the riverbank rose to fill her mind, she refused to answer.

"I rest my case."

"This is a very self-serving conversation, don't you think?"

"Of course. Goes with my so-called arrogance, and my not wanting you to be with someone who won't make love to you properly."

"So now, you're an authority on how I should be loved?" Mariah had had just about enough of him. "Stop the buggy."

"Why?"

"Because since you are such an authority I want you to show me what I need to judge a future husband by, and if he doesn't measure up, I'd like to be able to teach him what he needs to know."

Logan found himself speechless again. He studied her face in the moonlight. "You want me to make love to you so you can tutor another man?"

"You seem to think it's what I need, so yes."

"Do you realize what you're asking?"

"Yes, Mr. Arrogance, I do. Shall I move to your lap?"

He didn't know whether to laugh or be appalled. "Okay, how about we compromise. I'll show you, but I'll let you keep your innocence."

"Whatever you think is best, maestro."

He dropped the reins and the horse stopped. "Come here," he said softly and moved her onto his lap.

He studied the small, angry face with its feline gold eyes. She was the most spirited and fearless woman he'd ever had the pleasure to hold in his arms, and because of that, the lure of her was irresistible. He brushed his lips over her sweet, ripe mouth and coaxed her to join him. At first she sat stonily, but the more he cajoled and enticed, the softer her lips became until they parted with an invitation of their own. His tongue slipped inside and then toyed with the parted corners of her mouth. She trembled in response, her eyes slid closed, and he knew the anger was gone. Buoyed by her willingness, he continued to tempt her with fleeting touches of his mouth and began undoing the buttons on her blouse. "I'll give you a short lesson now, and more when we get home . . ."

And there in the shadowy interior of the buggy with the moon shining down, Mariah allowed him to open her blouse. She realized belatedly that in throwing down this gauntlet she'd let her anger override her good sense and now . . . *This was such a bad idea,* a small voice scolded inside, but his lips and the hot tongue flicking against the bared skin above her shift and corset melted the voice and her as well. His palms trailed across the front of her shift to move her blouse aside, and as they glanced over her nipples they bloomed to life and she let out a whispery moan.

"You want a man to go slow, *querida*. Real slow . . ." he voiced, while placing fervent kisses in the valley between her confined breasts. He burned a trail up her throat, lingering on the way to make certain the skin in between caught flame. And while his lips set her on fire, his hands did the same. Moving up and down the surface of her shift along her torso, he circled the flat of his palm over her breasts and wantonly teased the sheltered nipples. She didn't protest when he freed the three buttons on the front of her shift to expose her corset. "Undo your corset for me."

She held his burning eyes.

"Men like to watch."

His heat-filled voice flared like lightning over her skin. She'd never done anything so brazen before, but she'd started this, and something inside gloried in the idea of inflaming him the way he'd inflamed her. So, she slowly undid the series of frogs that held her corset closed from top to waist. When she was done, he pushed the halves aside and greeted the exposed twins with licks and sucks and bites from his gentled teeth. The play sent her soaring. The drum of desire pulsed between her thighs. As if he could hear the cadence, he slid her skirt up her thighs and touched her through her drawers. The orgasm shattered her like shards of glass, and her tortured cries filled the dark buggy.

Logan knew that if he didn't have this woman he would surely die, but he'd promised not to compromise her innocence. All he could think about was slowly impaling her on his erection and letting her ride him until sunrise, but her first time shouldn't be out in the middle of the countryside, and he considered himself a man of his word. So he watched her ride her climax instead and contented himself with savoring how wet she was and the taste of her nipples in his mouth.

When Mariah's body finally quieted and her eyes opened, he was above her smiling down softly. Her first orgasm, on the riverbank, would always be memorable, but there were no words to describe this latest interlude. She could feel the hard heat of him beneath her hips and wondered about the entire act. He'd only used his hands between her thighs and she couldn't imagine what it would be like to be fully loved.

"So?" he questioned quietly while worrying a slow finger over her damp nipples. "Was that enough?"

"No."

"No?" he echoed unable to keep the amusement out of his voice.

"I want to know it all."

He ran a worshipping finger down her cheek. "Do you know what that means?"

"I believe so."

"What about your innocence?"

"I'm supposed to be a widow, I don't need it."

Speechless once again, he laughed softly. "Okay. Let's get you to the house and finish your education."

Chapter 17

When they arrived home, they kissed their way into the house. They stopped just inside the door because passion wouldn't let them go any farther. Their mouths mated, hands roamed and flush bodies flared. Mariah assumed this second round wouldn't be as fiery as the first, but she was wrong. Each and every kiss and caress stoked her desire so high she thought she'd die from the bliss. He began divesting her of her clothing; first her still opened blouse, shift and corset, then came her skirt, slips and drawers. She'd been raised to view nudity as immodest, yet she was standing in his front parlor wearing only her stockings, garters and high buttoned shoes while greedily relishing the magic of his expert hands. It was decadent, dizzying, and so very wonderful.

Logan hoisted her into his arms and never once letting his mouth leave hers carried her down the hall to his bedroom. Laying her down in the center of his big four-poster bed, he ran his eyes ardently over her in the moonlight pouring through the window, and made short work of his own clothing. Nude and ready, he sat beside her and ran a bold hand over the peaks and valleys, playing special attention to the dark treasure between her thighs. Her eyes slid shut, her hips lifted in response to the silent tutoring, and unable to resist, he bent and showed her how carnally exquisite he thought her to be. She splintered almost immediately, bucking, rising, and crying out hoarsely.

When he rose and met her feline gold eyes, not even the shadows could hide the passion glowing there.

To his surprise, she whispered, "May I touch you, too?" Rising to her knees, she reached out and wrapped her hand around him. "Or is that improper?"

His growl of pleasure mingled with his amusement. Who knew she'd be fearless in bed, too? He placed his hand around hers and showed her the rhythm that opened the male soul, and because she was such an adept pupil, he backed away lest the hold of her small, hot hand end him too soon. "Nothing is improper if it brings pleasure."

He reached into his nightstand to retrieve one of the small sponges designed to keep his seed from finding root. He quietly explained its purpose and admittedly enjoyed slowly settling it into place. From her sinuous reaction, she enjoyed the insertion as well. He spent the next few moments restoking her fires and when she seemed ready, he positioned himself. Leaning down, he whispered, "This may hurt, but only this once."

Logan was a big man. He was also very skilled

in the art of love and he used those skills to the fullest. With slow strokes, he drew himself in and out, teasing her, filling her, until she began to feed herself on his rhythm. Lord knew, he wanted to storm her gates with everything he had, but the slow conquering, the kissing, the keeping her nipples ripe and hard, all added to his blistering need. When he finally pushed through, he held still for a throbbing moment to let her become accustomed to the size and feel of him. With her encasing him so tightly, not moving had to be one of the most difficult things he'd ever done, but he sucked in a shaky breath and held on.

For Mariah the pain was sharp, but just for a moment. He'd prepared her so well that all she could think about was how good he felt inside. And soon, his stroking became her focus and then her whole world, banishing the pain and replacing it with raw hunger. She slid her hands up and down his taut arms and instinctively locked her ankles around his waist. He increased both the force and the pace, making her want all he had to give. Growling, he raised her hips, and from somewhere deep in her soul the orgasm rose, white-hot. She heard herself cry out just seconds before her body broke apart. A heartbeat later, he shuddered with his own completion, and his low cry mingled with hers. Waves of sensation flooded her again and again, until finally, they both fell slowly back to earth.

Mariah was vaguely aware of him removing the sponge, but of little else. Her entire being was throbbing and pulsing. When he gently eased himself in against her back and wrapped her in his arms, she never wanted to move again.

As they lay there in the silence, Logan kissed the top of her hair and wondered what she was thinking. Foremost in his mind was making sure he hadn't hurt her and where they'd go from here. "Are you okay?"

"I am."

She slowly twisted around to face him. "You're a very good teacher, Mr. Yates."

"And you are an excellent pupil, *querida*. Did you enjoy your lesson?"

"I did. Very much."

He traced her mouth, then kissed her softly. He wanted her again, but it was probably too soon. "So, what happens next for us?"

"We go on as before. You've given me what I asked for."

The thought of her using what she'd experienced with him tonight to share passion with another man bothered him more than he cared to admit or face.

"How about that bath, now?" he asked as a way to escape his troubled thoughts.

"I'd like that."

"Be right back."

While he was gone, Mariah went over the

evening again in her mind and smiled. She was glad she'd tossed down the gauntlet. Who knew *it* could be so exhilarating? Did her enjoyment make her abnormal? Having no experience with things of the flesh she wasn't sure, but decided she didn't much care. She had no regrets about anything they'd done together, nor the lessons learned. Touching him had been a wondrous thing. Even now she could feel how velvety hard he'd felt in her hand. She felt bold and not the least bit shamed. Coming to California changed her in many ways and nothing on earth could make her go back to being the Mariah of before.

She was concerned however that he'd think she'd offered her innocence as a means of extracting a proposal of marriage. There in the dark, she honestly admitted to having feelings for him that undoubtedly equated to love, but she wasn't naïve enough to believe that admitting it to him would serve any purpose. Instead, she sealed their night together in a special place in her heart and left it there.

He returned and sat on the edge of the bed. "Regrets?"

"No," she replied truthfully. "None."

Silence rose between them.

Not sure what he might be thinking, she echoed his question. "Regrets?"

"No."

"I will always remember this night, Logan. And

please, don't let my ramblings from the sangria make you feel as if you need to marry me now."

"Hadn't crossed my mind."

She scooted to where he sat. Emboldened by the pleasure they'd shared, she raised up on her knees and cupped his face. "Good," she whispered and kissed him sweetly.

He gathered her in against him and before long the kisses led to another vibrant lesson.

The tub was large enough to hold them both. The feel of his manhood against her back made her slide against it sensually.

"Stop that," he said sucking in a breath. Logan was discovering that she liked to play, which aroused him even more, but she was going to be sore and he wasn't going to be able to walk if he didn't put a stop to her uninhibited shenanigans.

"Spoilsport."

He laughed. She reclined between his thighs giving him access to the secrets hidden between her own.

"You're going to be very sore," he warned, circling her softness.

"I'm only going to have this one night, so I'd like to experience all that I can. Is that brazen of me?"

"Yes."

It was her turn to laugh then and her head dropped with embarrassment.

"But I'm enjoying you enjoying yourself."

And Mariah was. His hand was making her hips rise in response to his call, and once again, she found herself filled with heat. "How many ways are there to do this?"

"Hundreds."

She swiveled her head around. "Truly?"

He nodded.

"Show me another."

He laughed aloud. "You are outrageous."

"And whose fault is that?"

He leaned down and kissed her passionately. "Mine, I suppose." He reached down to the floor and picked up the small copper box that held the sponges and extracted one.

"How many of those do you have?" she asked sounding amused.

"Enough. Now kneel up for me."

When she did, he slid it in slowly, then did the same with his arching manhood. As the slow rising and falling began, she gushed quietly, "Oh, Logan."

"What, *querida*?"

"I like this very much."

While maintaining the slow, lazy rhythm, he circled the brown aureole of her breast. "Do you?" He took the bud into his mouth.

Her flesh rippled around him. "I do."

She rode languidly while he feasted and caressed. It didn't take long for climax to stake its claim. Once they were able to move again, they rinsed off in the tepid water, padded back to his bedroom, and slept.

The following morning, Mariah opened her eyes. For just a moment, she was disoriented, then remembering where she was, looked around for the man who'd taken her to paradise so many times last night. He was beside her and propped up on one elbow watching her.

"Morning," he said. "Was wondering how long you were going to sleep."

She didn't want to admit how good it was to see him. "Morning. What time is it?"

"Just past eight."

He'd given her so much joy last night, and now, although she planned to go on with her life, nothing would ever be the same. Burying the small sadness and determined not to dwell upon how wonderful it would be to wake up each morning with him by her side, she sat up.

"Water's heating if you want your bath."

"I do, thank you."

In the light of day, she found it hard to believe her scandalous behavior, but again, she had no regrets. Knowing fully what it meant to be a woman and to learn it from his tender and selfless ministrations; every woman should be as lucky, however, she needed to reestablish her distance because it was in her best interest to do so. "I'm going to spend the day making patterns for the curtains and looking through my sketches for costumes for Feather. What are your plans?"

"I'd thought I'd see if I can't convince Andrew and Eli to help me with the bunkhouse, even though it's Saturday. Or?"

The tone made her smile suspiciously. "Or what?"

"Convince you to spend the day with me down by the river."

Shaking her head, she declined.

"May I ask why not?"

"It was to be just one night, Logan."

"Now who's the spoilsport?"

Because his jab was made in a teasing tone, she took it in the spirit in which it was given. Spending more time with him would be wonderful, but it would also make it harder to keep her heart from plunging further into love. So, no. Last night would have to suffice. She couldn't afford another.

Logan wondered if this is how the women he'd treated so casually most of his life felt when he moved on and left them behind. Although he was man enough to accept her decision to not take last night any further, he really wanted to kick and scream like a little boy until he got his way. Add to that the knowledge that sometime in the future she'd be sharing her sensual little body with another man, and he was decidedly unhappy, but he kept it all masked. As he'd noted before, he'd never begged a woman for her affections in his life, even though this golden-eyed beauty had him on the brink of doing just that. What gave him hope, however, was that she was as hot for him as he was for her. He'd give her a few days to let desire rise and claim her and see what happened. "I heated up the water while you were sleeping so you can go on in if you like. I took mine earlier."

"Thank you. And thanks again for last night."

"My pleasure. I'll see you outside for breakfast." Even though it had been his hope to make leisurely love to her this morning, he left the bed without touching her. Nude, he walked to his dresser to get fresh clothes.

She asked him, "Do you mind if I borrow your robe to wear to my room to get my things?"

"Not at all." He saw her eyes on his erection and told her, "It's hard for a man to disguise his feelings—especially after waking up beside a beautiful woman." And hard he was.

She took his robe from the end of the bed and quickly slipped it on. The desire in her eyes was plain to see, so he stood there and waited.

"I—I'll meet you outside," she said and beat a hasty retreat.

Smiling, he watched her leave. After dressing himself, he went over to the bed to strip the sheets. He paused in mid-motion at the sight of the small bloodstains. She'd given him her innocence. If that didn't make her his and his alone, he didn't know what did. Pulling the sheets off the bed, he said aloud, "This is not the end, *querida*. Not by any means."

Breakfast was ready when she stepped outside her door, and just the sight of his welcoming smile was enough to knock large holes in the defenses she was determined to erect. His nudity earlier hadn't helped either. Feasting her eyes on the part of his anatomy that had given her so much joy began the undermining. How she expected to maintain the distance she wanted when last night was all she could think about was beyond her, but she gathered her will and walked over to join him.

"Enjoy your bath?" he asked as he filled her plate with small helpings of potatoes, eggs, bacon, and sliced oranges.

"I did, thank you." She took her plate and sat down in the grass. She'd half expected him to join her while she was in the tub. The thinking, saner parts of herself were glad he hadn't, while the parts of herself aroused by his male display were disappointed. Integrating the two opposing forces was yet another conundrum she faced. Deciding for the moment to concentrate on eating, she did just that.

"Are you sore?"

Her eyes jumped to his and she stammered, "Um. A bit, but it isn't a bother."

"I'm asking out of concern, nothing more. We had a pretty spirited night, so the gentleman in me wanted to know."

"I'm sure it will pass in a day or so." Hoping she was right, she asked, "It will, won't it?"

He nodded.

"Good." She wasn't in pain by any means, but the aftereffects of their spirited play were there. What was more of a concern was the lingering thirst for more. Were it up to her body, she'd be back in bed letting him fill her with his magnificent desire. She wondered how long it would take for that to fade, but didn't dare ask.

They ate their breakfast in silence. As if he had the ability to read her thoughts again, he told her casually, "It isn't going to go away."

She wanted to feign ignorance but simply being near him made her nipples harden in wanton response.

He set his empty plate aside and stood. "I'll be over at the bunkhouse—if you need me."

She didn't respond verbally to the double entendre, but her body said plenty.

Alanza was seated in her courtyard enjoying the peacefulness of the morning. Two of her three sons were now home; the eldest more than likely in love, and her youngest would be arriving in a few days. She had a new woman friend whom she adored, and who might just be the mother of the grandchild she'd been longing for, and *Destino* was one of the most profitable ranchos in the county. What more could a woman ask for?

Bonnie stepped out. "Senora. Mr. Rudd is here. Shall I bring him out?"

Alanza shook her head at the ironic arrival, and wondered if God was sending her a veiled message. "Yes, Bonnie."

A few moments later, he appeared.

"Morning, Lanz."

"Max." She gestured him to a seat at the table. "Would you care for coffee?"

"Yes, thanks."

Alanza turned her attention to Bonnie, who replied, "I'll bring it out right away," and went inside.

They sat silently until her return. She placed the brimming cup on its saucer before him and left them alone.

He took his coffee black and while he stirred it idly to aid in its cooling, Alanza asked, "What brings you here on this beautiful morning?"

"Want to take a look at how Logan's bunkhouse is coming along, and to deliver a couple of crates that were at the station yesterday for the new housekeeper. They're on the wagon."

"That was very kind of you."

"Went to pick up some materials I ordered from San Francisco and Jess Hopkins asked if I'd bring them." Jess was a porter at the station and an old friend.

"Hopefully, it contains her sewing machine. A lot of women are wanting her needlework. Missed you at Feather's party last evening."

"Started planing the cabinets for Logan's kitchen and lost track of time."

So for the next few moments, she told him about the celebration: who was there, who wasn't; what she'd heard by way of the gossips; Mariah sitting with Reverend Dennis; and how proud everyone was of the guest of honor. "We'll miss her while she's away."

He nodded. "Yes, but she's going to do well back East."

Silence rose and he watched her over his raised cup. "The other reason I came by. Going up to the cabin in a few weeks to do some fishing. Wanted to know if you'd like to—"

Andrew suddenly appeared, and Alanza was admittedly relieved. The look on Max's face said he wasn't. Andrew must've sensed that, because he paused in mid-step. "Am I interrupting something?"

"No," Alanza said.

"Yes," Max countered at the same time.

Andrew glanced between them and a smile widened his face. "Well, what have—"

"Go," Max said firmly.

"Don't be rude," Alanza scolded. "Drew, you're more than welcome to sit and join us."

"No, you're not, because I'm officially courting your mother."

Andrew's grin widened.

"No, you aren't."

Andrew acknowledged Max's declaration with an inclination of his head. "I'll let my brothers know, and you have our blessings."

"Andrew!"

He leaned down and kissed her cheek. "I'll eat inside. I love you, Mama. Good luck, Max, and dare I say, it's about time." Ignoring Alanza's fuming face, he left them alone.

Max toasted her with his cup. "So, do you want to go fishing?"

She looked away and thought about all the reasons she wanted to say no, but because not a one held water, she turned back and met his eyes. "Yes."

"Then we'll leave right after your birthday."

Logan was at the bunkhouse adding more nails to the framing when Andrew rode up. "Morning, Drew."

"Morning. Came to see if you need any help before I ride out to San Francisco."

"What's in San Francisco?"

"A beautiful piece of love candy named Whilemina Wells. Calls herself Billie for short."

"I was hoping to get some help today, but you aren't exactly dressed for manual labor."

Andrew glanced down at his fancy Mexican suit, and admitted, "No, I'm not. Just offered my help to be polite."

Logan chuckled. "At least you're honest."

"Max is over with Mama. I'll bet he'll help if you catch him before he leaves." He then told Logan about Max's declaration.

"About damn time."

"Same thing I said. Mama put up a fuss of course, but he'll be good for her. Always has been."

"Yes he has."

"Speaking of fussing. How's your beauty this morning?"

"At the house working on curtain patterns."

"You really aren't going to let the reverend into the corral, are you?"

"You worry about Billie. I'll handle Mariah."

Drew inclined his head. "Whatever you say, big brother. I'll be back in a few days."

"Travel safe, and don't choke on the candy."

"I won't, and neither will she."

Logan laughed. "See you when you get back."

Drew turned his horse and galloped off.

On the heels of his departure Max drove up on his wagon. "Morning, Logan. Got some crates for your housekeeper."

Logan knew how anxiously she'd been awaiting their arrival. "She'll be pleased. Let's take them over to the house." He wanted to see the pleasure in her eyes.

Logan climbed aboard and once they were under way, Max asked, "Have you seen your brother this morning?"

"I have, and he told me about you and Alanza."

"Just want to make sure you don't have a problem. Not that it'd matter."

Logan always liked Max's plain way of speaking. "I don't. Drew and I wholeheartedly approve and I know Noah will as well."

"I'll be taking her up to the cabin for some fishing after her birthday."

Logan approved of that, too.

"How are you and the housekeeper getting along?"

"We're not arguing every five minutes any-more, if that's what you mean."

Max turned his way and studied him silently.

"Yes?" Logan asked suspiciously.

"I hear the reverend spent some time with her at Feather's party last night."

"He did."

"Good man, Reverend Dennis."

Logan didn't respond.

A ghost of a smile played across Max's face. Logan didn't respond to that either.

Chapter 18

Mariah was so pleased by the arrival of her crates, she could've kissed Mr. Rudd for his kindness in delivering them. "Thank you so much."

The two wooden crates were nailed shut, so he'd brought in a pry bar to help with unsealing them. The first crate held clothing and, wrapped protectively in an old quilt, her beloved Singer sewing machine and its foot pedal. Having it in her possession again was like being reunited with an old friend. The two pieces would need to be put back together, but once that was achieved, she'd be able to begin Feather's wardrobe and see about fulfilling the orders of some of the women she'd met at the party. She turned her happy face Logan's way and he met it with a smile.

Also inside were two letters. She recognized Kaye's handwriting on one, but the handwriting on the other wasn't familiar. Deciding to read them later when she was alone, she stuck both into the pocket of her skirt.

"How about Max and I take these to your room?" Logan asked.

"That would be wonderful."

They were just about to do so when the door pull sounded.

"Can you get that, please?" he asked her. "We'll

go ahead and take these to your room and be right back."

She nodded and went to answer the door.

On the porch stood a portly gentleman wearing a very nice gray suit and matching hat. She assumed he'd arrived in the buggy parked near Mr. Rudd's wagon, but she had no idea who he might be. "May I help you?"

"Ah, there she is," he purred. "The woman of my dreams. How are you, Widow Cooper?"

Mariah was a bit taken aback by the surprising greeting. "Have we met, sir?"

"Yep. Last night at the Indian girl's party. Name's Silas Cook."

She didn't remember him, but she'd been introduced to a large number of people. "Please forgive me for not remembering you."

"That's okay. Can I come in and visit for a spell?"

"Certainly. Let me get Mr. Yates."

"Didn't come to visit with Logan. Came to visit with you."

She stilled. "May I ask why?"

"Want to talk about you marrying me."

She stared into the mischief in his eyes. "Um. Would you excuse me for just a moment? I think I hear Mr. Yates calling. Why don't you take a seat on the porch. I'll be back shortly."

"Don't keep me waiting long now, sugar."

Sugar!

"I—won't."

Once assured that he was seated, she all but ran to the back of the house.

"Silas Cook?" she enquired of Logan and Mr. Rudd.

Logan spoke first, "What about him?"

"He's on the front porch. Says he's come to visit with me so he can talk about marriage."

"You did say you were looking for a husband."

Not the response she'd been expecting nor cared to hear. "Is he sane?"

Max chuckled. "Depends on who you ask and what day it is."

Another disconcerting response. Logan looked entirely too amused for her liking.

"He's not a bad sort," Logan offered. "Cattleman. Has a nice spread a few miles from here."

Max tossed in, "But he's also got two of the worst-mannered boys in the state. They're nine now. Mama died when they were babies. Silas's last wife took off about a year ago."

"Last wife? How many has he had?"

Max appeared to think a minute. "Let's see. The boys have run off three, maybe four?" He looked to Logan as if seeking help with his memory.

"Three at least."

"Oh my."

"He's pretty harmless," Logan assured her. "So have a good time. Max and I are going to work on the bunkhouse. I'll see you later."

Her eyes widened.

Logan touched his hat, and a heartbeat later, he and Max exited via her back door.

She did not have a good time. One, Silas Cook kept referring to her as "sugar," and two, when she told him she was flattered by his proposal but uninterested in becoming his next wife, he refused to take her seriously.

"Playing hard to get are you, sugar?"

She took in a calming breath and held onto her temper.

"I'm a pretty big bug around here, if you don't know. Girl with nothing in her pockets like yourself could do a lot worse."

She wasn't sure if he was trying to insult her, or simply relaying his version of kind advice. "Thank you for the visit, Mr. Cook, but I need to return to my duties."

He stood and picked up his hat. "Think about what I said, and I'll stop by again in a couple of days. Maybe we'll go into town and have a meal. I'll bring the boys."

Mariah closed her eyes and counted to ten. When she opened them, he gave her a wink.

He finally drove away. Hoping to never ever see him again, she left the porch and went back inside the house.

A second man arrived less than an hour later. He had nut brown skin and looked old enough to have died years ago. He, too, had on a nice suit but was standing with the aid of a cane.

"May I help you?" she asked, stepping out of the door and onto the porch.

"Morning. Are you the Widow Cooper?"

"I am."

"Name's Beattie McDowell." He had the kindest eyes she'd ever seen.

"Pleased to meet you, Mr. McDowell."

"Same here. Please forgive me for speaking so frankly, but you are the prettiest little thing I've seen in many a year."

"Why, thank you, sir. Would you care to take a seat?"

He chose one of the chairs and set his cane beside him. "Don't want to take up much of your time, but whenever a new lady comes to town, I pay her a call. Haven't gotten a one to say yes to marrying me for going on thirty-five years now, but I keep trying."

She found him sweet. "I'm going to have to say, no, too, Mr. McDowell."

"Figured you would." But he didn't appear angry or put out. "Being in your presence has been more than enough to make this old man's day, lovely lady."

They chatted for a short while longer about the weather and his work at the church. He looked pleased to hear she'd be attending come Sunday. "Reverend Dennis is a good preacher. Last one we had talked so long half the congregation stopped coming, and the other half used his sermons to catch up on their sleep." He stood. "It's been a pleasure meeting you, Mrs. Cooper."

"Same here."

He gave her a departing nod and made his way back to his buggy. That time, she reentered the house wearing a smile.

Next to arrive was middle-aged widower Orville Rose. He came carrying a framed photo of his stern-faced deceased wife, Maebelle.

"She was the finest woman on the face of this green earth," he explained. "Been gone eight years but she'll always be first in my heart."

That wasn't something a potential wife wanted to hear, but Mariah didn't say anything. She thought it best left to someone actually interested in succeeding Maebelle.

"Now, if we do get married, you have to understand it's Maebelle's house. I don't want nothing changed or replaced. Haven't moved not even a doily since the day she passed away."

"I'm very flattered by your offer, Mr. Rose, but I don't think I'd be able to fill your Maebelle's shoes."

"Haven't met a woman who can. Least you're honest." He stood. "Thank you for your time, Mrs. Cooper. Give Logan my regards."

"I will."

Shaking her head, she went back inside.

Over at the bunkhouse, Logan and Max watched Orville ride away.

"What's that now, three?" Max asked.

"Yep."

"Who's this riding up?"

Logan grinned. "Dex Sawyer."

"Got that banjo of his on his saddle."

Logan set his hammer aside. "This one I have to see."

Mariah sighed at the sight of the tall, thin young man on the other side of the door. He was wearing an old suit that was a couple of sizes too large and he had a battered banjo in his hand.

"You Mariah Cooper?" he asked eagerly.

"Yes." She prayed this wasn't another proposal but knew the prayer wouldn't be answered.

"Name's Dex Sawyer. Me and my folks raise pigs."

Unfortunately, her nose already knew that.

"Can you step out here for a minute? Got a song for you."

Mariah wondered if she were being punished for something. Putting on a pleasant face, she stepped outside just as Logan walked up.

"Hey Logan," the young man said. "You're just in time to hear my new song."

"I'm all ears."

The glint of humor in his eyes made Mariah want to box his ears, but she turned her attention back to the troubadour.

He strummed the banjo with more force than talent, and to the tune of "Oh! Susana" sang in a somewhat tuneless bass voice: *"Oh! Mariah. Oh won't you marry me?*

I come here with my banjo so please say you'll agree!"

She closed her eyes for a moment. When she opened them he was still standing there looking as eager as before.

"So, what do you think?" he asked as if she might actually say yes.

Logan's shoulders were rising and falling with silent laughter. She ignored him.

"I'm sorry, Dex, but my answer is no."

"No! I spent all night working on that song."

"I could tell, and I'm very flattered but I'm going to go lie down now. Thank you for visiting."

"But it rhymes and everything!"

Mariah entered the house and didn't look back.

When Logan followed her inside a few moments later, she warned, "If you say a word, I will find a hatchet and chop you into tiny little pieces and feed you to whatever will eat you."

Chuckling, he came over and took a seat next to her on his battered old settee. He draped his arm casually across the back. "Interesting cast of characters you had over today."

She shot him a look.

"Did Orville show you a picture of Maebelle?"

She massaged her temples in hopes of preventing the headache coming on. "Yes, and he told me should we marry I couldn't change anything at all in Maebelle's house. How he expects to find a new wife is beyond me."

"Same question everybody asks."

"And Mr. Banjo. Lord. And he has the nerve to tell me he spent all night on that so-called song. How many more will I have to endure?"

"Probably until you pick one out."

She leaned back and closed her eyes. "This would be comical were it happening to someone else."

"I'm having a good time."

She sent him another look.

"You wanted to find a husband."

She pushed herself to her feet. "I do, but I prefer one not employed by the circus, although Mr. McDowell was rather nice."

"As old as Beattie is, a wedding night would probably kill him, but he'd die happy."

Mariah laughed in spite of her mood. "That's an awful thing to say."

"Still true, though."

His words made her think about their night together. Because of the topsy-turvy day, she'd managed to put it out of her mind for the past few hours, but now, it was back along with all its vivid memories.

He asked quietly, "Did you get all your things put away?"

The tone of his voice and the way he studied her conspired to awaken the parts of herself that wanted to answer his silent call. "For the most part. The sewing machine is still unassembled but I can take care of that later."

"Do you need assistance?"

She shook her head. "I spent many a night before going to bed repairing my mother's machines. She didn't believe in spending money, whether it was needed or not."

A memory rose of something she hadn't thought about in years, and with it came old pain. "One time I was so ill the doctor had to be called. He told her what type of medicine he had for me in his bag and she asked the price. When he quoted it, she said it was too expensive, then asked what would happen if I just went without. I remember him looking at her for a very long time and then over at me in the bed. He reached in his bag, gave her the medicine without asking for any money, and he left."

"How old were you?"

"Seven. Eight." The terrible thought that her mother might've actually wanted her to die made her so incredibly sad, tears stung her eyes.

"'Riah," he said emotionally, but she slowly raised her hand and replied softly, "It's all right Logan. I'm here, she isn't."

His jaw throbbed visibly.

To ease his worry she walked over and kissed

him gently. "I'm very thankful that Alanza brought me here."

"Had I known, I'd've sent for you years ago."

The tears she was holding back almost burst free. She ran a finger across his strong jaw. She was in love with a man she'd met less than seven days ago. *Lord help me.* "I'm going to finish emptying my crates."

"Okay."

Only when she was out of sight did she allow herself to cry.

Logan sat there a long time. He was torn between finding her mother and tying her down on an anthill in the desert, and whether to ask Mariah to marry him now or wait for a better time. He refused to live the rest of his life without her. That he, who'd eschewed marriage his entire adult life would suddenly find himself determined to marry a woman he'd known less than a week was as baffling as it was humbling. He refused to contemplate her being with another man because it wouldn't come to be. She was his. Period. The reverend couldn't have her, nor could Beattie McDowell, Silas Cook, or banjo-playing Dex Sawyer.

His decision made, he left the house and went to see if Max was still around.

He was. "Didn't think you were coming back. She pick any of them?"

"No, because she's picking me."

Max chuckled. "Really?"

"Yeah, but she doesn't know it yet." Logan continued to contemplate the correct timing.

"I see." Max peered at him for a moment before asking, "You okay? She didn't knock you over the head with anything, did she?"

"No, but I am going to marry her. I'll figure out the details on the way. And don't tell Alanza. If you do, she'll head straight for Mexico City and buy every christening gown she can find instead of going fishing with you."

"Good point." Max studied him again. "You're real sure about this, aren't you?"

"Yes."

"Then I'll help if you need any."

"Thanks. How about we call it a day."

"That's fine with me."

"I'm going to grab my fishing gear and go catch some dinner."

"Good luck."

"Thanks."

Max nodded and departed.

Logan got his fishing gear and headed to the river.

Once Mariah had everything put away, her still somber mood was lifted by a surprise she found inside a small wooden box tucked into the bottom of one of the second crates. Opening the box revealed dress pins, pairs of embroidery scissors, threads, thimbles, and a fancy pincushion made to be tied around her wrist. There was also a short note inside that read: *To get you started.* It was signed Aunt Libby. And below the signature she'd added, *PS. I've also included two letters. One from Kaye and the other from a surprising source who wanted to send you good wishes.*

Mariah wondered who that might be. She knew her mother's handwriting, so the letter hadn't been penned by her. She set Libby's note aside for a moment to return to the contents of the box. She still needed things like buttons and frogs, and an assortment of hand needles for hemming and such, but she now felt closer to her goal of starting her own shop.

After placing the gift atop her dresser, she asked herself why Libby couldn't've been her mother, but it was a silly question, so she didn't dwell on it. Instead, she went outside to sit on the bench in her cleaned-up little courtyard to read the two letters. She was still curious about the one with the unfamiliar handwriting but saved it for last because she wanted to read Kaye's first.

Dearest Mariah,

I know you've been gone only a few days but I'm already missing you terribly. I am determined that we will meet again. Carson continues to love me, so our wedding is still on. Thank you from the bottom of my heart for my gown. I know I thanked you incessantly before you left Philadelphia, but it seems I can't stop. I'll be a very beautiful bride because of you. I hope you are well and that California is even more than you hoped it would be. Please write me back as soon as you are able. I'm looking forward to reading about all you're doing and seeing.

Your friend for life.

K.

Mariah set the letter in her lap and sighed. She missed Kaye dearly as well. Now that they were apart, their friendship seemed that much more precious. She made a mental note to buy stationery so she could write to Kaye as often as she wished.

She picked up the second letter. Opening it, she glanced down at the signature on the bottom and went still, seeing Tillman's name. "What on earth is he doing, writing to me?" she wondered aloud.

Dearest Mariah,

I hope this letter finds you well. I had no idea you'd left Philadelphia until after you were gone. In talking with your mother she expressed her worry that you were lured away by nefarious sources.

Her concern has affected her business and my mother worries that the gown she's chosen for my wedding will not be ready if your mother doesn't find peace. So to ensure that all goes well for everyone involved I have agreed to accompany your mother to California so we can bring you back to Philadelphia where you rightfully belong.

Yours always,
Tillman Porter

She read it again and her temper exploded.

Chapter 19

Logan returned home with four fat fish for dinner and a hankering for the woman he planned to marry. After unhitching the team from the wagon and turning them out into the pasture, he grabbed the bucket holding his catch and made the walk back to the house. The sight of her seated on the chair in her courtyard filled his heart with sunshine, and was a sight he hoped to come home to for a lifetime until she turned at his approach and he saw the fire shooting out of her golden eyes. Wondering what he'd done to deserve such an angry welcome, he slowed his steps, but with her he never knew, so he decided to confront her head-on. "What's wrong?"

She stood and thrust a piece of paper at him. "Read this."

He set the bucket down, and after scanning her furious face again, complied. The wording surprised him and not in a pleasant way. "Who's Tillman Porter?"

"A man I might have married had he the spine to stand up to his mother."

Logan found that surprising as well. Her anger made him wonder if Tillman had any idea what he might be in for should he have the bad sense to actually come after her. Logan read the letter again. "He's bringing your mother here, so they can take you back to Philadelphia and make his mother a gown?"

Her withering look told all.

He couldn't believe what he'd read. "Alanza won't react well to being called a nefarious source."

"Is she good with a firearm?"

"Exceptionally."

"Then I'll just have her shoot Tillman when he arrives and that will be the end of it."

That said, she sat back down in her chair and stared angrily out at the countryside.

Logan couldn't wait for them to arrive so he could have the pleasure of immediately sending them packing. "You know I won't allow anyone to harm you."

"I do. But even were I living elsewhere, they'd be returning to Philadelphia without me. They'll find out that I'm not the same Mariah."

Knowing what he did of her, Logan couldn't imagine her being weak or submissive enough to go along with such a ridiculous plan, but apparently, Tillman and her mother believed she would. The Mariah Cooper he'd come to love was fearless, fiery, and threw scrub water. Even though he was glad her anger wasn't directed his way, he didn't like seeing her so upset and wanted to lift her mood. "Are you hungry? I caught some fish for dinner."

"I am, maybe food will help lower my temper."

"Would you like to eat on the riverbank? I don't mind driving back."

She gave him a smile. "I'd like that."

"Then let's go."

After they ate, he showed her how to skip stones. It took her some time to find the right angle to send the stones skimming across the water's surface, but once she mastered the throw, she crowed with joy and he was pleased by her happiness.

"I've never done anything like that before," she told him. "There was no time for play while I was growing up."

"Then I'll have to make sure you have the time now."

"I always envied the lives of other children. They got to go outside after school to play, have birthday parties—"

"You never had a birthday party?"

She shook her head. "Waste of time and money. I was allowed to spend an overnight with Kaye on a few occasions, and I always enjoyed that."

Logan was so outdone by her revelation, he didn't know what to say. Even in the lean years, his family's birthdays were always celebrated in some way. That her mother didn't care enough to make her day of birth a special one angered him. "When's your birthday?"

"The second day of October."

"Then expect us to celebrate."

"That isn't necessary."

"Sure it is. Birthdays are special here. And so are you."

Mariah thought him very kind for wanting to grant her such a boon, but admitting she'd never had a party was embarrassing in the sense that it showed how little her mother thought of her yet again. However, she chose not to dwell on it. She had a new life now. "What other kinds of things did you and your brothers do for fun?"

"We competed to see who could find the best shapes in the clouds."

He apparently saw the confusion on her face. "Come, I'll show you."

Taking her by the hand, he led her away from the bank and back up to the grassy meadow where they'd eaten.

"Take a seat and lie back."

Suspicion filled her eyes.

He laughed. "You can't see the clouds if you don't lie back. I don't have nefarious motives. I promise."

The word *nefarious* was becoming a running joke. She sat and then stretched out on her back in the grass. He took up a position beside her.

"You've really never looked for shapes in the clouds?"

"No."

"We definitely need to get you more play-time."

She looked his way and laughed.

So, for the next little while, they searched the sky for cloud shapes, and she found it to be as much fun as skipping stones. She saw a horse, a castle, and a steamboat. He pointed out a tree and the face of an old man that reminded them both of Beattie McDowell. It was a wonderful carefree time together that she added to the other wonderful memories she'd accumulated so far. She sat up and looked down at him where he still lay stretched out by her side. "This was fun."

"Good. Part of my job as your employer."

"Not that I've done much work."

"No you haven't. Let's see. You've cleaned out the house, and done all the floors in under a week. You are one lazy, lazy woman."

She chuckled softly. Their easy time together made her wonder if this was what it might be like for a married couple. Did they skip stones, lie in the grass, and humorously argue about whether the clouds resembled goats or elephants? She knew for a fact that this wasn't something she would've done with Tillman Porter; he was entirely too proper for such foolishness, but now, because of Logan, she wanted a husband who enjoyed a bit of foolishness every now and again.

"Penny for your thoughts."

"Just thinking had I actually married Tillman, I doubt he would've ever done anything this silly or carefree."

"No?"

She shook her head.

"His mother didn't approve of him courting you, I take it?"

"No, I was too poor, and my eyes were too odd. She found the idea of having grandchildren who might look like me appalling, and Tillman didn't think enough of me to go against her. When I left Philadelphia he was set to marry a woman from Boston."

"This is the same wedding he referenced in the letter."

"Yes."

"He did you a favor."

"I realize that now, but at the time, I was just so angry at his lack of spine and then resigned when I learned he'd proposed marriage to someone more to his mother's liking."

"If he does show up here, I'll make sure he's sent packing immediately."

"Not until after I give him the tongue-lashing he's so richly earned. He'd better hope there are no rocks lying around."

All humor aside, she wasn't looking forward to the confrontation with her mother and prayed it would be over quickly so she could go on with her life.

He asked, "What would you like to do now?"

She shrugged. "You're the maestro of fun. You get to decide."

He sat up. "Since your cloud castle was the best shape of the day, I declare you the winner, and winners deserve a crown, so come on."

With her hand in his, they took off at a run. The surprised Mariah laughed and let him drag her along. They came to a stop in a stand of wild-flowers a short distance away.

"Have a seat," he instructed her.

She complied, and to her surprise he began picking the blooms and tying the stems together.

He explained. "My brothers and I used to make these for Alanza."

When he was done, he eased the circle of red flowers over her hair and set it to rest just above her brows.

"I crown you, Queen of the Meadow."

She reached up and gently touched her crown. No one had ever done such a sweet thing for her before. Emotion thickened her voice. "Thank you, Logan."

"You're welcome."

Time seemed to lengthen. She knew he intended to kiss her and when he did, she met him gladly and without protest. They both caught fire immediately and the passion made him drag her onto his lap. Mariah felt so right in his arms that thoughts of distancing herself melted in the heat flaring her blood. His lips left hers to place a gentle kiss on each of her eyelids.

"Your eyes are as beautiful as the rest of you," he whispered.

And she felt beautiful indeed. Were it her choice, she'd spend the rest of her days right where she was, so she contented herself with meeting him kiss for thrilling kiss. Soon her blouse was undone, and her corset, too, and her nipples were treated to a lazy loving that took her breath away and made her remember his vivid words: *I want to love you in a field of wildflowers beneath the sun and breeze . . .*

The ardent conquering continued. Her eyes slipped open for a moment. Through the haze of desire, she saw Reverend Dennis standing a few short feet away watching them. She stiffened with alarm. "Oh, Logan, stop! Please!" She snatched her blouse closed.

"What's wrong?" he asked against her ear.

"The reverend."

Confused, he studied her startled eyes, then turned his head just in time to see Paul Dennis stalking off stiffly.

Mariah watched him disappear below the rise and sighed heavily. "Well, that's that, I suppose." She'd been looking forward to their dinner tomorrow, and maybe to him courting her if things worked out between them. Now, because Logan's loving was capable of making her lose her mind, and with it all good sense of proper behavior, Paul Dennis would take his interest elsewhere. Disappointment filled her from her head to her toes.

Logan gently raised her chin. The sadness he saw reflected in her eyes made him say tenderly, "You didn't want to marry him anyway."

Misery in her voice, she countered, "Please don't make light of this."

"I'm not. There'll be another proposal."

"From whom, someone like Dex Sawyer?"

"No. Someone like me."

She went still and slowly searched his eyes for what he assumed were signs of trickery. "You don't have to offer just because of this."

"I know. But I decided earlier today that I'm in love with you, and can't live without you, Mariah Cooper."

Her golden eyes widened.

"I want to make love to you from sunrise to sunset—wake up with you every morning and sleep beside you each night, so we can have golden-eyed daughters who'll throw rocks at any boy who crosses them."

Her mouth dropped.

He chuckled. "Don't tell me I finally found a way to render you speechless."

"But you said you didn't wish to marry."

"A week ago I didn't. Now, I do, but only to you. So, what do you say? Will you marry me?"

She searched his features again. "This isn't a prank of some kind is it?"

"No, *querida*." He leaned down and brushed his lips over hers. "I'd never turn something as serious as this into a prank."

She still looked stunned.

He warned teasingly, "Either say yes, or I'll have Dex Sawyer come back and serenade you with his banjo again."

She laughed. "Then, yes, it is."

He pulled her into his arms and never wanted to let her go.

She leaned back. "Are you sure? I love you, too, Logan—but—"

"Lord, woman, stop talking and kiss me."

She grinned and did just that.

They went back to the house, kissing all the way. He carried her into his bedroom, slowly stripped her of everything except her crown of flowers, and made wild passionate love to her until neither of them could move.

Later, after a shared bath, another round of loving, and yet one more shared bath, Mariah lay beside him on his bed in the darkness. He'd fallen asleep a short while ago, but she was still too happy to do so. What an incredible experience coming to California turned out to be. She was happier than she ever thought possible. She couldn't wait to write Kaye and tell her the news. Some might question her sanity in agreeing to marry a man she'd known for such a short amount of time, but she didn't care. Logan Yates could be arrogant, difficult, and as pigheaded as any man alive, but he'd given her a crown of flowers today and made love to her with a tenderness and patience that spoke to who he was underneath all the things that made her chuck rocks at his head. He loved her and thought her beautiful, even her eyes, and that in itself endeared him to her. Earlier in the evening, as they were lying side by side, it was he who'd suggested she turn what was now her bedroom into her dress shop until she decided on a more permanent location. All in all, an excellent idea as far as she was concerned. That he wholeheartedly supported her dream to open her business was enough to let her know she'd chosen the right man.

Her eyes finally closed and she went to sleep looking forward to the future.

On Sunday morning, Mariah took great care with her appearance. The church service would be her introduction to more people in the community and now that she'd agreed to be Logan's wife, she wanted to make a good impression, not only for herself, but for him as well. She still found it hard to believe he'd proposed and she was certain she was the happiest woman in the country. She had a few concerns, however, over how she'd be received by Reverend Dennis, and hoped he wouldn't give a sermon on the sins of flesh in response to what he'd witnessed in the meadow yesterday. She was highly embarrassed, but since his happening upon them wasn't anything she could change, she chose to dwell on her happiness instead.

Logan stuck his head in the doorway. "Are you almost ready?" His nut brown suit, string tie and fancy hat made him look like the prosperous rancher she knew him to be.

"I am. Just give me a half minute more."

She put the last touches to her hair and added a plain pair of silver earbobs. She donned her hat and picked up her handbag that matched the fabric and color of her navy blue walking suit.

"How do I look?"

"Good enough to eat. Did you make the suit?"

She nodded.

"I'm impressed."

The coat fit snugly per the fashion and allowed the high collar of her best blouse to show above it. A row of black buttons graced the front, leading the eye to the coat's scalloped hem and the full skirt below. All in all, she agreed with his assessment; she did look nice. Drawing on her gloves, she hoped the congregation would think so, too.

They rode to church in a fancy black buggy she'd not ridden in before. He said it belonged to Alanza and she only used it on special occasions. The leather seats were comfortable and there was a curved awning attached to keep out the sun and the elements.

Because it was the sabbath, the ranch workers had the day off, and as he drove down the strip of road that led past Alanza's house and to the gates, she noted how peaceful the ranch appeared. "Does Alanza attend Reverend Dennis's church?"

"No. She and the Gutierrezes go to the Catholic church over in Sacramento. They left yesterday afternoon and will be back this evening. Lupe and her husband have family there, so they stay with them on Saturday nights."

He looked her way and asked, "Still want to marry me?"

She hooked her arm in his. "Of course."

Once the gates were cleared, he headed them out onto the main road. "How far away is the church?" she asked.

"Not very. Should be there shortly."

Mariah was admittedly nervous. She wanted the people to like her. She also had hopes that she'd find a few friends. She enjoyed Alanza's company, but she thought it might also be nice to befriend someone closer to her age, too.

Logan thought she looked very fetching in her blue ensemble and feathery hat, and knew the men at the church would agree. He wasn't looking forward to the sarcastic remarks surrounding his attendance any more than all the male eyes turned her way. He did look forward to letting it be known that they planned to marry, however, and that made him smile.

Chapter 20

They arrived at the church shortly before ten. Logan steered the buggy into the open field adjacent to it that was filled with parked buggies and wagons and the people who owned them. Their arrival drew much interest if the way the people stopped and stared was any indication. Sighing and determined to be pleasant and not to bark at anyone, he parked and handed her down.

The first person to approach was Naomi Pearl, the diner owner. Her gray ensemble showed off her curves and Mariah found herself admiring her very stylish gray hat. He did the introductions.

"Welcome, Mrs. Cooper," Naomi said, smiling. "Very pleased to meet you."

"Same here, but please, call me Mariah."

"Then call me Naomi."

Mariah admired not only Naomi's hat but her clear-as-glass velvet-brown skin as well. Her beauty glowed.

"Is Logan treating you well?"

Mariah looked to him and received a smile. She wanted to tell her they were going to be married but decided to let him make the announcement when he was ready. "He is."

"I hear you cleared out the mess in his house."

Before Mariah could answer, they were interrupted by a voice saying, "Well, hello. You must be the new housekeeper everyone's been talking about."

Mariah turned to see a short little man with a mustache that nearly dwarfed his face.

"Name's Jim Deeb. I'm the president of the cattlemen's association."

Beside him stood a very tall, terse-faced woman in a green gown, and wearing a hat way too large to be flattering. "And I'm his wife, Felicity," the woman stated clearly and coolly.

Mariah was a bit thrown by the woman's tone. "Pleased to meet you both."

"Likewise," Felicity replied. "Logan. Naomi."

Both nodded greetings, but Felicity didn't linger to chat. "Come James. Looks like the church will be crowded, and I don't want to have to fight to get a seat."

He didn't balk, but as he departed, he shot Mariah a bold wink.

That threw her as well, and she saw Logan's jaw tighten and his eyes narrow.

Naomi cracked, "If Felicity had seen that wink, he wouldn't be able to see out of that eye for a week."

Logan chuckled. "I agree."

Naomi added, "But Felicity's right about the crowd. Apparently word's gotten around about Logan being here this morning. Everybody's wanting to see if lightning'll strike."

Mariah turned to see how Logan was taking the dig. He was smiling. She decided then and there that she wanted Naomi Pearl as a friend.

Logan said, "Then let the lightning begin. Ladies?" He offered his arms to both. Naomi grinned and didn't hesitate. Mariah didn't either.

As Felicity predicted, the church's interior was full. They managed to find a seat on one of the wooden pews toward the back. Trying not to be overwhelmed by all the interest their entrance garnered, Mariah sat beside Logan while Naomi flanked him on the opposite side. Mariah recognized a few people from Feather's party who sent her smiles and nodded greetings, but most of the faces were unfamiliar.

Naomi leaned over and said quietly, "You and Logan are causing quite the stir, Mariah, but folks here are fairly nice, so don't be put off."

Mariah took the advice to heart, but in an effort to calm her nerves and not be intimidated by all the whispering and looks, she pretended non-chalance as she scanned the surroundings. There was a pulpit, a small choir box, and a beautiful wood altar rail, polished until it shone. The four windows, two on each side, were plain, not stained glass like those at her church back home, but they were opened to let in the morning breeze.

The organist was Beattie McDowell. He took his seat, and when he began the opening strains of the processional hymn, everyone stood. The small five-member choir, which included Dex Sawyer, slowly marched up the center aisle, singing as they went. They were followed by Reverend Paul Dennis. If he noticed Mariah, he gave no indication.

To her surprise, Eli entered their pew. He slid in next to Naomi, who acted as if he were invisible. He didn't appear to mind, and offered Mariah a polite nod.

Because the service was very similar to the ones she'd attended at her home church back in Philadelphia, she was familiar with the prayers and responses. When the time came, Reverend Dennis gave a nice sermon on the power of prayer. He stayed on message, and didn't go too long, just as Beattie promised.

After the sermon, the service continued, and Beattie stood up to read the announcements. He announced the times for the upcoming week's meetings of the usher board, the ladies' auxiliary, and choir rehearsal.

"Now, do we have any visitors?" He looked specifically at Mariah. "Mrs. Cooper, why don't you stand and introduce yourself?"

Everyone in attendance turned her way. She fought down her nervousness and stood. "I'm Mariah Cooper, and I'm originally from Philadelphia."

She was welcomed with applause. Smiling, she took her seat. When she glanced up at the reverend, she saw sadness in his eyes before his gaze slid away.

Beattie then asked, "Mrs. Cooper, who's that stranger sitting next to you?"

The congregation laughed.

Appearing amused, Logan nodded a greeting, then got to his feet. "Although Mrs. Cooper came out here to be my housekeeper, she's graciously agreed to be my wife. We'll be marrying in October and you'll all be invited."

A woman cried, "No!" which brought on a few snickers, but the deafening applause and words of congratulations that followed made it difficult to determine who the person might've been, and frankly, Mariah didn't care. Although she and Logan hadn't talked about setting a date, she assumed he'd chosen the month of October because it held her birthday. Such thoughtfulness made her love him all the more.

When Logan sat down, Eli leaned over and shook his hand.

Naomi said softly, "Congratulations, you two."

Eli turned to Naomi with a knowing smile, which she pointedly ignored. The reaction caused Mariah to wonder what their story might be.

Once all the hubbub died down, the service continued.

After church, Logan left Mariah in the care of Naomi and went in search of Reverend Dennis. He found him in the church's small office. "Paul?"

"What can I do for you, Logan?" His voice was as frigid as his eyes.

"Why'd you come out yesterday? Did you want something?"

"Frankly, yes. I came to make sure Mrs. Cooper and I were still on for dinner this evening, but I could see that she was, shall we say, occupied. My congratulations, by the way."

He didn't sound sincere in the least, but Logan didn't call him on it.

Paul removed his robe and hung it on the tree in the corner of the room. "Since it's common knowledge that I'm looking for a wife, I was naïve enough to believe you'd let me at least try and court her. Should've known better."

Logan's lips thinned. He wasn't going to apologize.

"And if you're worried about me telling anyone what I saw, don't worry. I won't. Anything else?"

"No."

"I'll let you know about the new teacher committee next week."

"Thanks." With that, Logan turned and walked out. He and Paul had always gotten along. Now, he had no idea what the future held.

Mariah was enjoying being introduced around by Naomi and Eli to the members of the congregation gathered outside. Eli soon left them to speak with some of the men, so she and Naomi strolled on. A couple of women they approached stuck their noses in the air and walked away. Naomi explained that they were among those who'd hoped to have Logan for themselves one day, but now that he was no longer on the market their hopes were dashed. "As if he'd paid them any attention before you came," she added sarcastically.

Mariah saw Dex Sawyer, but he walked by her without a word. She assumed he was still angry at her for not liking his song. Beattie McDowell sought her out and offered sincere congratulations on her upcoming marriage, as did Orville Rose. "Hope you and Logan will be as happy as me and my Maebelle were."

"Thank you, Mr. Rose."

He moved on, and Silas Cook approached. He looked angry.

"Hello, Mr. Cook."

"Don't you hello me, girl. You led me on."

Naomi eyed him with surprise while Mariah sighed. "I told you I wasn't interested."

"And I told you I was coming back so we could have dinner!" he shouted. His voice was loud enough to make people stop and stare.

"Don't you dare shout at me!"

"I'll shout all I want. Come here!" He grabbed her by the arm only to have a fist suddenly explode in his face. He was out cold before he hit the ground.

A seething Logan stood over him. "Are you okay?" he asked Mariah.

"I am."

"He didn't hurt you?"

"You didn't give him time," she pointed out.

Naomi chuckled.

"Good. I'm ready to head home."

"I think you are, too. Thanks for coming to my rescue."

He took her by the hand. She gave Naomi a quick wave. As he led her away, applause broke out.

After handing her up into the buggy and getting them under way, he cracked, "See why I don't come to church?"

That afternoon, she was seated in her courtyard working on Feather's sketches when Logan stepped out to join her. He looked at what she'd drawn. "I like that."

"I'm hoping Feather will, too."

"I spoke with the reverend. He's promised not to tell anyone about what he saw."

"That's kind of him," Mariah said. "Are you two still friends?"

"I'm not sure."

She stood and put her arms around him. "He looked very sad when you made the announcement."

"I know."

"I love you, Logan."

"I love you, too, *querida*."

Later, Logan left her to attend the monthly meeting of the cattlemen's association. The election of the new president was on the agenda and only two names were on the ballot. Logan's and current president Jim Deeb. The price of beef was falling. Logan and a few other ranchers wanted to explore agreements with distributors in the East as well as some in Mexico, but Deeb's ties to their current distributors and the kickbacks he'd been receiving for his loyalty were hemming in the members.

The meeting was held at Deeb's place and when Logan entered, he was greeted with congratulatory handshakes and pats on the back for his upcoming nuptials. He responded graciously and glanced around the room to see who was in attendance. The only man who appeared to be missing was Silas Cook. Logan hoped he was still out cold on the grounds of the church.

Eli approached and Logan asked him quietly, "How do you think the vote's going to go?"

"With any luck, the way it should. Everybody's had enough of Deeb and his strutting around."

Logan agreed. "So, are you any closer to a wedding day of your own?"

"Doesn't look like it, but I'm not giving up."

Naomi was making Eli pay for trying to keep her on a string with two of his other women, and his efforts to make her jealous by bringing another woman to her diner for a meal. "Have you tried writing Naomi a song?"

"A song?" he echoed sounding confused.

Logan chuckled. "Never mind. I'll explain later."

Deeb called the meeting to order. The old business was dealt with first, which included a discussion of the current legislation concerning water rights, bovine health issues, and landowner disputes. Logan thought about Arnell Wiley and his trespassing dairy cows. So far the repaired fence hadn't been breached. He was hoping Wiley had gone somewhere and bought himself some good sense.

Once the old business was taken care of, they moved on to the election. Deeb stood up to give a speech, but one of the ranchers, a man named Tom Foster who didn't care for the president any more than the rest in attendance, cut him off. "No speeches. Let's just vote."

Deeb looked angry, but a quick show of hands supported Foster, so the vote was held. When the ballots were counted, the final tally put Logan on top.

"I want a recount!" Deeb demanded.

Eli, who'd been one of the counters, shook his head. "You got three votes out of the thirteen here. A recount won't make much difference, Jim."

Eli looked to Logan. "You have anything to say, Mr. President?"

Logan met the eyes of the men counting on him to direct their economic future. "Thanks for the support and votes. We'll meet next month to talk about distributor alternatives. Until then, meeting adjourned. I've a woman I want to see."

Chuckles melded with understanding nods. They all said their good-byes and Logan rode toward home. He had one more stop to make, however. One he'd been looking forward to since proposing to Mariah the day before.

He found Alanza currying her mare in the stables and she greeted him warmly, "Hello, Logan. How'd church go?"

"Other than knocking Silas Cook out cold for trying to manhandle Mariah, it went fine."

She stopped. He explained how he'd seen Silas grab Mariah's arm, but he left out why Silas was upset with Mariah, for the moment. When he finished the abbreviated telling, displeasure filled her face. "Silas has always had manure where his brain should be."

He then filled her in on the cattlemen's meeting and his new position.

"That's wonderful. You'll be a much better leader than that tadpole Deeb."

He thought so as well. He then quizzed her for a moment about her day in church and when she was done, he said, "Now, I have some news."

"And it is?"

"I've asked Mariah to marry me, and she's said yes."

"Dios!" She grabbed him and began planting joyful kisses all over his face while speaking rapidly in Spanish about how happy she was, how happy they'd be, and her having grandchildren to spoil and love.

Then she stopped and eyed him critically. "You made me stand here and listen to all those other things about Silas and his manure for brains, and then that tadpole, knowing this is what I wanted to hear first? Shame on you, Logan."

He laughed.

She smiled and her voice turned serious. "She will be a wonderful addition to our name."

"Yes, she will."

"And I want at least one gold-eyed grandchild, okay?"

"I'll be sure to let her know."

She opened her arms and he stepped into the hug without shame. They embraced fiercely with a love for each other that had begun when he was six years old and she fifteen.

She whispered, "Since the day we met, you've always had a special place in my heart. Thank you for making me so happy, not just today but all these years. May God continue to bless you, my eldest."

"I love you, too, Alanza."

When they parted she wiped her tears. "Oh my. My heart is so full."

"So's mine. I'll head home now. Going to see if I can't convince Mariah to go to Sacramento in the morning, so we can get a few more things for the house. Do you want us to bring you anything back?"

"No. Your news has given me all I need."

"Good. See you when we return on Tuesday."

"Travel safe."

Outside, he mounted Diablo, and as he turned the stallion's head toward home, he heard Alanza back in the barn scream out happily, "Yes!"

When he entered the house the place was dark. It wasn't very late but he assumed Mariah was in bed asleep. He saw a faint light beneath the door to his bedroom. Easing the door open as soundlessly as he could so as not to disturb her, he entered and stopped at the sight of her in the tub.

"Good evening, Logan."

His manhood instantly returned her greeting in its own lusty way. "Evening."

"I think I'm in love with this tub."

"I think I'm in love with the sight of you in that tub."

"Care to join me?"

He was already undressing. While his eyes slid ardently over her dewy body and the way it glowed in the turned-down lamp, he wondered how he might convince her to greet him this way on a regular basis, but once he joined her and the kissing began, all his questions were forgotten.

Chapter 21

Logan didn't have to do much convincing to get Mariah to agree to a trip to Sacramento, so early Monday morning, they set out.

When they arrived, although the city was smaller than Philadelphia, Mariah enjoyed the many buildings and the traffic and the semi-crowded streets because in a way it reminded her of home. They spent the afternoon looking at furnishings and each purchase was loaded into the back of the wagon. When Mariah was first hired as the housekeeper, she'd resigned herself to furnishing his home for whomever he might marry in the future, but now that the future had come and he was marrying her, the choices would be for her home.

He spared no expense, which caused a few quiet arguments due to her efforts to be frugal, but he was having none of it.

"We can afford it, *querida*, so just buy the damn dining table, please."

She bought the dining table. And the matching chairs.

By the end of the day, the wagon was loaded down with her beautiful dining table and chairs, a couple of arm chairs, a curio cabinet, tableware and glasses made of fine crystal.

They spent the night at a small boardinghouse, and in the morning, the shopping resumed.

"Now, we shop for you," he told her.

She started to balk but the look on his face made her close her mouth and walk beside him quietly. He escorted her down the crowded walks to a shop he'd obviously patronized before, because the proprietor, a short, plump, older woman who appeared to be of Spanish ancestry greeted him enthusiastically. "Logan! How are you?"

"I'm well, Celestine. I want you to meet Mariah Cooper. She's from Philadelphia."

"Oh, she's so beautiful. Look at those eyes. Welcome to Sacramento, Mariah."

"Thank you." Mariah took a quick look around the shop and saw dresses and hats and other finely made female attire.

"Mariah and I will be marrying in October, so she needs nightwear and a few other things."

Mariah's eyes widened. *Nightwear!* She was more than a bit embarrassed by his request. Men didn't shop for nightwear for their wives, did they? "Logan, I—"

His eyes gave her that amused look again, so rather than argue in front of the beaming Celestine, she let him have his way.

"Such a lucky lady," Celestine told her. "Let me show you what I have."

The nightgowns brought out for her to inspect were thin gossamer pieces of confection that would never keep her warm on a cool California night, but it occurred to her that warmth wasn't the objective. Seduction was. Each beautiful piece was designed to entice and tempt the eye.

Logan asked, "Do you want to choose the ones you like?"

Mariah was speechless for a moment.

"Then I will."

While she looked on, he chose so many she wanted to protest wasting so much money on such frivolity, but remembering Alanza's words, she again kept quiet.

By the time he was done, she had more gowns than there were stars in the sky, and Celestine totaled up the bill with a smile.

"Is there anything else you want?" he asked.

She couldn't imagine she did, but walking around the shop, she saw bath salts. She picked up a small tin that held a lavender-scented variety and added it to the purchases.

The seamstress in her was impressed by the dresses on display. "Celestine, do you do your own sewing?"

"No. I buy them ready-made from a woman in San Francisco. I just wish she were closer, so that my customers wouldn't have to wait so long for their dresses to arrive."

Mariah shared a look with Logan before asking, "Would you be willing to look at some of my sketches?"

"You sew?"

"Yes. In fact, what I'm wearing I sketched and made myself."

Celestine evaluated her gray suit and hat and appeared impressed. "If your other sketches are all as beautiful as the costume you have on, I know a number of seamstresses who'd pay a good price for your creations."

They spent a few moments discussing the ins and outs, and Mariah agreed to return in a week or so to show her some of her work.

With that decided, Logan turned over the money for their purchases. Offering their good-byes, they left the shop.

"Now, one last stop and we can head home."

The stop turned out to be one of the city's finest jewelry establishments. Mariah stared up at him. "Who are you buying something for from here?"

"Diablo."

"Diablo?"

He shook his head as if she didn't have a lick of sense and opened the door so she could enter ahead of him. Inside, the shop's quiet atmosphere seemed to make all the beautiful gems on display and in the cases even more stunning. She saw emerald necklaces, diamond bracelets and lots and lots of pieces made of gold.

The salesman approached. "May I help you folks?"

"Looking for some things for my wife."

The man nodded a greeting to Mariah before resettling his attention on Logan. "What do you have in mind?"

"She'll need something for everyday. How about a solitaire on a chain?"

"We have an excellent variety."

"Earbobs, a few necklaces for special occasions. A bracelet or two, and oh, a wedding ring."

Mariah almost fell on the floor.

Logan told her, "Take a look around, *querida*. If you see something you like, let me know."

Look around! Mariah couldn't even move. While the salesman went to get his keys to the glass cases, she confessed, "Logan, I don't know the first thing about jewelry."

"Then let's look together, and no fussing about prices, okay?"

She nodded.

So for the next hour, a very stunned Mariah watched as the man she'd agreed to marry showered her with so much beauty that when she left the store carrying the bag of boxed jewels, tears were streaming down her face.

"What's the matter?" he asked softly. "And please don't ask me if I can afford it."

She shook her head. "It's not that. You are so incredibly kind to me."

He smiled. "Jewels for my jewel."

"But?"

"But, what? You are my love and my life,

Mariah Cooper. And because you are, I'd give you the moon should you ask for it. I'm going to spoil you for the rest of your days, so get used to it."

Then she really started to cry. She dug a handkerchief out of her handbag.

An elegantly dressed woman passing by them on the walk stopped and peered into Mariah's face. "Are you all right, miss?"

"I am. Thank you."

"Saw your tears."

"They're happy tears. This is my intended and he's so wonderful."

The woman smiled kindly, and upon giving Logan a quick once-over, said, "Honey, if he was my man, I'd be crying tears of joy, too."

With a nod, she moved on, and a happy Mariah hooked her arm into Logan's so they could walk to their loaded-down wagon to start the long journey home.

Alanza was in her sitting room reading the newspaper when Bonnie entered. "You have visitors, senora."

"Who is it?"

"The woman claims to be Mariah's mother."

Alanza was speechless for a moment. "Really."

"There's a younger man with her—a Tillman Porter."

"Is he kin, too?"

"I don't know. I left them at the door. Shall I show them into the parlor?"

"Yes, and I'll be right down."

Alanza wondered if Mariah knew her mother would be coming. Heading for the stairs, she hoped the woman had come seeking reconciliation, because if not, she and her companion would be back on the train before nightfall.

When she entered the parlor, a storklike woman was standing in the center of the room looking impatient and the man was staring at the vase he had in his hand.

"Sir, that vase has been in my family for generations. If you drop it, I hope you have the necessary funds to replace it."

He jumped. Seeing the cool anger on her face he quickly but carefully set it back on the shelf.

The stork looked her up and down and asked skeptically, "Who are you?"

"Alanza Maria Vallejo Yates, the owner of this house. Who are you?"

Once again Alanza was given a slow once-over. "I'm Bernice Cooper."

Alanza settled her attention back on the now very uncomfortable-looking man. "And you?"

"Um. Tillman Porter."

"Why are you here?"

Bernice answered. "To get my daughter Mariah and take her back to Philadelphia, where she belongs."

Tillman asked almost apologetically, "Do you know where she might be?"

"Sacramento."

"I was told she lived here," Bernice countered coolly.

"She does, but she's away on a shopping trip."

"When's she coming back?"

"Sometime today."

"Then we'll wait."

"Be my guest."

An hour later, Alanza eyed the two visitors with a barely veiled dislike. As far as she was concerned, she'd had to endure their presence in her home an hour too long. Knowing what she did of Mariah's pain-filled relationship with her mother, it took all Alanza had not to grab a shotgun and chase them both away. As it stood, she'd had very little to say.

But, because Alanza had been raised by a gracious mother, she'd had Bonnie bring out tea and a tray of macaroons.

"You have servants?" Tillman asked.

"Yes. I've had them most of my life."

Bernice glanced around at all the fine furniture and paintings. "And you own all this?"

Alanza sipped her tea. "I do."

"And you own this ranch?"

"Along with my sons, yes."

"And our Mariah works for one of your sons?" Tillman asked.

"That was the original arrangement."

"So what's changed?" Bernice asked.

"They're going to be married."

Bernice's eyes widened. "Since when?"

"I'm sure Mariah will explain when she returns." And Alanza hoped it would be soon, otherwise Logan might be forced to scour the bordellos of Yerba Buena in order to find Andrew so she could be bailed out of jail.

Mariah and Logan arrived home tired from the long ride. All she wanted was a bath and maybe a short nap. The day had been one of the happiest in her life. "Thank you again for all the lovely gifts."

"You're welcome."

They left the wagon parked out front and wearily climbed the two steps to the porch. There was a note stuck in the screen door. Logan took it out and read it.

By the look on his face, Mariah knew something was wrong. "What's the matter?"

He passed it to her and when she was done with the reading, her features matched his. "I suppose I have to go and see them."

"But not alone."

She was grateful for his support. "Let's just hope it doesn't take them more than a few minutes to grasp the meaning of the word *no*."

Sighing, she joined him on the wagon seat for the drive to Alanza's.

Bonnie ushered them into the parlor, where

the closed-faced Alanza sat on a chair facing Bernice and Tillman seated on the beautifully embroidered settee.

"It's about time," Bernice snapped.

Mariah saw Alanza's dark eyes flash angrily before she asked, "How was the trip?"

"Very pleasing," Mariah replied.

She turned to the unwanted visitors. "Hello, Mother. Tillman."

Tillman smiled widely in response and rose as if to approach her, but he must've seen something in Logan's stormy face because he stopped and sat down again.

Logan took the opportunity to walk over and place a kiss on his mother's cheek but there was no welcome in his eyes for the people on the settee.

Mariah made the introductions. "Logan Yates, this is my mother, Bernice Cooper, and Tillman Porter."

He offered a nod, nothing more.

"You the one she's supposed to be marrying?" Bernice asked while looking him up and down in the same way she'd done Alanza earlier.

"Will be marrying. There's no 'supposed to be' involved."

"Pretty uppity."

"Thank you."

Mariah saw Tillman viewing Logan with what appeared to be nervous fear. "Tillman, I received your letter, but sadly, you've come all this way for nothing. I won't be returning to Philadelphia."

Bernice countered, "Yes, you will. Get your things so we can leave."

"Did you not hear me?" she asked coldly. "I won't be returning." Mariah looked over at Tillman. "And how dare you lie to my aunt about your intentions so she'd send me your letter. After the way your mother treated me, you must be addled to believe I'd go back and help make her anything, least of all a gown for your wedding."

He looked down at his shoes.

"So both of you, get your things and go."

Bernice stood. "Do you remember what happened the last time you smart-mouthed me?"

"I do. You slapped me and knocked me down, but it won't happen again, believe me."

"Get your trunks!" Bernice demanded.

Mariah kept her voice evenly toned. "Mother, you may rant and rave all you like, but I won't be going. This is my home now, and these people are my family."

"What do you know about them? A bunch of foreigners, the lot of them. You've been here less than two weeks."

"And I've been given more love in these two weeks than I received in the thirty years I lived with you."

Bernice crossed the room with fury in her eyes. She raised her hand and Mariah snatched her arm and held. "As I said, you will never strike me again."

Bernice was taller and weighed more, but Mariah was angrier and that anger gave her strength. She leaned in to her mother's face. "For the last time. Go home!"

And she tossed her free.

Bernice looked at Mariah as if she'd never seen her before. "I'm your mother! You will obey me!"

"Or what? You'll make me get the strap, or send me to bed with no supper? You may be my mother, but I've seen dogs treat their puppies better than you treated me."

She slapped her.

Mariah slapped her back.

Bernice's eyes went wide as the moon.

Logan was across the room in a flash. Mariah stopped him. "It's okay. She's leaving, aren't you, Mother?"

Apparently, Bernice finally grasped the meaning of the word *no*. She eyed Mariah malevolently for a long moment, then snapped at Tillman. "Let's go."

He scrambled to his feet.

Logan's voice was cold. "I'll show you out."

They made their exit and Alanza opened her arms. Mariah went to her without hesitation and let the embrace salve the hurt she felt inside. More than likely, she'd never see her mother again, and in spite of the past, she'd hoped for a reconciliation. There seemed little chance of that happening now. "I think I'll be needing some ice, if you have any."

"So will Bernice if that's any consolation."

Alanza rang for Bonnie.

While they waited for her to return with the ice, Alanza said to Mariah, "You may have been her daughter by birth, but you are my daughter by heart. Always remember that."

Mariah had no doubts that she would.

Outside, Logan made sure the unwanted visitors got back into their rented buggy before issuing a warning. "Never bother Mariah again. If you return, I will shoot you for trespassing. Now get the hell off my land!"

Tillman set the carriage in motion and drove away.

That night, as she and Logan lay in bed, he asked quietly, "How are you?"

"Other than the pain in my face, I'm okay I suppose. The day started out so gloriously and then . . ."

He eased her back against him and held her close. "I know." He kissed the top of her hair.

"I'll not be like her. Our children will have more kindness and love than their arms can hold." She twisted around so she could make out his features in the darkness. "Thank you for loving me."

"You're welcome."

Chapter 22

In the weeks following her mother's departure, Mariah threw herself into her new life. She put up her curtains, positioned her new furniture, and filled her brand-new kitchen cabinets with all the items a kitchen would need. She also mastered driving, worked on Feather's wardrobe, and she and Alanza journeyed to Sacramento to show and sell four of her sketches to Celestine. In the evenings, she took her baths and made love to Logan.

By mid-July, the rancho geared up for Alanza's birthday party and her relatives began to arrive. Andrew stopped by one morning and had with him a particularly special one.

"Mariah, this is our little brother, Noah."

There was nothing little about him. He matched Logan in height but was leaner. He also had an ugly scar slicing his left cheek that gave his handsome face a sharp edge. "Welcome, Noah."

"Pleased to meet you, Mariah. I hear you're going to be a member of the family."

"I am."

"Not sure my big brother deserves someone so lovely, but welcome."

Andrew said, "We need to get back before Logan and Mama find out we're missing."

Noah added, "They have a list of work for us to do that reaches Los Angeles. It's been a pleasure meeting you, Mariah."

"Same here."

Drew said, "We'll see you later."

The brothers departed.

In a way, Mariah looked forward to meeting Alanza's family, but she was also very nervous because she had no way of knowing how'd they'd treat her or react to having a so-called servant marry into their illustrious family.

Later that day, Alanza arrived. She was carrying something draped over her arm encased in brown paper. When Mariah held the door open for her to enter, her friend and soon to be mother-in-law placed a kiss on her cheek. "Brought you something for my birthday dinner tonight."

They moved to the parlor and Alanza handed over the item she'd carried in.

"What is this?"

"A dress."

Curious, Mariah eased the paper off and her eyes popped. The dress looked like something from the closet of a queen. Made of beautiful blue silk, it dazzled the eye. "Where'd you get this?"

"Celestine. I didn't know if you'd have anything fancy to wear so I took the liberty of commissioning this. I hope I haven't offended you by doing so."

"Oh, not at all. This is gorgeous."

"You're my daughter-in-law, and I want you to stand out tonight like the beautiful woman that you are. You have jewels?"

"I do."

"Then make sure you put them on. The women in my family like to show off by dressing like they're at the court of Queen Isabella. There'll be lots of beautiful dresses and jewelry."

Mariah gave her a strong hug. "What would I do without you?"

"You'd manage."

"I met Noah."

"Ah. My baby. He's the most even-tempered of them all. I'm enjoying having the three of them home. I'm glad you like the gown. Now, I must get back. So many things to do. So little time."

She kissed Mariah's cheek and hurried away.

Later, at the dinner, Logan eyed his beautiful intended in all her finery and wondered how much trouble he'd be in if he spirited her away so he could take her home and make love to her. The dress she'd been given by Alanza made her look not only elegant but tempting as hell. The way the bodice cut across the tops of her breasts made him want to find a dark corner so he could ease it down and pleasure her to her heart's delight. The jewels at her throat and in her ears were equally as stunning.

Andrew sidled up next to him. "We may have to get you a hood."

"A hood, why?"

"If we don't get something to put over your eyes you may burn the place down the way you're looking at Mariah."

"Is it that obvious?"

He sipped his champagne. "Yep."

"You have to admit she is the most gorgeous woman around."

"No argument here."

Noah joined them. "Logan, Mama said she'll take a buggy whip to you if you sneak away with Mariah before she announces your wedding and cuts her cake."

Logan rolled his eyes heavenward and prayed for strength.

The large formal parlor was filled with women in luxurious gowns and men in evening wear. There'd been fifty people at the two dining tables.

Andrew noted, "This gathering seems to get bigger every year."

Logan silently agreed as he watched Alanza introduce Mariah to one of the late-arriving male cousins. Although he loved Alanza with each beat of his heart, he wanted this to be over so he could take his beauty home.

Alanza then called out, "Everyone, may I have your attention. Logan, will you join me please."

"Finally," he said under his breath.

Both brothers laughed softly.

He joined Alanza in the center of the room and took Mariah's hand.

"Logan and Mariah will be married in October."

Applause and cheers filled the parlor.

"I will be sending out invitations in a few weeks, so please plan on returning to join them as they start their new lives together."

The soon-to-be-wed couple was then mobbed. The aunts kissed them, the uncles and cousins shook their hands, and the servants circled the room with more crystal flutes of champagne.

Mariah had tears in her eyes. She'd worried about being accepted, but the outpouring of goodwill she'd experienced from the moment she and Logan arrived set her anxiety to rest. Thanks to Logan she was now a member of the biggest family she'd ever had the pleasure to meet. She looked up at the man she would be marrying in a few months' time and her heart was full.

"Happy?" he asked over the din.

She nodded but had no time to voice her happiness as more people came up to offer best wishes.

Then, Bonnie wheeled in the biggest, most beautiful birthday cake Mariah had ever seen. There were lit sparklers all over the top.

While the cake sputtered and blazed, Alanza yelled in Spanish for silence. The room stilled.

Addressing those gathered, she said, "My *nuera*

didn't have an opportunity to celebrate her last birthday, so I'm sharing my cake with her."

Mariah whispered to Logan, "What's *nuera* mean?"

He smiled. "Daughter-in-law."

Her eyes widened. Alanza looked her way and said with deep affection, "Mariah, come."

Her hands to her mouth and tears in her eyes, Mariah glanced first at Logan, and then at Alanza. Together, and hand in hand, the two *amigas* stood behind the big beautiful cake while calls of happy birthday, congratulations, and the toasts from the fifty guests filled the air.

Later, after the cake was cut and the slices passed around to the guests, Mariah snuck outside to the courtyard to get some air and reflect on her glorious new life. Answering the ad in the newspaper had been the best decision she'd ever made. Her past might have been filled with sadness and pain, but her future seemed as bright as the sparklers on her birthday cake and not even Queen Calafia could've asked for more.

A few moments later, Logan joined her. Mariah stepped to him and circled her arms around his waist. She placed her cheek against his heart. "Do you know how much I love you?"

He held her tightly. "Probably as much as I love you."

She leaned up and kissed him passionately. As

the kiss ended, she asked, "How long does this celebration last?"

"A couple of days. Tomorrow there will be jugglers and horse races, tons of food and a dancing bear or two."

"Really?" she asked with a laugh.

"I kid you not. By mid-afternoon there will be so many people here, it'll look like the whole state of California's been invited."

"Amazing. How about you take me back to the house and make love to me until I can't walk?"

It was his turn to laugh. "You're getting to be pretty outrageous, missy."

"But you love me for it."

"Damn right."

So they snuck away, and Logan filled her request until the sun rose in the sky.

Epilogue

On April 15, 1886, Alanza Yates stared down at the small face of her first grandchild. Her name was Maria Elizabeth. She had a head full of dark hair and was perfectly formed from her tiny toes to her beautiful golden eyes. Alanza could barely see the one-hour-old baby through her happy tears.

"Mariah, she's beautiful just like her mama."

"And her *abuela*," the very tired Mariah offered with a smile.

Being called *abuela* made Alanza's eyes fill with even more tears. "Thank you for her."

"You're welcome."

"I'm going to give her back to you, because I know Logan is going to lose his mind if we don't let him in."

So she handed the precious child back to her *nuera*, and after placing a kiss on the brows of both, made her exit.

Logan tipped inside.

"Hello," his wife called sleepily. "Come see our Maria."

He walked over and the sight of Mariah holding the product of their love nearly knocked him to his knees. He was so overwhelmed his emotions wouldn't let him speak. "She's so beautiful," he finally managed to say.

"Yes, she is. Do you want to hold her?"

He leaned down and Mariah very carefully transferred their daughter into her father's strong arms. "Hey, little miss," he said softly. "Welcome to the world. I'm going to teach you how to ride, and shoot, and all the things a girl needs to know. Uncle Noah will teach you to sail and to fight pirates. Not sure what your Uncle Andrew can teach but I'll make sure it has nothing to do with bordellos."

"Logan!" Mariah laughed.

Logan thought his daughter just perfect. "She has your eyes, *querida*."

"And will probably have your height. The midwife says she's quite long."

He tenderly handed Mariah back the baby and kissed his wife softly. "I'll let you two sleep. Get some rest."

"Logan?"

"Yes."

"I love you so."

"I love you more. I'll be back in a little while. There's something I need to do."

"What is it?"

"Start gathering rocks."

As he left the room, the happy Mariah looked down at her beautiful daughter, thanked heaven for both her child and her husband, and drifted into sleep.

· · ·

In a small boardinghouse in San Francisco, another baby was born—a little boy with dark hair and dark eyes. His tired mother, a stranger to Mariah and Logan, peered down at him sleeping so peacefully and smiled at him lovingly in spite of all her worries. Because of her profession, determining who the father might be had been a conundrum, until the midwife showed her the small birthmark on the child's back. It resembled a sunburst, and the mother knew of only one man similarly marked. He wouldn't be pleased to learn he'd fathered a child, especially not with her, but the baby was his, and she'd not let their son be denied. Kissing her son's tiny forehead, she snuggled him close, and she, too, drifted off to sleep.

Dear Readers,

Destiny's Embrace is the first of a three book series featuring Alanza Yates and her sons. My editor and I thought it might be fun to break away from the older characters we all know and love so well and create something new. This book, featuring oldest son Logan and his Philadelphia seamstress Mariah gave me a chance to not only bring a new family to life, but also allowed me to sprinkle the story with nuggets of the fascinating history unique to the State of California. As schoolteacher Daisy Stanton pointed out to Mariah, few people know about the great mythical Queen Calafia, but she's been depicted not only as the modern-day Spirit of California, symbolizing the untamed bounty and beauty of the land before European settlement, she's also been the subject of paintings, sculpture, stories, and films.

A 1926 portrayal of the warrior queen can be found in a mural in the Room of the Dons at the Mark Hopkins Hotel in San Francisco, and in 2004, the city's African American Historical and Cultural Museum put together a Queen Calafia Exhibit featuring works by various artists.

In 2001, Disneyland in Anaheim opened a twenty-three-minute multimedia attraction based on the founding of California titled "Golden

Dreams." The great Whoopi Goldberg narrated it as Queen Calafia. Sadly, in 2009, "Golden Dreams," which featured a bust of Ms. Goldberg as Calafia, was demolished to make way for a ride based on the Little Mermaid.

Demolished or not, her myth lives on and I hope you enjoyed learning about her as much as I.

Below is a partial list of the sources I consulted to bring *Destiny's Embrace* to life and that you can use to learn more about Estabanico, Biddy Mason, the Black forty-niners, and others.

Beasley, Delilah L. *Negro Trail Blazers of California*. University of Colorado at Boulder. 1918.

Graaf, Mulroy, Taylor. Eds. *Seeking El Dorado: African Americans in California*. Autry Museum of Western Heritage. 2001.

Lapp, Rudolph M. *Blacks in Gold Rush California*. Yale University Press. 1977.

Lapp, Rudolph M. "The Negro in Gold Rush California." *Journal of Negro History*. V. XLIX April 1964. No. 2.

Queen Calafia. Wikipedia: The Free Encyclopedia.

In closing, I send many thanks to my editor, Erika, and the great folks at Avon/HarperCollins;

my agent, Nancy, who works so tirelessly on my behalf; and last but not least, you, my readers. Without your support this author would be nothing. Peace and Blessings!

See you next time.

B.

Center Point Large Print
600 Brooks Road / PO Box 1
Thorndike ME 04986-0001 USA

(207) 568-3717

US & Canada:
1 800 929-9108
www.centerpointlargeprint.com